Praise for R. J. Lee and the first Bridge to Death mystery
Grand Slam Murders

"An attractive protagonist, plenty of Southern charm, a long
suit of colorful characters, and a plot that comes up trumps
at the surprising end, all bode well for future installments."
—*Publishers Weekly*

"A compulsively readable series debut, dripping in Southern
charm, for a clever sleuth whose bridge skills break the case."
—*Kirkus Reviews*

"R. J. Lee brings an authentic new Southern voice to the
mystery scene. He saturates his Bridge to Death Mystery
with colorful characters in a small town rooted in a more
genteel time in the Deep South. Lee's complex and
satisfying plot is woven with wit and grace. I look forward
to spending more time with the characters from Rosalie."
—Peggy Webb, *USA Today* bestselling author
of the Southern Cousins Mystery series

"The plot-driven story line is steadily paced and
the author cleverly uses knowledge of the game
of bridge to uncover what really happens—and
it all leads to one heck of a jaw dropping ending."
—*Mystery Scene* magazine

"An impressively original and deftly crafted mystery
from first page to last, *Grand Slam Murders* by R. J. Lee
will prove to be an inherently riveting read."
—*Midwest Book Review*

Books by R. J. Lee

GRAND SLAM MURDERS

PLAYING THE DEVIL

Published by Kensington Publishing Corporation

Playing the Devil

R. J. LEE

KENSINGTON BOOKS
www.kensingtonbooks.com

KENSINGTON BOOKS are published by

Kensington Publishing Corp.
119 West 40th Street
New York, NY 10018

All Kensington titles, imprints, and distributed lines are available at special quantity discounts for bulk purchases for sales promotion, premiums, fund-raising, educational, or institutional use.

Special book excerpts or customized printings can also be created to fit specific needs. For details, write or phone the office of the Kensington Sales Manager: Kensington Publishing Corp., 119 West 40th Street, New York, NY 10018. Attn. Sales Department. Phone: 1-800-221-2647.

Kensington and the K logo Reg. U.S. Pat. & TM Off.

ISBN-13: 978-1-4967-1917-1 (ebook)
ISBN-10: 1-4967-1917-4 (ebook)
Kensington Electronic Edition: February 2020

ISBN-13: 978-1-4967-1916-4
ISBN-10: 1-4967-1916-6
First Kensington Trade Paperback Printing: February 2020

10 9 8 7 6 5 4 3 2 1

Printed in the United States of America

For my Angel Boy

ACKNOWLEDGMENTS

I begin as usual with profound thanks to my superb agents at Jane Rotrosen in New York: Christina Hogrebe and Meg Ruley. They both have an unerring sense of timing and guidance when it comes to producing the best work I can.

So many people at Kensington Books, my publisher, contribute to my success; starting at the top, there is executive editor, John Scognamiglio, who has allowed me to develop my writing skills over eight novels so far. Kristine Mills and Sara Not of the Art department, Carly Sommerstein in Production, and Larissa Ackerman and Michelle Addo in Publicity also help me shine.

I am also indebted to Rocky Kennedy, Lafayette County Coroner in Oxford, Ms., for helping me understand certain procedures and guidelines regarding autopsies. And thanks once again to my attorney cousin, Bruce Kuehnle, Jr., for clarifying legal issues essential to the plot of *Playing the Devil*.

CHAPTER 1

It was with great anticipation that the inaugural meeting of the Rosalie Country Club Bridge Bunch was about to take place, and Wendy Winchester was so proud of herself, she thought she might pop just like a champagne cork. Following the untimely demise of the venerable Rosalie Bridge Club and its four wealthy society matrons more than a year earlier in the historic Mississippi River port, it was Wendy who had taken the initiative to form a club with fresh new faces devoted to the game. Because she had been on track to become a fledgling member of the old group, her interest in learning the game and becoming more polished at it had not waned. She had continued to practice online and believed she was getting much better as a player.

As a result, the *Rosalie Citizen*'s twenty-six-year-old investigative reporter had forged ahead bravely in her spare time. The strawberry-blond, blue-eyed "power magnolia" had approached Delia Dorothy Hornesby—"Deedah" to her friends, as well as the director of the RCC, itself—about forming a new club and had discovered a formidable ally for her efforts.

"I've always thought we should have a bridge club that meets out here in the middle of the hardwood forests instead of in town where everything is so crowded. We don't have to have all our activities within sight of the Mississippi River, you know," Deedah had told her when they had met in her office several months earlier. "We have tennis, golf, swimming, and Ping-Pong here at the country club, so why not bridge? As much as I like the game, you would have thought I'd have come up with the idea, myself."

Wendy had paid her the ultimate compliment with a gracious smile to seal the deal.

"You were too busy running the country club to perfection, I would imagine. You're a woman of priorities."

Deedah had leaned in across her desk and given Wendy a conspiratorial wink. "That's the truth of the matter, I'm afraid. It takes some doing to keep this place humming, what with all the conflicting personalities who belong and want their way in everything. It appears the method the late William Voss used was to give in to Brent Ogle all the time, and that was the only way to keep the peace. Well, I have other ideas about how to get around the high-and-mighty Mr. Ogle."

The first female director of the RCC, Deedah was no slouch in the "high-energy department." Against the sexist opposition of the club's most substantial contributor, Brent Ogle, she had won over the rest of the board when the previous director, William Voss, had keeled over unexpectedly from a heart attack and left an opening ripe for the taking. Had Brent campaigned against her? Not up front unless he had to. That was not his style. He preferred under the table and behind the scenes. At those tactics he had always excelled. Nonetheless, he had not succeeded in preventing Deedah Hornesby's ascent to the directorship, and that had made him more hostile than ever.

Meanwhile, Wendy and Deedah had managed to collect two other members to form the Bridge Bunch's first ever table: Hollis Hornesby, Deedah's gangly, "pushing forty" son, whose art gallery had just closed after nearly two decades of struggle on Royal Street in the New Orleans French Quarter; and Carly Ogle, the long-suffering wife of the notorious Brent, himself. There had been a few others who had expressed interest but had not followed through. Perhaps they would join at a later time when the Bridge Bunch had gelled. Rosalie was full of those who were joiners only after a project had gotten off the ground and made a success of itself. There was always tremendous pressure to conform socially and do the "acceptable" thing.

This first meeting of the Bridge Bunch would be taking place on a gray, overcast Saturday afternoon the week before Halloween, and Wendy was hopeful that the threat of severe thunderstorms would not affect attendance for bridge in any way. At least it shouldn't, she reasoned. It was obviously keeping most of the golfers and tennis players away, however, as there weren't many people meandering around inside or outside otherwise. The Bridge Bunch would have the multi-columned brick clubhouse with the classic portico to themselves, practically. In fact, the only other person visible inside at the moment was the RCC's longtime bartender, Carlos Galbis, who stood like a short, uniformed sentinel in his tux behind his marble-topped counter in a corner of the sprawling great room with its impressive vaulted ceiling.

The rest of the great room was unremarkable. There were sofas, chairs, and tables scattered here and there, some near the bar, others near the huge flat-screen HDTV mounted on the wall so that members could watch sports events of interest while they chatted and sipped their drinks. There was also a covered deck outside that wrapped around three sides of the building itself, offering rocking chairs to those who just wanted to enjoy frequent episodes of quiet laziness.

Wearing a pale-blue shift that she had bought at Lehman's

Department Store because she thought it matched the color of her eyes, Wendy had taken her place just inside the front entrance with its matching potted palms standing guard on either side of her. She was sipping on a glass of white Zinfandel, shifting it now and then to keep nervously checking her cell for the correct time at ever closer intervals. At least she knew where Deedah was, working as usual in her office in one of the building's two wings. But it was almost three o'clock—their designated start time—and Wendy disliked stragglers of any kind, a pet peeve she wisely kept to herself. She also firmly resisted the urge to text any of the fledgling group as a reminder, having already decided to resort to that only if anyone was unfashionably late.

Finally, at five after three, the stylish, leggy Carly Ogle rushed in with a downcast expression. "I'm so sorry I'm late, Wendy," she said, gasping. "Brent was supposed to fill up my car, but he apparently forgot, considering his golf date today with Tip Jarvis and Connor James. They're out there on the course right now, the three of them, even if it looks like the weather will chase them in any minute. It had already started to rain at our house downtown, and it's on the way. Anyway, I had to stop for gas, and wouldn't you know it? There was a line a mile long at every one of those pumps. Isn't that always the way when you're in a hurry?"

Wendy gave Carly a quick, reassuring hug and then drew back gently with a smile. "Calm down, dear. It's no big deal. Hollis Hornesby isn't here yet, so you haven't kept us waiting if that's what you were worried about."

"Oh, thank goodness for that," Carly said, finally catching her breath while fanning her face at the same time. "I hate being a problem."

"You are anything but. We're going to be about playing a relaxed rubber or two of friendly bridge while we forget the cares of the world for at least this afternoon."

Carly managed a mischievous smile. "Might I indulge in a drinkie-winkie before we start?"

Wendy graciously pointed in the direction of the bar. "Carlos is at your service over there. Help yourself. And there's a snack table next to where we'll be playing. I stocked it with mixed nuts, a couple of dips, some cherry tomatoes, and crackers in case we get the munchies. Maybe we'll bring some fancier food as time goes on."

"Yes, well, I think I'll have Carlos whip up a mint julep with his magic mortar and pestle," Carly said, her face lighting up immediately as she sashayed over.

Indeed, the RCC was known for its mint juleps, mojitos, and other exotic concoctions, and Carlos Galbis, whose father had escaped Cuba as a teenager just before Castro's takeover, had become somewhat of a fixture in his ten years of service as a bartender. That was all to the good, since the RCC didn't offer much in the way of food service—some store-bought sandwiches kept in a mini-fridge were about it—nor did it offer dancing and other formal social activities as most country clubs did. All of that was the exclusive purview of the venerable garden clubs who ran the Spring Tours and staged the Historic Rosalie Pageant for the tourists who appeared mostly in March and April in the midst of a thousand pink, purple, and red azalea blooms.

It was Wendy's observation that Carly Ogle was almost never without a cocktail of some sort in her hand in most social situations. Probably because she had to live in the same house with her husband, Brent, and his rude, overbearing personality that offended nearly everyone who had to deal with him. Otherwise, she was the epitome of a modern, chic woman. Given to designer clothes that always flattered her figure—her height always doing them justice—she had never been seen around Rosalie without just the right touch of makeup, an impeccable coiffure, and an ingratiating smile.

Wendy had thought to herself more than once that she hoped to be that "put together"—minus the cocktail crutch—when she reached the shank of middle age, but she was a good fifteen or twenty years away from that.

Wendy watched from afar with a combination of admiration and awe as the swarthy Carlos began his polished ritual of muddling the mint and lemon with his heavy but elegant Carrara marble pestle, then adding that fragrant mixture to simple syrup, good bourbon, and crushed ice in a blender to create the incredibly smooth but seductive julep that had brought him such fame in Rosalie. *Seductive* was the proper word—because drinking one seemed harmless enough, often leading to a second and sometimes even a third. That was when the bourbon became its own butler, standing up tall in the doorway and announcing itself loudly. If it could actually be heard, it would surely have said something like, "Time to put away those car keys and take a long nap."

At any rate, Carly was soon settled in at the bridge table, sipping her julep and sighing at the ceiling as if giving thanks, while Wendy eventually made eye contact, lending her support by waving playfully. They would soon be all set for the first hand once Deedah and her son were in place.

At ten after three, Hollis Hornesby made his grand entrance. Some might even have described it as *dramatic*, as in Shakespearean, as in having his own follow spot in an off-Broadway production.

"Here I am at last in this too, too solid flesh," he announced to Wendy, while not bothering to look her straight in the face. He seemed to be playing to some phantom balcony off in a corner of the room where Juliet was delicately waving her handkerchief.

In fact, Hollis was anything but too, too solid. No one had ever seen him eat anything in public, and he had always been notoriously underweight. "I couldn't do anything with this long, mousy brown hair of mine today, so I put it up in a ponytail. I assume there'll be no dress code with this group. I'm definitely not up for a Joan Rivers–type assessment."

Wendy laughed appreciatively. Hollis had that effect on most people—Brent Ogle being the most notable exception. Hollis's flamboyant gesturing and posing were perfect accompaniments to his artistic temperament, his speech always leaning toward hyperbole. Furthermore, he dressed as if he had just been spit out of a time warp grounded firmly in the turbulent late sixties. He wore a psychedelic T-shirt with a pair of ripped jeans and sported sandals on his feet. All that was missing was a hand-lettered protest sign with a peace symbol scrawled on it for good measure.

Since his return to Rosalie, Hollis had been somewhat disgruntled about life in general, but Deedah had stepped in and footed the bill for a new art gallery on Locust Street. Not to mention giving him his old room back in his childhood home. At least he had a second chance at selling his art—a collection of oils and acrylics that consisted mostly of people hanging out under lampposts or hanging over lacework balconies throwing Mardi Gras beads and doubloons to the fevered crowd below. His was a somewhat one-note talent, and that had not served him well so far in his career.

"You're just fine, Hollis," Wendy told him. "Why don't you go on over to the table and talk to Carly Ogle while I round up your mother? You need to get her to lighten up with one of your patented anecdotes. She was beating herself up way too much because she was just a few minutes late. You and her mint julep are bound to do the trick and bring her around for some expert bidding."

"I'm sure I'll be up to the challenge." Then Hollis pointed to the office wing. "Is Mother holed up in there again with her number crunching? She never takes even a nanosecond off from her work. Why she won't hire a secretary is beyond

me. She says it's because she wants to control everything herself. I keep telling her that if she continues on her current
path, she will go to an early grave just like Father did. Then
it will be me all alone in the universe. Lost in the stars, as the
song says. Was it Frank Sinatra whose version I remember and
admire so much? Anyway, I'm nowhere near ready for that."

"I'm afraid it takes the kind of effort your mother is putting in to run the RCC," Wendy said, smiling at Hollis's last
couple of comments. "Your mother shared a lot of the details
with me while we were putting the Bridge Bunch together.
But I wouldn't be concerned about her health if I were you.
She's a very robust woman."

"That's certainly one way of putting it," Hollis said,
smirking. Then he turned on his heels and sped off, while
waving at Carly Ogle in the distance as if she were his long-
lost playmate.

Wendy was about to head over to Deedah's office when
the director, herself, suddenly appeared in the doorway to the
office wing. "Everyone here, Wendy?"

"All accounted for. We are ready to play."

"Even Hollis? He's always late for everything. I seriously
considering renaming him 'Dawdle' by the time he was in his
teens."

"Even Hollis," Wendy said, somewhat amused.

"Then let's deal the cards."

"Did you want one of Carlos's cocktails before we start?"

Deedah waved her off vigorously. "Not yet. Let's see how
the cards go first. I may be driven to drink if I have an afternoon of passing on every hand I'm dealt."

"Maybe the cards will take turns being good to us."

As the two women moved together to the bridge table,
Wendy marveled once again at the foursome who had formed
the new bridge club. How different they all were—particularly
the women. Where Carly was constantly drowning her sor-

rows, Deedah was the quintessential "take charge" personality. A retired accountant who had put her skills to good use after her husband's death, she was eminently qualified to run the RCC, making quick decisions and apologizing to no one.

Unlike Carly, however, she disdained the latest fashions, preferring voluminous caftans that had the virtue of covering all of her significant figure flaws. Decidedly matronly in appearance, she usually just pulled her graying hair back into a knot or French twist and left it at that. Nonetheless, hers was a pleasant-enough round face that was far from off-putting. Wendy wasn't quite sure how the four of them would get along as bridge players, but she was certain their time together would be anything but dull.

Finally, it was time for the Bridge Bunch to get things started, and it was Wendy who did the honors after everyone was seated. "Well, here we are," she began, smiling at the look of anticipation on their faces, "and I trust we will become the only game in town after a little time has passed. We're only four right now, but we can always hope that we will grow to four or five tables with two dozen regulars. Maybe we can eventually hold our very own championship that will mean something."

"That would be lovely," Deedah chimed in, and the others nodded approvingly.

"Before we begin," Wendy continued, "I'd like to offer a helpful pointer. I thought it would be fun for one of us to take turns explaining one particular element of bridge that's not used as much as it could be. I'll be the one this first time, and we'll go around the table as the weeks pass."

She paused and then drew their attention to a hand she had already arranged for herself, separating it by suits and displaying it in the center of the table. "If you need to get up and stand behind me while I discuss this, be my guest."

The other three did exactly as she suggested, and then

Wendy began explaining. "Today's pointer is the preemptive bid. Take your time to look it over."

There were, in order:

7 6 4 of spades
K Q J 10 9 6 2 of hearts
9 of diamonds
J 4 of clubs

After a short period of time had passed, Wendy resumed her presentation. "As you all can see, this hand does not have very much in the way of high card points—just seven, counting the four face cards. It does not have the thirteen or fourteen points normally required for an opening bid. But what it does have is length in hearts—seven of them, in fact. This is the perfect hand for a preemptive bid."

The others agreed by nodding their heads or making soft noises that showed they understood.

"Although it's possible that the heart suit might become the trump suit, depending upon what your partner has in the way of support, the primary purpose of a preemptive bid is to give the opponents trouble, to disrupt their communication. You *preempt* by opening at a high level. Thus, if they should get the contract, they will probably be at a much higher level than they would prefer to be. So, you would bid three hearts here, and your partner knows you do not have strength, you have length. The preemptive bid is a defensive bid, but you take the offensive even though you are in a weak position with point count traditionally."

Wendy allowed a few more moments to pass and then said, "Any questions on the preemptive bid?"

It was Hollis who spoke up, applauding her softly a few times. "You did that beautifully, Wendy. I've always understood about preempting, but I must confess, I'm always nervous about actually using it. I'm afraid I'll actually get caught playing the hand and messing up. You know, going down in flames."

"Probably not, though," Wendy said. "At the very least, you will likely rob your opponents of a legit contract they could have had if you hadn't thrown them off the track and gotten them out of their comfort zone." Wendy then asked for further questions, but as there were none, the foursome again took their places around the table, and the Bridge Bunch began their very first deal.

The expected deluge that Carly had described upon her arrival began just as Brent Ogle, Tip Jarvis, and Connor James were finishing up the RCC's ninth hole sometime after the bridge game had started. An explosion of thunder and a spidery bolt of lightning against the frowning black sky had them stuffing their clubs into their bags quickly and jumping into their golf carts as if their pants were on fire. Seconds later, sheets of heavy rain drenched the course, but the men did not have far to go to reach the clubhouse. The trio had been well aware of the forecast, yet had decided to see if they could get in a round anyway.

For the first time ever in their years of casually playing together, the much more athletic Brent had finished behind the others by three strokes—even if they hadn't managed the full eighteen. Incredibly, he had double-bogeyed the eighth hole and then followed that with another bogey on the ninth. Until this afternoon, he had never been bested by either of the other men by even a stroke at the end of nine or eighteen, even if they were all thoroughly middle-aged. Tip and Jarvis had whooped and hollered over their long-awaited triumph at the hole and on the way back in their carts. They were like giddy little boys in bumper cars. If they could have rammed Brent, they would have. Tip even raised his fist in the air, and Brent reacted to the gesture with a pronounced scowl plastered across his angular features. If he could have instantly grown a mustache and twirled it, he would have.

"You guys both know the score wouldn't have held up if we'd gotten to play the back nine. I just had that crazy slump there at the end," Brent insisted as they entered the back door of the clubhouse off the wraparound deck and headed down the long hallway toward the locker room, lugging their clubs. Their intention was to put their clubs away, do a quick toweling off of arms and faces, and then avail themselves of Carlos's services in the great room. The term *designated driver* was simply not in their vocabulary, yet they had somehow managed to avoid traffic tickets and car wrecks in all their outings together. The gods of the golf course were evidently looking after them.

Brent decided not to drop the subject of his milestone loss, however. "I mean it. You fellas act like you won the US Open or something. Get over yourselves."

"Hey, we'll take what we can get," Tip said as an afterthought as they all sat down on the changing benches with their towels. He meant the reply as a joke, but Brent's frown indicated that he was clearly not taking it in that spirit.

They were perhaps Rosalie's most unlikely trio of recreational friends. Not because they did not enjoy their cold dranks, as they preferred to call them, at the bar after golfing; and not because they never failed to swap "dumb blonde" and other juvenile sexist jokes in the locker room. It was anyone's guess as to why undressing and showering within shouting distance of each other brought out this macho trait in them. Could they all really be that insecure?

No, the puzzler was that Brent—who still had a full head of dark hair and was enjoying an incredibly successful career as a personal injury lawyer—was a graduate of Rosalie High

School, while Tip, now a portly dentist with an old-fashioned, graying crew cut, and Connor, a balding pediatrician with a habit of slapping his friends on the back too heartily—had both graduated from St. Mark's Academy, an Episcopal private school that attracted wealthier Rosalieans to its corridors.

The rivalry on the football field between the RHS Devils and the St. Mark's Saints was as fierce and loaded as the biblical implications of their nicknames and mascots. All three men had played the game for their respective schools, but Brent had been RHS's most accomplished quarterback ever, winning a scholarship to LSU for his dazzling athleticism. Tip and Connor had never been better than second string for St. Mark's and had spent most of their time playing in mop-up situations after games had gotten out of hand.

Over the years, there had been many showdowns when an invitation to the state play-offs was at stake. Victories against the other team were rubbed in, and losses were taken with bitter resignation and resentment. It was public school versus private—the less privileged versus the snobs—perhaps a concept officially left unspoken but branded upon the brains of everyone following the games.

The most controversial of all the contests between the two schools was the one that had become known as The Four-Second Game, which had taken place quite a few decades earlier. St. Mark's had led for most of the game, and the score was 16–10, St. Mark's, with four seconds left. At the time, it had been nine years since St. Mark's had beaten its public school rival, but it appeared that a breakthrough was at last at hand. Brent had thrown a pass into the St. Mark's end zone for what would have been a tying touchdown for RHS, but the ball was batted down expertly by a Saints defender.

Game over. Brent and company had finally tasted defeat in the series for the first time in a good while. Along with

Saints fans in the bleachers, Tip and Connor had both jumped up and cheered wildly from their vantage point on the bench.

But as it turned out, the game was not quite over. Saints fans and players looked up at the scoreboard clock, which somehow had one second left on it. But the pass play surely had taken at least four seconds. Not according to the clock, however, which was the assignment of the clock operator who sat in the press box. When Brent got off one last play in that final second and scored a touchdown when his receiver grazed the very edge of the left pylon, then won the game 17–16 when the extra point was kicked with time expired, Saints fans cried foul, insisting that the clock operator had kept the clock from running out by putting his thumb on it and giving RHS and Brent that one extra second to pull the victory out of the fire.

"Sour grapes," was the rallying cry of all RHS fans, including Brent, himself. "Get over it. You lost again. That makes ten in a row." For his heroics, Brent earned the nickname of "The Baddest Devil of Them All."

As a result of that tenth consecutive loss, St. Mark's longtime coach, P. J. Doughty, was fired for his inability to defeat his school's archrival, leaving Rosalie in disgrace. It was likely for the best and also a relief, as he and his wife and daughter had been taunted mercilessly for years by their own fans for Coach Doughty's lack of success against RHS. The sobering fact of life in the Deep South then as now was that football at whatever level enjoyed the status of a religion and its worship was taken as seriously as a heart attack. There had even been fans at the collegiate level who had been shot and killed over what had taken place on the football field. Imagine that. Taking a human life because of what a teenage kid had done with a pigskin.

In the present moment, Brent had decided not to let go

of his unexpected defeat at the hands of his inferior golfing buddies. As an athlete and a lawyer he had rarely lost, and he detested the feeling now as it gripped and squeezed him like a great boa constrictor. It was making it difficult for him to catch his breath. He quickly devised a strategy, preempting Connor by rising from the bench and slapping him on the back first. Then he repeated the gesture with Tip.

"Let's just forget about today out there and have a cold drank or two or three, why don't we?" he told them both.

"Sounds good to me," Tip said, while Connor nodded and returned Brent's backslap.

Once they were all dried off and settled in at the table nearest the bar, Brent started barking in his customary fashion at Carlos Galbis. "Hey, Chico, stop posing over there and come take our coldo dranko orders. You're not there for show, you know."

Under his breath and out of the side of his mouth, Tip said, "Why don't you let up on him this once, Brent? He does a good job."

Brent's tone was stoic, and he made no effort to keep his voice low. "Hey, if he can't take a joke, it's not my fault."

"I don't think he appreciates you calling him Chico and teasing him about needing a green card all the time," Tip continued, almost in a whisper. "You know his family's been here for a long time."

Brent was laughing now, and there was a cruel edge to it. "I don't always call him Chico. Sometimes, I call him Pablo. I'll make a point to do it, just for you."

Carlos moved to their table quickly, pretending not to hear their conversation, and said as professionally as possible, "What would all of you gentlemen like to drink this afternoon?"

"I want bourbon on the rocks, but easy on the rocks,"

Brent said. "And keep 'em comin'. Keep your eyes peeled over here. When I snappo my fingers, you'll know I'm ready for another one, Pablo."

Carlos took a calming breath and nodded eagerly. "Yes, sir."

Tip screwed his mouth up and ordered a mint julep, while Connor opted for a beer.

Craning his neck as they waited for their drinks, Brent said, "I see my wife's busy playing bridge across the room with Her Highness Deedah and that sissy son of hers. Oh, and that reporter from the *Citizen*, Bax Winchester's daughter. She's a looker with that strawberry-blond hair of hers."

Tip squinted. "What do you have against Hollis Hornesby all the time? He hasn't done anything to you."

"You mean to tell me that since he started coming out here recently you don't feel the least bit uncomfortable when he comes into the locker room?" Brent said, narrowing his dark-brown eyes. "He doesn't even play golf or tennis. I think he comes in to get an eyeful."

"He comes in to use the bathroom after swimming a ton of laps in the pool," Tip said. "Do you want him to do what all the little kids do right there in the water? Hey, we all know they do because we all did it growing up."

Brent's left eye twitched a couple of times, and he looked bored. "Whatever. Deedah Hornesby is turning the RCC into a ladies' club with all these card games and whatnot. Carly's all excited about getting more of her garden club friends out here to dress up and gossip. She was like a canary out of its cage this morning, flying all over the place getting ready. And then there's that female golf pro Deedah hired who refuses to use the ladies' tee—that Missy Stone."

"It's Mitzy," Tip reminded him.

"Missy, Mitzy, po-tay-to, po-tah-to. Anyway, what's she doin' with a man's job? I warned all a' you that this kinda thing would happen if Deedah got to run the show. This place has hit rock bottom." Brent made a face in the direction of the bar. "Yo, what's the holduppo over there?"

"Coming right up, Mr. Ogle," Carlos said, quickly raising his hand. "It takes a little more time with the julep order."

When the drinks finally arrived, Brent chugged his bourbon while the others looked on in disbelief. "Another one. And make it snappy," Brent said to Carlos, who hurried off to the bar once again.

"That was quick," Tip said, after taking a sip of his julep. It was always a drink to savor. "What's the hurry?"

"I feel like getting drunk this afternoon, fellas," Brent said. "You're both welcome to join me."

Both Tip and Connor continued their sipping and said nothing, however.

It was after Brent had made short work of his third drink and the others were well into their second a good forty minutes later that he went into action. "In case you fellas have forgotten . . . this is the thirtieth anniversary of The Four-Second Game."

Connor put down his beer and groaned. "No, I didn't realize it. But not that again."

"Yes . . . that again," Brent told him, sounding quite boozy. "There's something you guys should know, that . . . uh . . . The Baddest Devil of Them All has . . . uh, well . . . I've been keeping it a secret from you since . . . forever."

Connor didn't even pretend to be interested and exchanged shrugs with Tip. It had been many years since Brent had brought up the subject to them. If he had kept at it constantly, they would likely have dropped him altogether. "I suppose you're gonna tell us whether we want to hear it or not," Connor said.

"You got it, Connor. . . . Since you and Tip . . . you think you're such big shots for beating me today . . . this is the perfect time to get this, you know, off my chest," Brent continued. "You'll never look at that game . . . uh . . . the same way again. What I'm gonna tell you will add ten strokes to your golf game and take ten years off your life."

"Go ahead and tell us, then," Tip said, making a grim slash of his mouth, while Connor took a deep breath and braced himself. Something was warning them both that what would follow was going to be a trial by fire.

CHAPTER 2

Over at the bridge table, Wendy and her partner, Hollis, had just taken the first rubber after making game in spades. It had taken an hour and a half to accomplish that feat. They were having spectacular luck, and everything they had tried had worked from cross-trumping to finesses and even to the preemptive bid that Wendy had discussed earlier. Carly and Deedah had managed one paltry leg—a one club bid they had barely made—but that had been cut off by their opponents. Wendy could see that Deedah, particularly, was becoming more and more frustrated with every deal. This was not how Wendy had envisioned their maiden voyage as a club. It was never fun to play bridge when the same partnership got all the points all afternoon. It was always more fun if the deck contained "equal opportunity" cards.

"Well, Wendy," Deedah said, "looks like I might have to go visit Carlos after all. If this is the kind of fortune I'm going to have all afternoon, I might as well get a buzz on. You all very cleverly robbed us of our only chance at a game with that preemptive bid of yours. So, I think I'm in a very bloody Bloody Mary sorta mood. That means two jiggers of vodka, of course."

"I don't blame you with the cards we've been getting. So I think I need another julep," Carly added, pointing to her glass—empty except for the flecks of mint that were sticking to the sides of her tumbler. "Would anyone be interested in taking our drink orders over to the bar, pretty please?"

"I will," a female voice chimed in from just behind her.

It belonged to Mitzy Stone, who had been kibitzing the bridge table after quietly approaching from her office in the pro shop off the front hallway. It was right next to Deedah's in the same wing connected to the great room.

"I thought I'd check up on all you guys and see how it was going," Mitzy continued, "and it looks like my timing is perfect. I don't mind playing barmaid one bit. So, who all wants what?"

Wendy raised her hand and said, "I believe I'll take another glass of wine. I'm having white Zinfandel."

Mitzy snapped her fingers. "Got it." Then she pointed to Hollis. "And you, sir?"

"A mimosa, I think," he told her after a brief pause. "I need the vitamin C, so tell Carlos to throw in a couple of lime slices if he has them. He usually does that for me."

Mitzy looked down and counted the drinks on her fingers. "So, that's another julep, a stiff Bloody Mary, another white Zinfandel, and a mimosa with extra lime, right?"

Everyone nodded, and Mitzy started to head over to the bar; but at the last second, she turned around. "I'm just curious. What is this preemptive bid y'all were talking about? Sounds intriguing."

Wendy spoke up and quickly explained the requirements for such a bid.

"Bridge is a more devious game than I thought," Mitzy said.

Wendy smiled politely and said, "More cerebral than devious, I'd say."

Mitzy nodded and then headed toward the bar again, but

she had only gotten halfway there when Tip Jarvis shot up from his chair at his table and grabbed Brent Ogle by the collar of his blue polo shirt while uttering profanities. Connor James also leapt up and appeared to be trying to enter the fray but was pushed away when Brent freed himself from Tip's intense stranglehold.

More snatches of profanity began filling the air, and Tip actually landed a glancing blow to Brent's cheek, but it didn't appear to break his skin. Then Brent managed to push Tip to the floor. Mitzy hurried over in an attempt to try to put an end to the face-off. She was every bit as tall as any of them and in much better physical condition than even Brent Ogle was. When other golfers had observed her opening drive from the men's tee at a distance, she had often been mistaken for a male golfer with her short dark hair and colorful plaid pants that she always wore. Yet up close, there was a softness to her features and her voice that clearly indicated she was a woman; and though she did not lack confidence, she made no attempt to lord it over anyone—male or female. She considered that it was her job to be a good golf pro to everyone.

"Stop this, you two!" Mitzy shouted, devoting all her energy to restraining them both as Tip got to his feet and tried to lunge at Brent again.

When she eventually succeeded, Brent glared at her with an intensity that was nothing short of murderous. "This is none of your bid'ness, Missy."

"That's *Mitzy* to you," she told him. "We don't need this kind of childish conduct here."

Brent briefly maintained his hostile posing and then plopped into his chair. "Yeah, right. Who are you supposed to be now, our mother? Gonna put us in time-out?"

Tip stepped away from the confrontation, exhaled noisily, and said, "Come on, Connor. Let's get outta here. He's not gonna sober up anytime soon."

Brent was obviously continuing to feel the effects more than ever of all the bourbon he had guzzled. "You mean, you guys . . . you don't wanna stay here and get roarin', screamin' drunk with me?"

"Nope," Tip said. "I think we've heard just about enough from you this afternoon."

Brent began laughing and pointing in Tip's general direction. "I guess you can't take the truth, huh?"

"I thought we'd called a truce years ago about all that high school stuff," Tip said. "But evidently not. He's all yours, Miz Stone. And thanks for the help. I was ready to wring his neck."

"And if Tip hadn't pulled it off, I would've tried," Connor added.

"Oh, yeah?" Brent told them, sounding like the proverbial bully on the playground. "I would've liked to see either one of you make that happen. Big talk."

Tip got in the last word under his breath. "I knew coming out here to play with this bad weather forecast was a lousy idea." Then he and Connor huffed off toward the men's locker-room hallway, looking back over their shoulders and shaking their heads.

By then, the altercation had broken up the bridge game across the room, causing Wendy and the others to join Mitzy and surround Brent's table. He eyed the four players contemptuously after yelling at Carlos for another drink.

"What was that all about?" Wendy said to no one in particular.

"Let me handle this," Carly said to her friends, moving to stand closer to her husband. "Brent, people have had about enough of your boorish behavior."

He laughed at her with a look of surprise. "*Boorish?* Now there's a word you . . . don't hear every day. What—are you carryin' a dictionary around in your purse now?"

Carly quickly turned to Carlos and made a throat-slashing gesture. "Cut him off, please, Mr. Galbis. He's had more than enough."

Brent continued his contemptuous tone. "So . . . now *you're* my mother? First . . . Missy Stone over there and now . . . well, who lit a fire under you?"

"Ignore him, Carlos," Carly added.

"Chico, you better keeppo 'em comin' . . . if you know what's good for you," Brent cried out, making a fist.

Carly shook her head again at Carlos, mouthed the word, *No,* and then began lecturing her husband. "You embarrass me constantly everywhere we go. If you don't get your way in everything, you act like a spoiled child. I'm at the end of my rope with you. I've held my tongue long enough. This has got to come to an end, as God is my witness."

"Whoa, what's that s'pose to mean? You couldn't stand on your own two feet . . . without me," he said, shrugging his shoulders. "You're used to all that . . . consumption, you know. The kind with credit cards . . . and I know you wouldn't want me to cancel 'em."

"Never mind that. Why did you and Tip and Connor get into it? Too much to drink, I guess," she continued. "They're about the only two people left in Rosalie who can put up with you, and that's the God's honest truth."

Brent tentatively touched his cheek where Tip had grazed him with his knuckles and examined his fingers. There was no blood, and Brent looked slightly disappointed. Macho men liked to broadcast the fact that they could survive any injury. Then he wriggled around in his seat for a moment and gave his wife a wicked smirk. "Hey, they started it."

"Good heavens, you sound like you're five years old. What did *they* do?"

His smirk turned into a sneer. "They beat me on the front nine . . . and they were . . . they were actin' like they'd actually done something. They're such losers. They're nothing but a couple a' jock sniffers."

Everyone looked puzzled, and Carly said, "What's that?"

Brent's laugh quickly morphed into a drunken cackle. "It's . . . it's men who didn't make it as athletes . . . so they hang around with other men who did . . . hoping that it'll rub off on 'em. Kind of a macho thing, you know. I figured that out about 'em a long time ago. So I went along with it because I got a kick out of it."

"That ego of yours is as wide as the Mississippi River," Carly said, giving him a look of disgust.

Wendy could hardly believe her ears and eyes at Carly's sudden transformation. She had never seen her self-effacing friend so strong and determined, so she decided to try to lend her a hand.

"Maybe some fresh coffee would help, Carly?" she said. "Carlos could brew some for us."

Brent turned on her immediately. "Who asked you? Are you a registered nurse or somethin'?"

Then Deedah got in on the act. "Mr. Ogle, I'm well aware that you went out of your way to oppose my directorship, but now that I'm running things, I'm going to have to insist that you conduct yourself properly when you come to the club. It doesn't belong exclusively to you."

"It ought to," he told her, turning up his nose. "I've forked over enough money all these years to keep it in the black. All a' you . . . seem to forget that. Hell . . . I've been successful at everything I've done . . . from football to lawyering. You can't be a wimp like your Little Miss Hollis here, Miz La Deedah, and get anywhere in life, you know." He corrected his slumping posture and cleared his throat, trying to enunciate a bit better. "Anyway, I don't have to keep contributing, ya know. Not if this is the way it's gonna be. I need some respect around here."

Hollis bristled at the insult directed his way. "Don't threaten Mother like that, and I am not a *Miss*."

"And you'll do what about it, Nancy?" Brent added.

"Never mind these threats you're making," Carly said. "So Tip and Connor beat you on the front nine. Was there more to this playground fight?"

Brent continued his cackling. "You asked for it. I told 'em that Daddy had paid Claude Ingalls, the clock operator of The Four-Second Game . . . and all the other officials . . . to do anything they could to make sure that RHS won the game. I told them that Claude really did put his thumb on the clock or whatever . . . to keep it from running out. I told 'em RHS cheated to win the game . . . thanks to my dear old dad, who was loaded as y'all well know. I told 'em . . . I said there were coaches in the stands from both LSU and Ole Miss that night . . . and a football scholarship was on the line for me. Hey, and as everybody knows . . . I got that scholarship. Money well spent. All due to a stolen extra second."

Carly exchanged flabbergasted looks with the others and said, "You told me you were going to take that bribery story to your grave, Brent David Ogle, and you swore me to secrecy."

"Looks like I changed my mind, doesn't it?" He surveyed the gathering around him and rolled his eyes. "Because now, all of you know. Hey, why shouldn't I have a little fun at everybody's expense now and then? Ah, the secrets to my success."

"Are you proud of yourself for causing all this trouble?" Carly said, bearing down upon him.

He ignored her comment and waved her off. "Proud, schmoud. I have decided that I need to . . . I'm gonna jump in the hot tub out on the back deck for a while and relax. Listen, all you losers—that is the deal . . . so all y'all can go back to your silly women's card game . . . and, you, Missy, can go back to pretending you're a man." He pointed in Carlos's direction once again. "And, hey, I'll want you to bring me another bourbon out there on the decko, Chico. If you don't, I'll have your jobbo pronto . . . you understand me?"

"You've had enough," Deedah insisted, while Carly nodded vigorously.

Brent managed to get to his feet, even if he had to hold on to his chair during and afterward. "Let me put it to you straight then. I know for a fact that you need my money . . . Miz Deedah Director. I'll cut you off cold turkey if that wetback over there doesn't do what I just told him to."

Deedah threw her hands up in the air. "I give up. Ladies and Hollis, let's all go into my office and talk this over. We can't go on like this another minute."

"Yeah . . . that's right . . . you do that," Brent said. Then he snapped his fingers at Carlos. "You in the penguin suit . . . another bourbon . . . out on the deck pronto. I mean it. *Vámanos.*"

And as everyone headed toward Deedah's office and Brent managed to make his way unsteadily toward the hot tub on the deck, Carlos busied himself making yet another drink for a man who had thoroughly disrupted everyone's afternoon and thrown the RCC into chaos once again.

The storm that had hit Rosalie and vicinity in the early afternoon had continued to wreak havoc intermittently, and the RCC did not escape its wrath. There was even a brief period during which opaque chunks of hail danced around on the greens, fairways, and front lawn as if they were living, sprightly creatures that had fallen to earth on a lark. It grew increasingly dark outside, what with daylight saving about to go off just around the corner; but the activity inside the clubhouse doggedly persisted as the minutes crept along.

Out on the covered deck, Brent was stewing in the swirling waters of the hot tub while Carlos dutifully served him the last drink he had ordered. As Carlos approached, he noticed that Brent's eyes were definitely half-lidded and his head was swaying back and forth slightly as if he were listening to a tune inside his head. The man remained certifiably drunk, still slurring his speech, and largely oblivious to his surroundings.

"Izza 'bout time," Brent said with a scowl as Carlos handed him the glass. "Where'n hell . . . you been?"

There followed a string of profanities that made Carlos wince, but he did not move from his spot. Instead, he gathered up his courage while carefully avoiding eye contact and said, "Will there be anything else, sir?"

"Just keep . . . you check in . . . umm, uh . . . check every five . . . no, ten minutes . . . if I need . . . uh . . . just do it. . . ."

Carlos said he would do what was asked of him and scurried off to avoid any further confrontation.

Meanwhile, Tip and Connor had checked their smartphones for the status of the violent storm cell stalled over Rosalie and decided to wait out the storm in the men's locker room. Tip retrieved a deck of Bicycle cards from his locker, and they began playing gin on one of the changing benches rather than venture out and risk hail damage, a car wreck, or worse.

In Deedah's office, the discussion about Brent Ogle had become quite animated, though still civil, and the five people seated around the room had divided informally into two camps. Deedah, Hollis, and even Carly were of the opinion that drastic action needed to be taken at once to keep Brent out of the RCC for good, if at all possible. They were all fed up with his inexcusable behavior and excesses, and Deedah was leading the charge without hesitation.

"I have allies on the board who'll see things our way.

They're the same ones who voted me in over Brent's objections," she said.

Surprisingly, Mitzy took a different approach. "Don't get me wrong. I'm fed up, too," she began. "But the reality is that we need his money to keep things running. You know that as well as I do, Miz Hornesby. I suggest we hold off on kicking him out until we're sure we truly have alternative ways in hand of keeping things running the way they should. The RCC doesn't operate on goodwill, you know."

Wendy thought carefully and agreed. "We can always let some of the others who've contributed in the past know about the current situation and go from there. That way we don't leave ourselves high and dry. I think Mitzy's point is well taken."

"I also think we're being way too emotional about this right now," Mitzy continued, though she had actually raised her own voice in the moment. "I suggest we reconvene when we've had time to think things through. We can e-mail, text, and talk to each other over the phone in the meantime."

That seemed to shut down the discussion, and after a prolonged silence Deedah said, "All right, then, let's get together sometime next week and revisit this here in my office. We can decide on a date and time later."

Everyone agreed, and then the five of them began focusing on their smartphones, displaying weather radar for Rosalie and vicinity on their screens.

"I'm not about to venture out in this mess right now," Deedah said, holding up her phone. "Everything's either red or purple, and it says a tornado even touched down in Woodville, thirty miles south. I think this clubhouse is sturdy enough to protect us in the meantime."

After a good ten minutes or so had passed, restlessness seemed to overtake the group. "I need a breath of air," Hollis said. "I don't care what it's like out there. I think I'll pop out under the portico for a while before I get the vapors and faint." He fanned himself dramatically and headed for the door.

"Sounds like a good idea," Carly said. "Wait up, and I'll go with you." And the two exited together with their phones in hand.

Mitzy echoed their anxious sentiments as well. "First I have to visit the ladies' room, and then I have some online ordering of supplies and filing to do. I've been putting it off long enough. So I think I'd better get started." And with that, she made her exit, too.

"Well, it's just the two of us for a while, sitting in my apparently stale office," Deedah said to Wendy with a chuckle. "I'm beginning to feel like I should get out the air freshener."

Wendy flashed a smile. "When your son and Carly get back, we should resume our bridge game. Everything's over there just the way we left it. It's the perfect way to pass the time until this terrible weather lets up."

"I can only hope the cards come my way after this long break," Deedah added. "Carly and I had that one tiny little contract, and then you and my son cut off our leg. But you and I are determined to make this bridge club thing work. Maybe this isn't the good start we expected, but we can't let the weather defeat us, now can we? There'll be another day when the sun is actually shining outside and even on the cards I get inside."

Wendy was about to answer when an earsplitting crack of thunder accompanied by a near-atomic flash of lightning produced the inevitable—the dreaded loss of power. The clubhouse was plunged into utter darkness, and smartphones instantly turned into flashlights throughout the building. Wendy glanced at her screen, and it prominently displayed: 6:13.

"I think we should stay right where we are until the lights come back on," Deedah said. "Meanwhile, I'll call Rosalie Power and Light, report this, and see if they can tell me what's going on. Of course, I'll probably get a busy signal."

"Ordinarily, I would agree about waiting," Wendy said. "Except that it could take a while and I need to use the ladies' room. Wine always does that to me. Not that this is the perfect time to go by any means—in the dark, of course. What an afternoon. It's hardly what I'd envisioned."

A few minutes later, Carly and the light from her phone entered the room, and she was hyperventilating. "What else can happen to us after all this?" she managed. "This is like a nightmare."

Deedah craned her neck and said, "Where's Hollis?"

"Still out there," Carly told her. "There's not much wind, so it's not raining in under the portico. He said he heard another one of those transformers popping off somewhere in the distance, and then he said he wanted to stay a little longer and soak up the dark ambience or some such phrase."

"That's my Hollis," Deedah said, unable to suppress her amusement. "There's no one on earth who talks like that but him."

Wendy took Carly by the arm gently. "Good timing. I was just headed to the ladies' room. We would have to give up our official female cards if we didn't go together. Isn't it a requirement—you know, two or more?"

Carly nudged her. "At least. I was just about to tell you that I wanted to go with you. And I might as well check on that drunken husband of mine while I'm at it. He's liable to fall asleep and drown himself or try to climb out of that tub and hit his head."

"Don't you think he'll stay where he is under the circumstances?" Wendy added.

Carly's sigh was plaintive. "You'd think so, wouldn't you?

If he doesn't get all the booze he wants, though, he'll probably get out and stagger around until he crashes into the bar."

"You're exaggerating, right?"

"Sweetie, you have no idea what he's resorted to over the years to get his way."

It took some time for the two women to reach the ladies' locker room, but when they finally did, Wendy was surprised that Carly wanted to peel off first instead of accompanying her farther, as women often do on such occasions. "I want to get checking on Brent out of the way. He doesn't deserve it, but it's just a reflex action on my part, I guess. The deck's not far away. I'll see you in a few minutes."

"Be careful, please," Wendy told her. "Are you sure you don't want to wait and go together?"

"I'm sure. You're not used to him. I am."

Those few minutes that Carly had mentioned seemed like an eternity to Wendy once she was inside the bathroom alone. She noted for not the first time that darkness definitely slowed time down. It was a matter of sensory deprivation, she supposed. But not being able to see things clearly created an alternate reality of sorts. There was no depth perception, no sense of up and down, right and left, to speak of. There was just darkness, except for the paltry glow of her smartphone; and even that added nothing more than a ghostly element to the setting. To say that there was something of a Halloween haunted house present in the ambience was an understatement. All that was lacking were the spooky sound effects and the screaming children.

The other thing Wendy noticed was that her hearing was being heightened greatly by the absence of any real illumination. Little from the eyes, much from the ears. Every little noise from afar that drifted her way seemed to take on a life of its own. There was occasional rumbling still going on outside from the storm. Then, there was an eerie quiet, broken by a brief shriek and a thud; then the sound of someone running in the hallway outside. Then nothing but silence.

Had someone stumbled and hurt themselves? She had warned Carly to be careful. Where was Carly right now? Was she in some sort of trouble? Was she the person who had shrieked?

Alarmed, Wendy finished up, quickly washing her hands at the sink, and was about to open the locker-room door when Carly beat her to the punch. She stood there in the doorframe, limply holding her smartphone. At any moment it looked like it might fall out of her hand onto the floor. The expression on her face was blank, her eyes widened in zombie-like fashion. But she said nothing.

Wendy took Carly's free hand and pulled her inside, closing the door behind her. "What's the matter? I heard all these strange noises. Did you fall down? I hope you didn't hurt yourself."

Carly managed to shake her head, speaking almost in a whisper. "It's Brent. I think he's dead out there. It's his eyes. They're not blinking. He won't answer me. You go and see. I'll wait here. I tried to rouse him. I moved his head from side to side. It's the look in his eyes. Go see for yourself."

"Are you crazy? I'm not leaving you alone, and I'm not going out there by myself, either. Come on, we'll go together."

Carly backed away from her slightly. "I don't know if I can do that. I think I might faint."

"Then you don't have to look. But you'll hang on to me while I check everything out. I need to keep an eye on you."

Wendy hooked her arm through Carly's, and the two of them walked slowly toward the end of the hallway, then through the door and out onto the covered deck. Brent's head was tilted back awkwardly, resting on the shelf of the acrylic hot tub, his eyes staring at the ceiling above, while the rest of his body remained submerged in the water, no longer swirling due to the power outage, but still giving off steam into the surrounding cooler air.

"Brent?" Wendy managed while holding on to Carly tightly and shining her smartphone down on his face. "Brent?" she repeated.

But there was still no answer, and even in the limited light available to her, Wendy could see the deep, ugly gash on the crown of his head. She loosened her grip on Carly, leaned down, and lightly put her fingers on Brent's warm neck, but there was no pulse. For an instant, it flashed into Wendy's head that she probably shouldn't have touched him; but without having to think any further, she contacted 911 on her phone to report the emergency. Then she texted both her father, Captain Bax, and her boyfriend, Ross Rierson, with the disturbing news.

Now there was nothing to do but wait.

CHAPTER 3

Power had been restored to the RCC by the time the Rosalie Police Department arrived upon the scene, though the weather continued to be uncooperative and delay their journey. First responders were also quick to confirm that Brent Ogle was indeed dead—the visible cause of death being blunt force trauma to the crown of the head. Something heavy had been wielded violently with ugly results. That something was easily retrieved when spotted at the bottom of the hot tub: it was the pestle used by Carlos Galbis in creating his julep and mojito specialties. There was no blood on it, however, as the soak in the hot tub had obviously acted as a dishwasher, cleaning it perfectly. Also found near the drain was the glass from which Brent had been downing the booze Carlos Galbis had been serving him all afternoon. It, too, was spotless, with no prints or DNA on it.

As processing of the entire clubhouse was continued in earnest by various members of the Rosalie Criminal Investigations Division, it was determined that Brent had also been dead less than an hour, according to his liver temp. No surprise there. The longtime, gregarious coroner, Tommy Cantwell, arrived soon after and agreed with blunt force trauma as the preliminary COD. Interestingly, he had barely survived the last election cycle when his opponent had pointed out some irregularities that the public was not privy to.

"But we'll have to send the body down to Merrill Higgins in Jackson for an autopsy, fellas," Tommy said to those surrounding him. "We obviously have some foul play here. This is one for the medical examiner."

Meanwhile, some of the officers began separating the various witnesses or suspects, seating them well away from each other on the various sofas and chairs around the great room.

There were eight people in all to consider: Deedah Hornesby; her son, Hollis; Carly Ogle; Tip Jarvis; Connor James; Carlos Galbis; Mitzy Stone; and even Wendy, herself, for the obvious reason that she was in the clubhouse at the time the murder had taken place. As the police would soon lament, the odd thing about it all was that none of those people— other than the actual murderer—could accurately be termed "witnesses," since the entire building had been plunged into darkness when the murder had been committed. The time of both the loss and restoration of power had already been confirmed helpfully by the utility company. Power lost—6:13 CDT. Power restored—6:44 CDT. Approximately one half hour of a lack of stage lighting, so to speak. The theatrical aspect of it all seemed like something out of a play, but the dead body was real enough, and the blood was no mixture of corn syrup and red dye conjured up by a prop crew.

Yet how reliable could what any of these eight people had seen—or thought they had seen—truly be, assuming they would be telling the truth to start with? That aspect aside, they all had to be classified as suspects, since it stood to reason that one of them was the likely murderer, unless some unknown person had managed to slip in from outside, do the deed, and then slip away unnoticed. No need to take on such paranoia at this early stage unless absolutely necessary, though.

The lead detective on duty was Ross Rierson, who had played the same role during the infamous Grand Slam Murders case the previous year, which his girlfriend, Wendy Winchester, herself, had helped the department solve. Thus, it was beyond awkward—even surreal—that Ross had to approach Wendy as if she were a viable suspect, even though he knew that she could not possibly turn out to be a person of interest. He already knew that she had gone to the RCC to play bridge that afternoon because she had texted him as a reminder that morning. The two always stayed in touch throughout the day with their smartphones.

Furthermore, Ross knew that, as the daughter of the highly respected Chief Bax Winchester, she was on the side of the angels. In fact, so angelic was she to him that he had proposed marriage to her last year, even though she had politely told him that she was not ready to walk down the aisle quite yet. They had continued to see each other, however, and she had assured him she needed time to become accustomed to her important new position at the *Citizen* and her new boss and editor, Lyndell Slover.

Just before Deedah Hornesby agreed to make her office available to Ross so that he could do his preliminary questioning of everyone in private, one at a time, he took Wendy aside and spoke to her discreetly.

"This is going to be a first—and last, I hope. Me questioning you this way, I mean," he said, giving her that disarming smile that had lulled many a suspect into a complacency that had eventually resulted in a confession. "You . . . and then Miz Ogle will be the first two, since you both discovered the body."

"I can hardly believe it myself," Wendy said out of the corner of her mouth. "It's like a throwback to some old film noir. You know, the lights go out for a while and then when they come back on, somebody's been murdered." She snapped her fingers smartly, but she was hardly smiling.

Ross managed a slight tilt of his head, showing off his shock of dirty-blond hair to great effect. "I can only hope this gets solved as easily as those old plots did."

Wendy caught his gaze intently, her tone one of resignation. "You're not gonna like hearing this, but I think just about everyone here—with the possible exception of me—hated the man's guts. And even I think I would have eventually gotten there had I spent much more time out here with him around. Whoever actually did it won't be a shock to me."

"Hold that thought," Ross said, lifting his index finger in the air. "I'll want to explore that further with you."

Ross wanted to get his interrogation of Carly Ogle out of the way as soon and as painlessly as possible. She still seemed to be in shock. Or was it the effect of the sedative she said Deedah Hornesby had given her to help calm her nerves? First, he lost no time in expressing his sympathy for her loss. She had then explained to him that Deedah and her son, Hollis, had insisted that she go home with them to spend the night and that they would be looking after her in her time of great distress.

"You have no idea how much I do appreciate that. My son, David, lives way away up in Wisconsin. It might take him a day or two to get down here for services," she concluded in somewhat mumbling fashion, working her fingers together into a nervous knot.

"If you could, Miz Ogle," Ross continued from behind Deedah's desk, "just give me the sequence of events as you remember them that led to the discovery of your husband's body. And try to speak up a bit more so my recorder gets everything. Thank you so much."

Nestled on Deedah's sofa across from him, Carly took her time, her words coming with great difficulty. "I'll . . . try." There was a long pause. "As near as I can recall . . . I . . . well, I . . ." She briefly put her hand over her mouth. "Maybe you should start with Wendy Winchester first."

Ross gave her his most sincere smile, not the exaggerated one he used to intimidate suspects. "She's up next, Miz Ogle. But I need you to tell me what happened as best you can. It will be vital to our investigation. You are the person most affected by this, and we want to see that justice is served."

Carly continued to sound ill at ease. "It's just that . . . it all seems like a blur to me now. I'm not sure I'll get everything right."

"Do your best, do your best. I assure you, I am on your side."

Finally, Carly put together a hurried sequence. "I went down the hallway after I left Wendy at the ladies' locker-room door. Then I went out onto the deck and found Brent like that. He was lifeless; he wouldn't answer me. I was in shock. The rest seems like a blur. I think I stood there, not believing what I was seeing. Then I headed back into the hallway, but I remember being frozen in place for a while, unable to move forward or backward. Then someone came in from the deck and tackled me, knocking me to the floor. They ran away, but I didn't see who it was." She paused for a breath and then slowed down somewhat. "And then . . . and then I went back inside the locker room and told Wendy to come look. And she did. And we both knew . . . he was dead. We just knew. But that gash on his head—I just couldn't get over it. I know I'm still in shock."

"And that was when Wendy called 9-1-1 and texted me?"

"Yes . . . I think so. She told me she was going to text you and her father."

Ross nodded sympathetically. "And she did. You said someone practically tackled you and knocked you over. From behind, or did they come directly at you?"

Carly looked him straight in the eye for the first time. "They were . . . coming at me directly from the end of the hallway. Maybe they'd been out on the deck all along hiding and I hadn't seen them; I don't know. I was looking down at the light from my smartphone when it happened. I guess we've all gotten used to wandering around, looking at those tiny screens. I wasn't paying attention, and . . . I certainly didn't expect to be knocked down. I remember being startled and screaming, but it wasn't loud or long. I wasn't hurt or anything like that."

"Do you remember what time it was when you looked down at your phone?"

"I'm not sure," Carly said. "Maybe 6:30. But I really can't be sure. I was in shock."

"And you didn't get a good look at whoever knocked you down at all? Even at a piece of clothing they were wearing?"

Carly squinted for a few seconds. "No, I didn't get a look at anything. It all happened so fast. Suddenly, I was on the floor, and by the time I got up, whoever it was had disappeared into the darkness down the hallway in the direction of the great room."

"Do you think it was a man or a woman?"

"I . . . really couldn't say. It was just a body that threw itself against me. I suppose it could have been either a man or a woman."

Ross was shaking his head. "That's where the power being off didn't do us any favors. I have my own little saying— *lots of people get away in the dark.*" Then he made a clucking noise and moved on. "What about the sound the shoes made when whoever it was ran off?" He gave her his most expectant gaze. "You see where I'm going with this, don't you? A woman's heels make a different sound than a man's golf shoe with cleats or sneakers and so forth."

"Yes, I see what you mean." Carly drew herself up in an attempt to recall. "The only thing I remember is that those shoes didn't make much of a sound. They sounded . . . well, soft."

Ross's tone became more animated. "As in sneakers, maybe?"

"No. Just as in . . . soft."

"You're going to think I'm a bit off here," Ross continued, keeping his tone lighthearted. "But I want to cover all the senses. What I mean is, when whoever it was tackled you, was there a unique odor of any kind? Perhaps a perfume or cologne you detected or even recognized?"

Here, Carly seemed confident. "Now that you mention it, there was no odor of any kind that I can recall." She put a finger to her temple and screwed up her mouth for a moment. "And all of us women playing bridge today were wearing different fragrances. So does that mean I was thrown to the floor by a man?"

"Possibly," Ross said as evenly as he could manage.

"I hope that makes things easier for you, Mr. Rierson."

He nodded quickly, but there was a sober aspect to it. "It might narrow things down a bit. But it's possible that whoever knocked you down wasn't the person who killed your husband. Perhaps you surprised them as much as they surprised you."

"I don't quite get it."

"What I mean is—suppose whoever it was had just discovered the body right after you did and wanted to get out of there as fast as possible. You just happened to be in their way."

Carly looked confused at first but then shrugged. "I guess I understand. Well, I'll leave figuring it all out up to you."

"Before we wrap this up, was there anything else you wanted to add to this interview?" Ross said.

"Yes, there was." Carly seemed to have acquired a second wind and spoke with certainty. Perhaps she was becoming more comfortable with the interview at last. "There was almost a fight between my husband and his golf partners, Tip Jarvis and Connor James. They'd all been drinking heavily after their golf game, and Brent revealed that my father-in-law had paid off all the officials to do whatever they could to make sure RHS won what became The Four-Second Game against St. Mark's. The clock operator, Claude Ingalls, was the one who made that happen when he kept his thumb on the clock at the end of the game."

Ross whistled sharply. "Wow! Everyone in Rosalie knows about that game. You're right—it is a legend in local sports. There were always rumors among the St. Mark's folks that something fishy happened that night, but the RHS fans just said it was all sour grapes and there was nothing to it."

"Brent bragged about it to me all the time, but I never thought he'd actually admit to it publicly. I guess Tip and Connor got under his skin this afternoon."

Ross thought for a moment and said, "Miz Ogle, let me applaud you on your composure. I know this was a shock to you."

Now Carly was leaning in as if they were old friends. "Mr. Rierson, my husband was not a very pleasant man to deal with. I ought to know, but anyone can tell you that. He started out popular enough with everyone here in Rosalie because of his athletic prowess at RHS and LSU. But as the years went by, he let his ego run wild, and he rubbed in a lot of his courtroom victories as if he were still playing football games. He loved playing with people's heads. I know he played with mine enough, and I have to tell you, it's taken its toll."

Ross shut off his recorder and stood up. "Thank you, Miz

Ogle. I think that's enough for now. If we need to question you further, we'll get in touch after we've checked out everyone's DNA and fingerprints. And once again, please know that I'm very sorry for your loss."

As Carly stood up and he walked her to the door, she turned and said to him, "Don't take this the wrong way, Mr. Rierson, but it wasn't so much a loss as it was a relief for me. I don't mind telling you that ours was not a happy marriage for a very, very long time. I didn't kill my husband, but I should have left him a long time ago."

Wendy was sitting across from Ross on Deedah's floral print sofa, waiting for him to start his interrogation. He had just fingerprinted her and collected her DNA. She noted that the creases on his forehead had come out to stay and he kept moving his lips as if trying to confirm something in his head.

"What is it?" she said finally. "You look like you're trying to memorize the Pledge of Allegiance. You've even got your hand on your chest. Did you realize that?"

He came to and pleasantly caught her gaze. "Do I?" He looked down and put his hand on the desk. "No, uh, I was trying to convince myself of a particular observation. I might as well let you in on it. Was it . . . or is it now your impression that Carly Ogle was and is not all that upset over her husband's death?"

Wendy considered for a moment and drew back slightly. "Is that what you really think? My impression is that she's just in shock. I mean, who wouldn't be, losing a spouse that particular way? The whole thing is so brutal." She paused and chuckled under her breath. "Who knows, though? Living with a man like Brent Ogle was probably brutal, too."

Ross nodded, but his expression indicated he did not necessarily agree with her. "What I'd like to do is try and match up your details of what happened there in the hallway and out on the deck with Miz Ogle's."

"You do understand that my perspective will be different from hers," she said. "At least part of the time. We were together there at the end, but we were in two different places for a while."

"Precisely the point," he said. "I want to see if there are any real discrepancies and go from there."

"Right. Who's the detective here?" They both enjoyed a brief chuckle, and then Wendy added, "But you might as well know that while I was waiting for you to finish up with Carly Ogle, I did text Lyndell Slover about what was going on out here. First thing Monday, she and I will be discussing making this my next big investigative assignment. After all, I've been right in the middle of it from the get-go, and I've already gotten lots of inside info on the RCC since Deedah and I formed the new bridge club. It should make for an interesting article. Something with *Murder* in the title might fit the bill, I was thinking."

"That'll be the headline in the Sunday paper. Old news by the time this feature of yours comes out. You'll have to find a different angle."

Wendy pretended to take offense. "I beg your pardon. Lyndell will rein me in if I go too far, I assure you. I've never enjoyed working with someone so much in my life." She displayed her crossed fingers. "Total symbiosis."

Ross's smile diminished slightly. "So you will be playing detective in a manner of speaking? Just like you did last year during The Grand Slam Murders?"

"I won't be getting in your way, of course, but I'll be happy to share any insights I can turn up as I interview certain people for the feature."

"You know what I think?" he began, leaning in and

managing a wink. "You're gonna end up being on the police force after all if you keep this up. Your daddy'll be so pleased. Bax mentions it to me every now and then that he thinks that's what you're really up to. You know, that you're skating around the edges of what he's done all his life. Like father, like daughter."

"Ha! I've got my dream job now, and I intend to keep it. Anyway, let's get on with this, shall we? You've got lots more people to interrogate."

"So I do." He turned on the recorder again with an expectant expression. "All right then. Give me your version of you and Carly discovering the body. Start wherever you like."

Wendy straightened her posture, cleared her throat, and began. "Well, the five of us were—"

"Wait. Who are 'the five of us'?" he interrupted. "I need the specific names, of course."

"Oh, yes. Myself, Deedah Hornesby, her son, Hollis, Mitzy Stone, and Carly all went into Deedah's office to discuss Brent Ogle's behavior and what to do about it for the good of the RCC."

"Miz Ogle went in, too?"

"Yes. I know for a fact that he had embarrassed her many times over here at the RCC. Brent Ogle spared no one."

"Where was Carlos?"

"He stayed at the bar. I don't think Deedah invited him to come along. Not sure why, because he was one of Brent Ogle's biggest targets. I guess because he had drinks to serve to Brent and she didn't want to make trouble for him."

"Understood. Did you get very far in your discussions?"

Wendy shook her head emphatically. "Somewhat. We began by rehashing the altercation that Brent had instigated, and there were two different opinions about the best way to proceed, and then the power went off. That changed everything. Smartphones were the only illumination any of us had after that. Even the streetlamps in the parking lot weren't working, and it was pitch-black outside. I remember that Deedah suggested we stay right where we were until the power came back on."

"And did everyone do that?"

Wendy took her time, shifting her eyes trying to remember what had happened before the outage and what had come after. "I forgot that Hollis and Carly said they needed some air after a while and headed off together for the portico. That was before the power went off. Mitzy said she needed to do some paperwork in her office next door, also before the power went off."

"How long do you think this 'after a while' was? Five, ten minutes?"

"Maybe closer to five? But as for me, I wasn't about to sit still in the dark a little later. I'd had some wine, and I had no way of knowing how long it would be until power was restored. So I intended to head off to the ladies' locker bathroom with my phone. Carly came back in not long after that, and I asked her to go with me."

"Do you remember the time?"

"It's all running together now," Wendy told him, looking exasperated with herself. "Maybe 6:21, 6:22? I keep seeing all kinds of numbers in my head now."

Ross was nodding and said, "So far, so good. Did you see anything or anyone on the way to the bathroom?"

"Actually, we didn't. But our eyes were locked on to our phones. Now that I think about it, we should have seen the light from Carlos's phone at the bar, but I don't remember it. If he'd been there, we would have spoken to him. We did run into him on the way back from discovering Brent's body, though. He said something about being out on the portico to talk to his wife."

Ross looked puzzled and stopped the recorder. "Well, it

seems the portico was quite popular tonight. Carlos and Hollis and Carly all out there at one time or another. Interesting." Then he turned the recorder back on and pointed to Wendy. "Let's pick up where we left off."

"Right, back to discovering the body. Carly and I didn't stay together once we got to the locker-room door. Carly said she wanted to check on Brent out on the deck. She said it a bit begrudgingly, if you want my interpretation. She complained about him every time I saw her. So I spent the next couple of minutes in one of the stalls, and I have to say it was kinda creepy."

"I'll bet it was."

"I heard all sorts of strange noises, mostly from the weather outside. But then, coming from inside, I heard a thudding sound, then a short little shriek—or maybe it was the other way around—and then the sound of someone running down the hallway. I was worried that Carly might have fallen and hurt herself. I finished up as fast as I could but met up with Carly in the doorway. She was looking like she'd seen the proverbial ghost and said she thought Brent was dead out in the hot tub. I pulled her inside to calm her down. Then, I took her by the hand, and we went out on the deck. I took one look at him and knew she was probably right about him being dead when I saw that gash." Wendy paused and bowed her head slightly. "Oh, and I did reach down and touch his neck with my fingers, hoping for a pulse. If my fingerprints show up, that's the reason."

"Everything you've said so far checks out with everything Carly told me," Ross said. "But I do want to ask you about the footsteps you heard. Did they have a distinctive sound? Loud or soft?"

Wendy was surprised by the question and cocked her head. "Now that you ask me that, I have to say that I couldn't give you a definitive answer. They just . . . sounded hurried."

"Like high heels, perhaps?"

"No. Not like that. Definitely not. I know the sound of heels."

"Okay. Anything else you'd like to add to the events of the afternoon?"

"Yes, quite a bit. Brent Ogle insulted practically everyone in the RCC great room today, except me. And I'm not even sure about that. He probably mumbled something about me under his breath while he was doing all that drinking over by the bar. His reputation for rudeness preceded him and was justly deserved. At the end of his testosterone display today, he threatened Deedah with the withdrawal of his funding of the RCC, and if you ask me, I think he was serious about it. I'm not sure they could run the place without his contributions. He wasn't getting his way like he used to when William Voss ran things for him. He bitterly resented Deedah becoming the director and treated her like a stranger off the street, he didn't like Mitzy Stone being hired as the golf pro, and he even complained to Deedah once to the effect that the RCC was becoming a hideout for sissies like her son and all her gossiping biddy friends. He was a man who never minced words. His mouth cut like a machete."

Ross's jaw dropped, and his eyes widened. "That's quite a mouthful in itself. I'm surprised someone didn't knock him off long before now."

"Offhand, I'd say he tempted fate once too often."

Ross checked his phone for the time and said, "Appears that way. Well, I think that's all I need from you right now, sweetie. Have Ronald Pike send Carlos Galbis in when you go out, will you?"

They met each other at the door and embraced, followed by Ross giving Wendy a peck on the cheek. "I'll be more than happy to," she said, looking back over her shoulder as she walked out.

★ ★ ★

A little over an hour later, Ross finally finished interrogating, fingerprinting, and collecting DNA from everyone. After that, he continued to sit at Deedah's desk and make a sketch of the interior of the RCC, placing an X where all eight people had said they were during the blackout period. Although his sketch was no blueprint masterpiece, it was clear to him that the case was not going to be easy to solve—barring something conclusive turned up by DNA or fingerprints. He knew Wendy had not committed the murder; and if Carly had not done so, either—despite her lack of emotion regarding her husband's death and remarks about her marriage—then someone else had to have been sneaking around at some point during the outage to get to Brent Ogle. He began reviewing in his head the highlights of the rest of his interrogations, playing back snippets of his recordings when needed.

Carlos Galbis, for instance, had presented a time quandary of significance. "I was having trouble getting a signal to call my wife from the bar," he had said at one point. "That sometimes happens because that part of the roof interferes. So, I was at the bar most of the time, but I also went outside for a little while to get a better signal under the portico. I probably need to get a newer phone."

Ross listened to the ensuing recorded sequence with great intensity. "And did you get a stronger signal?"

"Eventually. I told my wife everything that was happening," Carlos had said.

"Do you remember what time that was?"

"I remember saying some not so nice things to my phone when it just wouldn't cooperate with me at the bar as usual. I was able to get through once, and I actually heard my Elena saying hello. But then the call dropped. I want to say when I headed out to the portico, it was around six-twenty. But I didn't pay much attention to the time after that because I was so happy to get through to her to see if she was all right. I also didn't want her to worry about me being late. She always likes to know where I am."

It did not take long for Ross to conclude that Carlos would be brought in for further questioning. The murder weapon had surely been the pestle that Carlos routinely used to make his famous concoctions. Who would have had better access to it than he? Yet the revelation that he had left the bar for a decent period of time also opened up the possibility that someone else could have gotten to it and used it to off Brent Ogle. Unfortunately, the power outage would have enabled that to happen. Without that, it would not have been as easy.

Ross advanced his recorder to Deedah's interview.

She claimed she had remained in her office after the great room altercation until Wendy and Carly had arrived later to deliver the disturbing news about Brent; but her tone on the tape suddenly rose a decibel or two, and Ross recalled the sour face she had made at that point in the interview.

"Everyone was complaining about my office being stuffy, including my son. So I can't account for his whereabouts the whole time, or Carly's, or Mitzy's, or even Wendy's. They all abandoned me at some point to go elsewhere—porticos, offices, bathrooms, you name it. They were all scattered to the wind."

Then Ross played the sequence about the altercation near the bar. "Yes, it's true. After the brawl was over—if you want to call it that—Brent Ogle did threaten to withhold his financial contributions to the RCC," Deedah had said.

"Did you believe he would?" Ross had said next.

"So much so that I told everyone to convene in my office—this very one we're in right now—to come up with a plan of action. I was not about to let him hold the RCC hostage like that. No one puts a gun to my head like that. I wasn't going to sit idly by and let that happen."

"Yes, Miz Ogle and Wendy have already mentioned that to me. So you were plenty fed up with Brent Ogle, is that right?"

"Everyone was. He was the Devil, himself."

"Interesting choice of words."

"I'm a firm believer that when you end up playing the Devil on his own terms, you always lose. You have to be smart about it in just the right way. Brent Ogle was the sort of man that brought out the worst in people. There was an aura he had that was nothing short of destructive. So you have to come up with a strategy of your very own to win out."

Ross rewound and listened to Deedah's phrasing again: ". . . when you end up playing the Devil on his own terms, you always lose. . . ."

Ross paused the recorder. He couldn't seem to get those words out of his head. Exactly what strategy had Deedah been contemplating? Had it been emerging over a long period of time, or was it spontaneous and possibly executed during the blackout?

Next up, Ross listened again to his questioning of Hollis Hornesby. Particularly of interest was Hollis's admission that he had left his mother's office to get some air.

"It's because Mother doesn't have a window in here, as you can see," he was saying. "It really does get stuffy. I'm surprised you aren't yawning yet. If you ask me, I think it puts Mother to sleep half the time. That's why it takes her longer to do everything. I don't know why they didn't put at least one window in here. They bothered to put them everywhere else, like around the great room and next door in the pro shop. Who designed this place—a drunken monkey? But anyway, the time I spent under the portico revived me, as it did Miz Carly, since she was with me for a while. Then when we had that power outage, she went back in first."

"But you stayed?"

Hollis's voice suddenly had a nervous edge to it, even cracking at one point. "A little bit longer. I can't say how long. By the time I reached my mother's office, she told me that Wendy Winchester and Miz Ogle had gone to the little girls' room together. Mother also said that Miz Ogle would be checking up on that husband of hers. Why, I don't know. She'd just told him off in no uncertain terms, and he did everything to ignore her. I can't tell you how odious that man is . . . or rather, was."

"Care to go into detail?"

Hollis had struck one of his dramatic poses at that point, Ross recalled. "I'll cut to the chase, as you police types like to say. He enjoyed picking on me because he didn't like the fact that I was out of the closet. I didn't stare at him, but he would always stare at me when I went into the locker room to use the bathroom or change out of my swimming trunks. He went out of his way to make a big to-do out of my very existence. Like I had no right to be anywhere near him. Paranoia, thy name is . . . or was Brent Ogle."

Ross had exhaled noisily at that point and said, "Seems he went out of his way to find something not to like about everyone. By the way, was Carlos Galbis out on the portico with you and Miz Carly at any time?"

"Nope. Miz Carly and I were alone the whole time we were out there."

"Thank you very much for your time," Ross had said, ending the interview.

Next, Ross reviewed his talk with Tip Jarvis. Particularly the sequence where the altercation between himself and Brent Ogle had become physical.

"Why did you attack him, Mr. Jarvis?" Ross had asked.

And Tip had not answered immediately. Ross remembered that Tip had hung his head, looking somewhat embarrassed before finally speaking. "Because I just lost it, Mr.

Rierson. The three of us had been drinking, and Brent was so cocky about what he said his daddy had done. I just . . . I just wanted to strangle him for being such a pompous ass about it all."

"Or hit him over the head with a pestle?"

At that point, Tip had protested vehemently. "That never happened. Connor and I never left the locker room after the lights went out. We passed the time scrolling on our phones to keep our sanity, since we couldn't keep playing gin."

There was a pause in the tape, and then Ross said, "Did you and Mr. James hear any peculiar noises out in the hallway during the blackout?"

There was another pause. "Noises? Afraid not. Just the weather outside is all we heard."

Connor James's interview produced the same results largely. But Connor's reaction to Brent's revelation about paying off the officials to win the game was slightly different.

"I thought Brent might be telling the truth about the clock operator," Connor said. "Of course, he was really drunk. We all were to some extent. So I tried to pull Tip off when he went for Brent's neck. It was a knee-jerk reaction on my part, but I have to admit, I could understand why Tip was so upset. As for me, I kind of hold things in when I shouldn't. Sometimes, that backfires on me."

"And neither of you left the locker room during the blackout?"

"No. We resigned ourselves to sitting on the bench and scrolling on our phones. It was boring as hell."

To be sure, Ross found it somewhat puzzling that neither man claimed he had heard anything at all out in the hallway. No thuds, no shriek, no sound of someone running. But the men's locker room was farther away from the deck than the ladies' locker room was. And when Ross and his partner, the

burly Ronald Pike with the buzz cut, inspected the lockers after all the interrogating was over, they discovered that on the
one hand, the changing benches in both were deep inside near
the showers and well away from the door. The stalls, sinks,
and several mirrors off to the right, on the other hand, were
the first thing people saw when they walked in. It then stood
to reason that someone in a stall like Wendy was would have
heard more than the two men sitting on one of the changing
benches could have.

In Ross's final interrogation, Mitzy Stone had expressed
great consternation that the power outage had temporarily
deprived her of getting some long-overdue online inventory
ordering and also some filing done that she had been post-
poning.

"We're running out of golf tees for one thing, and I've got
to get a new supply in fast," she had added. "I take great pride
in my job. I did agree to participate in a discussion with the
others in this very office about Brent Ogle. But it was delay-
ing my getting to my real work. I really wanted to get the
discussion over and done with."

"And how did you pass the time when the power went
out? Did you leave the pro shop and your office?"

"No. I kept up with all the college football scores on my
ESPN app. As you well know, Saturday is huge during the fall
in the South. Everybody roots for one team or another. If you
don't, you're practically considered a pariah or an alien from
another planet."

At that point, Ross had abruptly changed the subject.

"What was your experience with Mr. Brent Ogle?"

Ross remembered that Mitzy had closed her eyes and
shaken her head. "Unpleasant. He made it clear to me that he
thought I had taken a job away from some man and his family
somewhere. I'd taken food off that man's table. There's always

that nebulous fellow out there who came first in everything for people like Brent Ogle. You know, the usual male chauvinist bull."

"And how did that make you feel?"

Here, Mitzy had laughed. It seemed strange and exaggerated upon playing it back. "I shook it off like the professional I am. If I allowed myself to let that kind of thinking bother me, it would affect my job performance, and that's the last thing I'd want. Don't think Brent Ogle is the first man who has resented me, by the way."

"I can imagine," Ross had said, noting the intensity of her tone.

"You just do what you have to do," Mitzy said. "Sometimes I wish men had to try as hard as we women do to succeed."

After taking a brief stretching break from all his winding and rewinding, Ross sat back down and referred to the notes he had made of the type of shoes everyone was wearing during their interviews, along with a few observations from his questioning:

Wendy—flats (she's so practical but still looks good)
Carly Ogle—heels (those really high ones—yikes!)
Carlos Galbis—men's dress shoes (to go with tux)
Hollis Hornesby—sandals (I don't like seeing toenails!)
Deedah Hornesby—heels (but lower than Carly Ogle's)
Tip Jarvis—sneakers (said he changed from golf shoes w/cleats)
Connor James—sneakers (changed from golf shoes also)
Mitzy Stone—sneakers (did not play golf because of weather)

As Ross reviewed his list, he immediately saw another major discrepancy. Both Wendy and Carly had claimed that the running footsteps had not sounded loud but muted—even "soft." Yet Carlos Galbis, his leading suspect at the moment, was wearing heavy black dress shoes during his interview. That particular hitch did not last long, however, as the obvious quickly occurred to Ross. It ran across the front of his brain like a ticker tape: *Shoes can be removed or changed entirely . . . also, people running in socks make much less noise . . . for that matter, people running barefoot make even less noise. . . .*

Ross shut down his thought process, stood up, and rubbed his eyes. Were the sounds that shoes made that important, after all? Perhaps Carly's claim that there was a lack of a fragrance in the air had more bearing on the case. At any rate, he was very tired of talking and listening and trying to make fine print out of raw chunks of information. Then, a text came through from Wendy to lift his spirits:

r u through yet?

He sat back down and replied, though his thumbs seemed as if they were operating in slow motion.

just about
wow! another murder of a mover and shaker
yep . . . headed home now
take care
u 2, hugs

CHAPTER 4

It wasn't so much that Wendy enjoyed having a woman as her editor and mentor at the *Citizen* as much as it was that the man who had hired her originally, Dalton Hemmings, had been a three-year trial by fire. The seventy-ish curmudgeon had kept her on a short leash, the one he particularly reserved for females under his command, whereas Lyndell Slover asked for her input at the very beginning of every assignment and took her contributions seriously. What was not to like? At last, her journalism degree from Mizzou was being utilized as fully as it was supposed to be. It was the ultimate accompaniment to her sleuthing and mathematical problem-solving skills, and it was a pleasure for her to go to work every day.

The gold and silver plaques that had replaced those of Dalton Hemmings on the walls of the editor's office were impressive, indeed. Numerous awards from the state press associations of Arkansas, Alabama, and Tennessee; and now Lyndell Renee Slover was continuing her tour of the Deep South in Rosalie, Mississippi—a spot many considered to be the "deepest" in the region.

As Wendy and Lyndell huddled in her office on a late October Monday morning to discuss the murder of Brent Ogle at the RCC over the weekend, they both realized that the slant they chose for her proposed investigative feature was crucial. In retrospect, Wendy felt that perhaps she had been a bit too cavalier about Brent's murder with Ross on Saturday, and she had figured out why. No one at the RCC, including Brent's wife, Carly, had really liked the man much, and to Wendy's way of thinking, he appeared to have no saving grace. He was a bully, a chauvinist, a homophobe, and a xenophobe, all rolled into one. She had to try very hard to push the thought out of her mind that he had finally reaped what he had been sowing for a very long time now. It didn't quite amount to *he probably deserved it*. But the phrase came perilously close to justification, and Wendy did not like herself for considering it even briefly. She had always believed in deferring to her better nature.

"What I think we need to do," Lyndell was saying from her comfortable leather chair with a coffee mug in her hand, "is paint a picture of the dynamic out there at the RCC. Not having visited even once, it's my understanding that it is much more of a sports-oriented club rather than a social watering hole. For the longest time, it was dominated by men, but that's no longer the case."

"That's absolutely correct," Wendy told her. "In Rosalie, you have to belong to one of the garden clubs if social standing is what you want for yourself and your family. But if it's tennis or golf or swimming you're after, you join the RCC and get the exercise. Of course, Deedah Hornesby and I just recently introduced the game of bridge into the mix." Wendy paused for an ironic grin that she didn't hold very long. "None too successfully, I might add. As it turned out, we were upstaged by a pestle and a dead body in a hot tub. A bit grisly."

Lyndell nodded sympathetically. "It certainly wasn't the unveiling you imagined, I'm quite sure."

For not the first time, Wendy appreciated the woman's patient, low-key personality—a welcome change from Dalton Hemmings's bombastic, throat-clearing directives and ultimatums. Lyndell was also easier on the eyes by far than Hemmings with his wrinkled clothes and face had ever hoped to be. The only thing they remotely had in common was that both were unmarried. Where he was bloated and sloppy, she was trim, wore business suits to perfection, disdained a lot of makeup, and wore her hair in a sensible short cut. Yet she was no glamorous model, either. Her middle-aged face was a bit too long and angular, and her smile was slightly crooked but hardly off-putting. It all meant that everyone took her seriously, but she generated no fear and loathing from her employees as Hemmings had done universally.

"I'm starting to think that I should stay away from bridge entirely," Wendy added. "It's been a matter of life and death for some of the people involved in it with me these past couple of years."

"Are you implying you're somehow cursed?"

They were both unable to suppress a chuckle, and Wendy said, "Maybe that should be the slant of our feature. A paranormal piece."

"I realize we aren't too far away from Halloween," Lyndell said with a quick wink. "But I think we won't go there."

Then she leaned in, and the previous levity in her tone disappeared. "Seriously, do you think you've gotten to know how everything runs out at the RCC to get a human-interest angle on this? That's what I think we should aim for. I'm quite sure we can afford to leave the solution of the crime to the Rosalie Police Department. Do you have any brilliant ideas?"

Just where the inspiration came from, Wendy did not know; but suddenly—there it was full-blown, and she was quick to run it up the flagpole. "What about the female angle? I mean, here you sit in front of me, the *Citizen*'s first female editor doing a bang-up job. Meanwhile, out at the RCC, Deedah Hollis has become the first female director, and Mitzy Stone is the first female golf pro. In a nutshell—the times, they are a-changin'. Even in a conservative outpost like Rosalie. And by the way, Brent Ogle was bitterly opposed to both of those hirings, and he let both women know it in no uncertain terms many times over."

Lyndell looked intrigued. "So we're back to the Devil angle again, are we?"

"It's interesting that that keeps coming up in my conversations with everyone. You may or may not have heard this, but Brent Ogle's nickname around town was The Baddest Devil of Them All because of his quarterbacking ability for the Rosalie High School Devils back in the day. And he acquitted himself well at LSU, too."

There was the slightest hint of amusement in Lyndell's voice. "As a matter of fact, someone did mention it to me. I forgot who and where. One of those good ole boys, probably. Rosalie seems to have minted a thousand of them, like those collector coins you can buy in hopes they'll improve in value with age. But I thought it was because of Mr. Ogle's reputation as Mississippi's preeminent personal injury lawyer. You know, the 'I'll get you five hundred thousand dollars for stubbing your toe' type. Whoever it was said the man almost never lost a case and that some people thought the Devil was actually on his side because of that."

Wendy's sigh seemed to have a great deal of thought behind it. "Under those circumstances, someone played the Devil and won Saturday night. But since it was murder, it was also a legal and moral loss."

Lyndell was moving her lips now, clearly repeating to herself what Wendy had just said.

"That seems a bit convoluted, but as I said before, I think we should leave the detective work to your father and his officers. I like your female slant on your assignment very much. I want you to concentrate on explaining the changes that hiring women in positions of responsibility have produced at the RCC. There will probably be some sidebars that result from your research, and we can run with them as they arise and as we see fit."

Wendy nodded with a measured enthusiasm, stood up, and shook Lyndell's hand crisply. "Understood."

What she did not say was that she fully expected that her interviews might very well turn up clues to the identity of Brent Ogle's murderer. She might even end up solving the crime herself. It had worked that way for her the year before when preparing her features on the four wealthy matrons who had been simultaneously poisoned in what Rosalie had called The Grand Slam Murders. For that achievement, Dalton Hemmings had promoted her from society columnist to full-time investigative reporter. Now she found herself fully inspired by the feminist angle that Lyndell Slover had embraced, and she knew that neither Deedah Hornesby nor Mitzy Stone were wallflowers where their careers were concerned. They would be a rich source of material, and she was certain she could mine it to perfection.

"I'll set up appointments with Deedah and Mitzy as soon as possible," Wendy said. "I know they'll be more than happy to cooperate."

"And I'm more than confident that you can get the job done."

"One last thought," Wendy added. "Shall we include you in this piece as the *Citizen*'s first female editor?"

Lyndell was very emphatic as she shook her head, took a stack of papers, and straightened them with authority. "Let's not make this about me. When I came aboard, there was an adequate description of my résumé. Let's just concentrate on the RCC for now."

"Understood."

The next morning was Merleece Maxique's day to clean Wendy's little bungalow out on Lower Kingston Road. Merleece—she of the high cheekbones, winning smile, and rich brown skin—and Wendy had become good friends while Merleece was cook and housekeeper for Liddie Langston Rose, one of the four Gin Girls who had been poisoned last year at one of their bridge club luncheons. As it turned out, it was something that Merleece had said to Wendy that had helped her solve the crimes when the entire Rosalie Police Department—including her father, Captain Bax, and her boyfriend, Ross Rierson—had been stumped.

Wendy and Merleece had become so close by then that neither wanted to lose contact. So Wendy had decided to broach the subject over the phone one day. "I've been wondering," she had begun, "do you think you could squeeze one morning every two weeks out of your schedule for Miz Crystal there at Concord Manor for you to clean my little house for me? I'd pay you the same hourly rate you're getting from Miz Crystal, and that way, we could have a little visit and catch up with each other as friends. After all, I'm your Strawberry and you're my Merleece, and nobody can keep us apart."

Merleece had not hesitated. "Lissen, *my* Strawberry with that pretty hair a' yours, I don't even have to ask Miz Crystal. I'm 'a tell her I'm gone do it, and that's that. She knows they's nobody like me in Rosalie to keep up that fancy mansion a' hers the way she like it—and who'd also put up with her nonsense."

Wendy had pursued the subject out of irresistible curiosity. "What's her latest nonsense?"

It would surely be another priceless story. The widowed

nouveau riche, supremely lacquered Crystal Forrest was always up to something preposterous, as she labored mightily to portray herself as a sixth- or seventh-generation Rosalian when everyone knew quite well she had arrived from Al-*benn-y,* Georgia (she had explained to everyone that that was the correct pronunciation) a mere three years earlier to restore the dilapidated Old Concord Manor.

"I tell you," Merleece had replied, barely suppressing her amusement, "I don't know where Miz Crystal come up with this stuff. She got it into her head now that she gone find one a' them historical names at the courthouse for her gardens that Arden Wilson tend to so well. I mean, she tell me that if she come up with the right name, the tourists who come every spring, they gone think her gardens, they been there since the Civil War. Lord help me, that woman think we all born yesterday. But she do pay me well, so she can pretend all she want. I know the truth."

Wendy's laughter was not meant to be at Miz Crystal's expense, but she couldn't seem to help herself. "I think she should run a contest and offer a prize."

"I wouldd'n put it past her, Strawberry," Merleece had answered.

And then, Merleece had agreed to get everything straight with the very social-minded Miz Crystal so they could see each other every two weeks, with a little bit of cleaning on the side. Wendy had also gotten permission from Lyndell Slover to come in a little late on Tuesdays, something she was certain Dalton Hemmings would never have let her do. He might have let a man get away with it, but never a female employee. Wasn't it heavenly to be working for a woman?

In the present moment, Wendy and Merleece were sitting down once again at the kitchen table, chatting amiably and sipping coffee before the dusting and vacuuming began in earnest.

"Strawberry, maybe you could help me with somethin' that I cain't seem to figure out."

Wendy gave her a bright smile. "Happy to. What's the deal?"

"Miz Crystal again. She got this fussy poodle that think it went to college and all, and don't even bother me 'bout all the things she do for that dog. She treat him like a human, and feed him steak and make him wear sweaters and pajamas and all like that, and he look ridiculous, but I just bite my tongue. But anyways, she call him somethin' that sound like it spelled H-a-r-r-y for the first name, and then C-o-f-a-i-r for the last name. *Harry Cofair*. That's what I think it is, but I could be wrong. So I say to her once why she name him that, and she say, 'It was after the vegetable, of course.' Now, I pretend I understand what she sayin' to me right then and there, but I really don't. Can you tell me what vegetable Harry Cofair is s'pose to be?"

Wendy put down her coffee cup and frowned. Her lips moved as she repeated the words several times. Then, there was a slight gasp, followed by a prolonged burst of laughter. "You are absolutely right, Merleece. Miz Crystal *is* something else. But we already knew that."

Wendy paused and leaned in for effect. "What she did was name her poodle after the French term for green bean— *haricot vert*. I'm sure that's how she spells it, too. That's a ridiculous name for a dog, but then, Miz Crystal is rather a ridiculous person from all I've heard from you and everybody else in Rosalie. Just as long as she keeps paying you well, I'd continue to put up with her quirks."

"You know I will. And thank you for clearin' that up for me. It was botherin' me no end." Merleece took a breath and went down in the mouth. "I read in the paper yesterday 'bout that poor man bein' murdered out at the country club. And in a hot tub, no less. What *is* the world comin' to?"

Wendy closed her eyes for a second and put her cup down. "I wouldn't exactly call him *poor,* but I know what you mean. And I guess you also know I was there at the time—not in the hot tub, of course, but trying to play bridge. I say trying because I didn't get to play nearly as much as I wanted to."

Merleece grinned and eyed her intently. "Now, I know murder not the least bit funny. I'm a God-fearin' woman who go to church erry Sunday. But it seem like erry time you set out to learn how to play bridge, somebody up and die. Now I'm not imaginin' that, am I?"

"My editor said practically the same thing to me. It's not funny at all, but it's the truth."

Merleece rose up slightly in her chair. "Well, you tell the *po*-lice that Miz Crystal and her poodle name after a vegetable can vouch for where I was that day. She got one of her big luncheons comin' up soon, so I was polishin' her silver all day and even into the evenin'. They can take me off that list right now."

Both women laughed, but there really wasn't anything funny at all about what had nearly happened to Merleece after the four Gin Girls had been poisoned last year. Circumstantial evidence had almost done her in as the killer, but Wendy's clever solution had exonerated her just in time.

"As a matter of fact," Wendy continued, "*I'm* actually a suspect this time, believe it or not."

Merleece's brown eyes widened even farther. "You? Now you really talkin' nonsense. Who on earth say you a suspeck? You tell 'em to come to me, and I'll set 'em straight."

"It's just a formality, really," Wendy told her, waving her off. "I was there in the building when the murder took place. Ross knows I'm not really a suspect, but my fingerprints and DNA had to be collected just like all the others'."

"How many others they got?"

"Seven, leaving me out."

Merleece changed the subject with a sly grin. "You and that handsome detective still seein' each other? He so tall and rugged, and his smile light up the room."

Wendy hesitated but finally brightened. "Yes, I guess he is all that. And we're still seeing each other, yes. But we still haven't gotten engaged or anything like that. We're not rushing into anything."

"Now don't wait too long, Strawberry. You gotta know you not the only fish in the ocean."

"I'm aware of that little cliché. Just don't you worry about me and Ross right now." Wendy took a big sip of her coffee and exhaled. "Anyway, enough about me. What's the latest on your son?"

Merleece looked and sounded exasperated. "Well, you know Hyram got that job with the fire department, and he seem to like his new apartment, even though he won't let his mother in to see it. How 'bout that? But now he tryin' to win back Charice Robinson. She the same girl that press charges against him when he slap her around a couple a' years ago. Seem she just broke up with the man she was seein' behind his back the first time around. If you want my opinion, that girl nothin' but big trouble, but Hyram not gone listen to his mama. No way. I guess I should be happy he stayin' down here in Rosalie for now like he say he would, instead a' bein' up to no good up in Chicago."

"Maybe this time the two of them will get it right."

"Maybe." But Merleece hardly sounded convinced. She glanced up at Wendy's owl kitchen clock that she'd found at a flea market and gasped. "Oh, the time getttin' away from me, Strawberry. And you got to head off to the newspaper to work, too. We both gotta get it together."

They both rose from the table quickly, and Wendy said,

"You're absolutely right. I need to get cracking on my latest assignment, and I have a couple of important interviews this afternoon to get it off the ground."

"You gone solve this one, too?"

Wendy couldn't resist delivering a prolonged wink. "Well, you never know. I just might."

Because the RCC was still considered a crime scene and off-limits to everyone except the Rosalie CID, Deedah had suggested to Wendy that she come to her house for their interview. Although Wendy had had a great deal of contact with Deedah as the two of them had worked hard to create the Bridge Bunch over the past few months, all of those meetings had all taken place in Deedah's office at the RCC. Thus, Wendy had never been in Deedah's house before and was looking forward to it.

As it happened, Deedah and her late husband, Jake Hornesby, had disdained restoring one of the Spanish Provincial town houses on iconic Minor Street. Instead, they had bought an already-restored Victorian raised cottage on Lambert Street, which was also considered a fashionable address in Rosalie.

As Wendy parked her car at the curb, she had to admit that Hornesby Cottage, as it had been christened by its owners, had great curb appeal. There was a row of mature crêpe myrtles lining the walkway leading up to the multi-columned porch; and even though their pink summertime blossoms were all but gone until next season, there still remained the majestic dignity of their gnarled branches to delight the eye. The traditional white clapboard and green shutters completed the impeccable ensemble, even though Deedah had never put the house on tour.

Wendy had gotten as far as the front stoop when Deedah swept out through the front door to greet her. "You're right on time," she said, as the two women embraced warmly. "I've been watching for you from the window, and I have tea and sugar cookies for us in the front parlor. Hollis has just left for the art gallery to see if he can scrounge up some bid'ness, so we'll have the entire place to ourselves."

As Deedah led the way in her colorful floral caftan, Wendy noted how sumptuously but properly appointed the house was: Great Persian rugs over polished hardwood floors, dignified ancestral portraits on the walls, rose-colored window treatments, Waterford crystal chandeliers, and there was even a very delicate-looking harpsichord in one corner of the parlor. Wendy wondered if anyone at Hornesby Cottage had ever played it or if it was there merely as an upscale conversation piece. She leaned toward the latter interpretation.

After Deedah had served them their Earl Grey tea from the coffee table next to the rose-colored Belter two-seater, Wendy complimented her hostess on the elegant Southern ambience. Then, the interview began in earnest.

"I'm excited about this opportunity to strike a blow for the achievements of Rosalie women," Wendy began. Then she explained the decision she and Lyndell Slover had made together regarding the slant on the feature. "I don't think we should ignore progress like this."

"You've come to the right woman, then," Deedah said. "There's so much I've wanted to say about how difficult it was for me to get the board on my side in the first place. It's common knowledge that Brent Ogle opposed my getting the directorship with every fiber of his being. The man very seldom failed to get what he wanted."

Wendy poised her pen above her notepad and said, "Yes, I've heard that. But what I don't understand is why he just didn't run for the directorship himself. Didn't he think he could win?"

Deedah quickly put down her teacup as a stern expression

and rigid posture overcame her, muscle by muscle. "That's not his style. He's too lazy . . . or was, rather . . . to do the actual work or put in the hours the directorship requires. He preferred to run things with a puppet in place, and he had that very arrangement in William Voss. I think William was a little soft in the head, if you ask me. He was little more than a glorified secretary. Apparently, he didn't realize that he was also there to take the fall for any improprieties that came to light. Then, poor William up and died of a heart attack, and Brent was no longer in control of the RCC. That's when I decided to make my move, and it took all the courage I could muster to do so. Fortunately, my late husband, Jake, had made friends with several of the board members back in the day, so Brent Ogle's thuggery didn't work like it usually did. I can tell you that he was furious."

Wendy finished up what she was writing and changed the subject. "Did everyone out there cooperate with you once you took the reins, or did you have to work to win them over?"

"Every single person stepped up to the plate and played ball with me," Deedah said, puffing herself up. "Mitzy Stone loved the changing of the guard, she told me. Mitzy's tough, don't misunderstand me. But she also told me how difficult it was dealing with the ghost of William Voss and Brent at the same time. She understood in retrospect that they were one and the same. Carlos Galbis felt the same way about me when I came aboard. It was a welcome and respectful change for him. And then there's poor Gerald Mansfield, of course."

Wendy looked puzzled and cocked her head. "I've heard the name before, but I'm not sure I know who he is."

"He's the greenskeeper," Deedah said. "He takes care of the course, the greens, the pin placements, everything. Hardworking young man. His office is out in the equipment shed. He works closely with Mitzy. Brent Ogle was hell-bent on having him sacked, always complaining that he didn't like the way Gerald was maintaining the sand traps and the rough, too. Brent thought it was . . . well, too rough and too overgrown everywhere. What that really meant was that Brent couldn't hit his way out of it like he used to. His game was starting to fail on him, Mitzy told me from her observations of him on the course. And she would certainly know what she was talking about being the talented golfer that she is."

Deedah paused and started to say something, then backed off.

"What is it? Remember, this is your chance to truly make an impact in this feature," Wendy said.

"Just that . . . Brent would get furious every time he saw Mitzy using the men's tee. If you want my opinion, I think it threatened his masculinity, or his version of it, anyway. It really seemed to drive him to drink even more than usual, and he'd come into the clubhouse and verbally abuse Carlos even more when he ordered from the bar on those occasions."

Wendy's expression was glum. "Not a pretty picture of manhood, is it?"

"It certainly isn't. Anyway," Deedah continued, "getting back to poor Gerald, Brent and William Voss had this case built up against him, and they were going to the board with it to get him fired. But then, William had that heart attack, and then . . . as you well know, someone conked Brent over the head this weekend with that pestle." Then Deedah gasped. "I just realized. That doesn't put Gerald in a very good light, does it? I mean, Brent's out of the way just in time."

"Offhand, I'd say you're right about that." Wendy thought for a moment. "But Gerald wasn't in the building Saturday, was he? I don't remember seeing anyone I didn't recognize."

"No. I believe he had the day off. Mitzy started not to come in herself because of the bad weather. She was surprised that Brent, Tip Jarvis, and Connor James ventured out with that forecast." Wendy could see the wheels turning in Deedah's head. "But now that I think about it, Gerald could have come out here on his own unseen, even in the bad weather. Do the police know about him?"

"That, I don't know. But if Mr. Mansfield doesn't have a solid alibi, it would appear there's another suspect for them to consider. I can ask Ross or my father if they have him on their list to interrogate."

Deedah offered the plate of sugar cookies to Wendy, but she declined politely. "Well, I trust the police have taken me and Hollis off the list," Deedah said while helping herself to a cookie and taking a bite.

"I don't know. It's still a crime scene out there. I know they're still processing inside and around the perimeter, too. They're going over everything and every room. You may be asked to come down to the station for further questioning at some point. And Hollis, too."

"But surely you . . . I mean, surely they don't think either of us killed Brent Ogle, do they?"

Wendy took a deep breath and patted Deedah's shoulder reassuringly. "As the daughter of a police chief, I can only tell you that following the evidence is what always counts in law enforcement. If nothing comes out that points to you or Hollis, then you have nothing to worry about."

Deedah took another bite of her cookie and then a sip of tea to chase it down. "I'll admit to you that there were times I devoutly wished Brent could be banished from the face of the earth. And he gave my Hollis nothing but holy hell all the time. Hollis is who he is, and apparently that was also threatening to a macho man like Brent. I know for a fact that Hollis never made a pass at him, though. Hollis told me he wasn't the least bit interested, or in anyone else out at the club. So why did Brent get so riled up all the time about his mere presence? Makes you wonder, doesn't it? Carly told me more than once that theirs was not a happy marriage by a long shot."

"I know this much," Wendy said. "Brent Ogle was an equal opportunity offender. I know he made Carlos's life miserable, and now you're telling me that he was on Gerald Mansfield's case hot and heavy."

Deedah managed a strange little shiver. "I guess from the police department's point of view, there are plenty of suspects."

"That's an understatement." Wendy looked down at her notes and a question she had printed beforehand got her attention. "I know that you were a C.P.A. at one time. Do you find that that has come in handy in running the RCC? I would imagine it makes you extremely qualified."

Deedah seemed delighted with the question. "Ha! That's another thing you should mention in this article of yours. People don't regularly associate women with the C.P.A. profession all that much. But I can assure you we are there and there's nothing in our brains that prevents us from managing the bottom line with the best of them." Then her face darkened slightly. "Would you believe Brent even brought that up when he was trying to derail me as director at the last minute? I can still hear him in that boozy voice of his: 'What does a woman know about crunchin' numbers, now I ask you? What? What? What?'" She let out a contemptuous little snort. "I'm not the least bit sorry that someone got the last word on crunching his number, so to speak."

Wendy nodded, but she was not smiling. "A word of advice, though. If you should get called down to the station for interrogation, I wouldn't joke around like you just did there at the end with the police. They might take you seriously and read more into what you say than you intended."

"Duly noted," Deedah said, "but I have to tell you honestly, when Hollis would tell me about the things Brent Ogle would say to him, I wanted to go after him like a tiger or a bear protecting her cubs. It made me so mad because some people seem to think that someone like my Hollis is fair game for their constant insults and rude behavior. But Hollis is a gentle soul trying to find his way in life, and it's the Brent Ogles of the world who stand between him and the right to go about his bid'ness like everyone else."

Wendy noted the passion with which Deedah spoke. It was clear that the woman had a firm grasp of the reality of the darker side of human behavior. After all, she had prevailed against it in becoming the RCC director. She was no pushover.

A half hour later, Wendy found Mitzy Stone's modest little apartment nestled inside a complex in the Rosalie suburb of Whiteapple Village to be in sharp contrast to impeccable Hornesby Cottage. Where Deedah had filled her spacious cottage with period antiques and designer décor items, Mitzy's theme was obviously one of straightforward dedication to sports. The shag carpet and the low popcorn ceilings with sprinklers quite visible fit right in with the pictures of golf tournaments, football games, players, and coaches all over the walls, and what furniture there was had a "rent to buy" look to it. Wendy browsed them all as if she were in an art gallery, smiling at photos of Mitzy herself teeing off or sinking a putt with her arms raised in victory. Mitzy's hospitality was much the same as Deedah's had been, and the two women were soon seated at her kitchen table with Wendy sipping coffee while Mitzy enjoyed a beer.

"I've always wanted to succeed at some sport," Mitzy was saying as they settled into the interview. "I tried nearly everything, including basketball because I'm so tall. But I found my niche as a golfer. I even went to qualifying school for the

LPGA tour. That's a tough one, and I never quite made the cut. But being a pro is where I landed, and I'm grateful to Deedah for giving me the chance here in Rosalie."

"This wasn't your first job, was it?"

"No, indeed," Mitzy said. "I'd been working at the Red Stick Country Club in Baton Rouge for a while, and before that, on the Mississippi coast. I do have considerable experience."

Wendy finished up her notes and said, "Talk to me about life out at the RCC. I think you know what I mean by that, too."

Mitzy put down her beer and leaned in confidentially. "I was happy to help people with their swings and how to select their clubs for various shots—the usual stuff. Most people were friendly and cordial to me. What I hadn't counted on was a monster like Brent Ogle hanging around all the time. He seemed to be obsessed with me, and I tried my best to avoid him after a while. He told me he particularly didn't like the fact that I used the men's tee. I told him I wasn't trying to show off, I was just challenging myself; but he implied that I was infringing upon his rights as a man. Now, you figure that one out."

"Everyone and everything bothered him, it appears," Wendy said. "He made many enemies. One too many, I'd say."

Mitzy returned to her beer, taking a healthy swig. "He got riled up all the time, and he riled other people up as a result. It turned out to be a lethal combination but hardly a surprise."

"Let's move on," Wendy continued. "What did you think of the changes Deedah was making at the RCC? I was involved in one myself in trying to introduce bridge to the club offerings. We were convinced it would catch on. We still are, once we get past this awful murder."

"I've never been a big fan of card games, myself," Mitzy

said. "But I've had friends who were devoted to poker in all
its many versions, and I know what kind of fun they had,
making their small bets and scoping out each other's tells and
such. Deedah felt that there weren't enough social events at
the RCC, and she wanted to bring some of the fun inside.
There was more than enough going on outside with the golf,
tennis, and swimming. I'm sure you felt the same way."

Wendy's sigh was full of exasperation, as she shook her
head in slow motion. "All I've been wanting to do is to learn
enough about bridge to be able to play it halfway decently.
But the gods seem to keep preempting me." Something in
Wendy's head seemed to click, bringing the hint of a smile to
her face.

Preempting.

It had an entirely different meaning in the game of bridge,
one she had tried to illustrate in that first meeting of the
Bridge Bunch. Odd, that the word had caused her to pause
and acknowledge it.

"I'm assuming you and Deedah will keep the Bridge
Bunch going after all this dies down," Mitzy said.

"I'm game, and Deedah hasn't said otherwise to me."
Wendy referred to her prepared notes once again. "Do you
mind my asking if you intend to stick it out with your job
here in Rosalie?"

Mitzy took her time, taking another swallow of beer first
and then tactfully suppressing a belch. "When I came here, I
had one thing in mind. To make a success of myself as a golf
pro. To make a success of myself in general here in Rosalie."
Her face darkened a bit. "Maybe that'll be a little easier now
that . . ." She paused and shrugged, and then Wendy finished
her sentence.

"Now that Brent Ogle is gone?"

"Why should I deny it?" she answered with a renewed

confidence. "He was after me and practically everyone else out here. All of us will be able to breathe much easier from now on."

"Did you have anything else you wanted to add?"

Mitzy drew herself up with a look of determination. "Just this. I've heard people say that women can't work together in positions of authority. That their egos get in the way the same as men's do. But I'm here to say that Deedah and I have been working together perfectly to make this clubhouse run smoothly from the get-go. It's all about teamwork. It's an old wives' tale that females are at each other's throats all the time in business or otherwise. Certainly not when we have a common enemy."

Wendy continued her note-taking; but even as she was writing, she was struck by Mitzy's tone. Was there an element of unnecessary hostility in it? Wendy remembered much the same attitude from Deedah regarding Brent Ogle. Undoubtedly, the man had put everyone around him on the defensive, and those tactics had obviously cost him dearly.

Then Wendy thought about Ross, her father, and the rest of the CID. What progress were they making in unraveling this murder? It was a bit early, but was the finger pointing to anyone in particular yet? The undeniable fact was that there were plenty of people with motive and opportunity under cover of darkness to have done the deed. It was also imperative that she get together with Ross soon to tell him about the existence of Gerald Mansfield, in case he did not already know. It might turn out to be a game changer for everyone.

So. It was back to eight suspects again, since Wendy knew she was innocent. Yet within her mind and according to her moral compass, it was difficult to accept the reality that one of those eight people had actually picked up that pestle and laid into Brent Ogle's skull with it. The act seemed too primitive, too uncivilized, and, more than that, a crime borne of great passion and rage. How much unbridled hatred had been engendered in one of those eight people—a list that still included Deedah, Carly, Mitzy, Tip, Connor, Carlos, Hollis, and the latecomer, Gerald Mansfield?

CHAPTER 5

Down at the station, Ross and his Captain Bax were discussing the report from the crime lab, now that processing of the RCC and its immediate surroundings had been completed. Previously, there had been Ross's notes from his taped interrogations and a diagram of the clubhouse to consider. Bax had his big feet up on his desk, and his sturdy arms were folded across his chest as was his customary position much of the time; while Ross sat off to one side in a comfortable leather chair, turning to the next page of the preliminary CID report before he resumed their discussion.

"Basically, everyone's DNA and fingerprints are everywhere around the building," he said with a hint of consternation. "That was no surprise. But there was nothing in or around the hot tub that doesn't belong to the deceased. Of course, any prints or DNA on the pestle were completely erased by the hot water in which it was submerged. Ditto the glass that was also found near the drain. So the crime scene was spotless with all the humidity and steam surrounding it, except for a few hairs in the drain that belonged to Brent Ogle."

Ross paused and gave his mentor and the father of his girlfriend a pained expression before continuing. "We thought we might find Wendy's prints on Brent Ogle's neck because she told us she had checked it for a pulse when she and Carly Ogle found him. But the humidity, the steam, and his sweat obviously compromised them completely, because we found nothing we could use. So that really wasn't helpful at all, even though Wendy volunteered the information thinking it might be."

Bax took his feet off the desk and sat back properly in his chair. Now he looked like a Chief of Police should—square jawed in his navy-blue uniform, unusually fit for a man in his fifties—with just that touch of gray at the temples to give him that aura of authority and experience. But there was a hint of sadness in his voice when he made some observations.

"You know, I'm about five years older than Brent Ogle. Although I'd graduated and was in college about the time he became big man on campus with all the girls after him, I still kept up with RHS athletics. I remember his heroics in that Four-Second Game decades ago. That's where he got the nickname The Baddest Devil of Them All, and I also remember the controversy surrounding the game. More than one St. Mark's fan claimed that RHS had somehow cheated. But how could anyone prove such a thing? I do recall that the clock operator vehemently denied at the time that he had tinkered with the equipment to give RHS an extra second. What was his name again?"

Ross quickly rifled through his notes and finally located what he was looking for. "Claude Ingalls."

"And Brent Ogle claimed his father had paid him to influence the outcome of the game?"

"And the other officials as well, if they got the opportunity. Sounds like the ultimate conspiracy theory to me."

Bax tapped his finger on the desk absentmindedly. "Completely improbable. But you know as well as I do that football truly is a religion in the South and people have been known to do crazy things and throw sportsmanship in the trash, all to get a victory. The thing that really surprises me the most is what an obnoxious and ruthless person Brent Ogle had become, according to your summary of these interrogations. I knew he was a successful personal injury lawyer. Good gracious, he had enough billboards and cheesy TV spots promising people hundreds of thousands of dollars if they'd hire him. Whether it's justified or not, some folks think there's a stigma attached to that 'get rich quick' approach, and just maybe Brent lived down to that stigma and forgot all about just being a decent human being."

Ross was nodding eagerly as he thumped his notes with his finger for emphasis. "Wendy spent some time out at the RCC trying to get her new bridge club going, as you know, and she insists that what all the others said about Brent was absolutely true. She saw some of it for herself. He was incorrigible to everyone, except maybe those golfing pals of his. And there at the end, he even managed to provoke them. But somebody finally had enough of it all and took him out to the woodshed for the last time on Saturday."

"So, which of the others sent up a red flag to you? Or at least bears our further scrutiny."

Ross confidently explained his priorities. "Well, we have to focus on Carlos Galbis first. It was his pestle—the one he used to make his juleps—and from all my interrogations, including his, it was apparent that Carlos was treated shabbily by the deceased. The bar where Carlos worked was not very far from the locker-room wing, and it was a straight shot to the deck and the hot tub from there. We already know that Carlos served Brent Ogle a drink or two while he was out there. We can't ignore the most obvious suspect, and the fact that Carlos admits he made a few trips out to the deck. Maybe Brent insulted him one too many times and Carlos just lost it out there. He could easily have returned in the darkness with the pestle and bludgeoned Brent in a fit of rage."

Bax nodded his approval of the analysis. "And then after Carlos? Where do we go next?"

"I hate to say it, but it's a roll of the dice. None of them had anything positive to say about Brent Ogle, as you've seen, and they all had the opportunity to sneak around in the dark and do him in. I've put together an overview or composite from my tapes of where everyone says they were during the blackout and who was with them at the time; and the fact is that with one exception, there were periods when most of them were by themselves with no one to observe them. I'd say they all pretty much knew their way around the clubhouse, even in the dark."

"Have you been able to establish a timeline?"

Ross had a slightly equivocal expression on his face. "Rosalie Power and Light provided us with the blackout timeline. So we have the power loss down to the second and likewise the restoration. It was about a half an hour that we're talking about. But after that, things get a bit sketchy. They all had their phones on, of course, but not a one of them was focused on the time all that much—not even Wendy. At that point, they were using their phones as flashlights or for following the storm on weather radar to see when it might let up so they could leave and get home. And not to sound too dramatic or corny about it, but one of them had to have used it to light the way to murder."

Bax's face lit up in what appeared to be an aha! moment. "Have you considered the possibility that more than one person could have been involved in this murder? Two, maybe even three? Makes sense if Brent had made nothing but enemies at the RCC, and we know that for a fact."

Ross looked perplexed but soon forged ahead. "Frankly, I hadn't gone there. Because it seems to me that if more than one person was involved, that would almost imply premeditation. The fly in the ointment there would be that an elaborate conspiracy after being plunged into darkness would be a stretch. How could like minds have gotten together easily and quickly under those circumstances? How could anyone have counted on the power outage in the first place? It wasn't peculiar to one transformer and the RCC so that someone could have somehow manipulated it. Rosalie Power and Light confirms that the outage was citywide. That was a monster of a storm that spared no one. Fortunately, there were no fatalities. Plenty of property damage, though. The city has some cleaning up to do."

Bax put his elbows on his desk and brought his hands together. "You make good points, but just file that thought away. We might need to revisit it later. Meanwhile, I want to hear more about that exception you spoke of where someone was not alone all the time."

"That would belong to Tip Jarvis and Connor James," Ross began. "They were the two golfers that went out on the course with Brent Ogle that stormy afternoon. They also had a physical altercation with him in the clubhouse great room that everyone witnessed. I have several blow-by-blow accounts of it that are almost exactly the same. The three of them had been drinking heavily. Then both Tip and Connor claim that they stayed together in the men's locker room both before and during the blackout. They said they started out playing gin until that was no longer possible."

Ross got up and again showed Bax the diagram he had made of the RCC with its great room and bar and also the two wings—one near the front for the offices and pro shop and the other near the rear containing the locker rooms. That rear wing, of course, led to the covered deck where the hot tub was located.

"By the way," Ross continued, "that hot tub has not

helped us out in the least. The RCC doesn't use chlorine or bromine to keep it sanitary. I asked Deedah Hornesby about it, and she said they just shock the water on a regular schedule. It might've been helpful if chemicals had been in the water so we could detect it on anyone. But from that aspect, the water's clean, and so are all the suspects."

Bax wrapped up his examination of the diagram for the second time and said, "Heh. So much for that. But we were just discussing more than one person being involved. Well, it appears that these two men were even closer to the deck and the hot tub than this Carlos was. I think you should make them your next interrogations after you finish up with the bartender. Obviously, they are vouching for each other, and they may be telling the truth. But see if you can catch one of them in a discrepancy and take it from there. One could have done the deed while the other was looking out for him."

"Will do," Ross said. Then he glanced at his watch and gasped. "Oops! I'm supposed to meet Wendy at the Bluff City Bistro for a quick lunch. She said she's turned up something as a result of her interviews and wants to let us know about it in detail. She said it was too involved for a mere text."

Bax's expression exuded the pride he'd been feeling for his only child since she'd solved The Grand Slam Murders the previous year. "You know, despite her protestations, I think that daughter a' mine is gonna end up on the force one a' these days. And, yeah, I know, she's finally got that investigative reporter gig at the newspaper she's always wanted. But if she keeps solving cases, I may have to make her an offer she can't refuse."

Ross hesitated for a moment but then expressed what was really on his mind. He thought he had nothing to lose. "And I hope I can do the same when it comes to getting her to marry me."

"Don't lose heart, son," Bax told him. "Her mother was the same way. She was no pushover in the romance department. I had to work hard to earn every bit of Valerie's affection and respect, but I can tell you, it was worth the wait. All I have is my memories now of that sweet woman—and some of her wonderful paintings that had her on the way to a distinguished career, I'm quite sure—but they're the best memories a man could ever ask for."

At the brick and lacework Bluff City Bistro overlooking the Mississippi River on scenic Broad Street, a smiling, energetic young waitress had just taken Ross's and Wendy's orders, removed their menus, and headed toward the kitchen. Ross had fallen back on his old standby—the Bluff burger, stuffed with blue cheese—while Wendy had gone for a Cobb salad this time around.

"So what's this inside info on the murder case you say you have for me?" Ross asked, taking a sip of his ice water and then putting his napkin in his lap.

"Two words," she said cryptically while holding up two fingers. "*Gerald Mansfield.* Mean anything to you?"

Ross frowned while searching his brain. "Nope, I don't think so. Who is he?"

"Well, he could be a new suspect," Wendy said. "He's the greenskeeper out at the RCC."

Then she told Ross the rest of what Deedah had mentioned to her during their recent interview.

"But he obviously wasn't in the building Saturday night, and Miz Deedah said he had the day off," Ross pointed out.

Wendy gave him that kittenish look of hers when she wanted more out of him in an official capacity, that look when she expected him to cross the line ever so slightly and divulge things that properly belonged to the CID and not the general public. But she was not the general public. She was the daughter of the police chief, and Ross's girlfriend as well. As a result, she was always the beneficiary of lagniappe and leaks.

"So, let me guess. There were lots of unidentified prints and DNA out at the RCC, and there were no hits on any of them."

Ross nodded with a sly grin, obviously wise to her line of questioning. "Yes. But that was to be expected, since RCC members are always out there doing things. I'm sure the custodian can only do so much in a busy place like that. And, by the way, he wasn't there on Saturday. We've confirmed that, and he has an alibi."

"Then there'd be no harm in interrogating Gerald Mansfield on his whereabouts Saturday as well. Particularly if he has no alibi."

Ross reached across the table and patted Wendy's hand. "Don't worry. I'll follow up." Then he managed a barely audible chuckle and a brazen wink at the same time. "I appreciate the lead, but you are incorrigible. Your father's right. You sure you don't want to switch from newspaper reporter to detective? We could be a husband and wife team like Nick and Nora Charles from the thirties. You know how much I love old movies." He paused and calmly added as an afterthought, "Eventually . . . husband and wife, I mean."

Wendy gave him her best sideways glance, but she was only playing at being displeased. It had been over a year since he had last proposed and she had turned him down; and in that year, she had learned a great deal about investigative reporting—the main reason she wanted to postpone anything as monumental as a wedding engagement. "We both have our pressing agendas, don't we?"

Then Ross withdrew his hand and took another sip of water, gazing at her earnestly. "While I have your utmost attention, I'd appreciate any insights you've gathered from your interviews so far."

"From Deedah and Mitzy, you mean, since they're the only ones I've gotten to talk to so far."

"Yep. Anything you have would be appreciated," he said. "You have very good instincts about people."

Wendy thought for a while as she sipped her water and then said, "Mitzy Stone seems completely devoted to her golf pro career, and she's very good at what she does. Offhand, I'd say she was way too strong a woman to let snide remarks from the likes of Brent Ogle bother her. Deedah seems to swear by her as well. It's hard for me to picture Mitzy letting Brent get the better of her under any circumstances. She's already proven her point at the RCC, and that means everything to her."

"And Deedah?"

"Same story," Wendy said. "She bucked tradition and went after the directorship after William Voss keeled over. She beat the odds. It takes a strong woman to do something like that and succeed, and I can tell you that she's been doing a bang-up job at the RCC. If I hadn't had to meet with her so much over the past several months to organize our Bridge Bunch, I wouldn't know that. But she's well organized and efficient and very pleasant to work with. Both women are perfect examples of professionals who get things done the right way."

Then Wendy hesitated for a moment, and her mouth twitched to one side. There had been moments when Deedah had made her a bit uncomfortable. "I will say this, though. Deedah is very protective of her son, Hollis. He's her project, and I know she didn't appreciate the way Brent Ogle treated him. The typical mother hen—or even tiger—in that respect."

"Those two are very different creatures," Ross pointed out. "Hen is one thing; tiger is another. So it would not be a stretch to say that just as you and Deedah worked as a team successfully, you could easily picture Deedah and Mitzy working together as a team the same way."

"Of course." Then Wendy eyed him intently. "Wait. . . . I have a feeling you're going somewhere with this. Do you mind sharing this particular theory of yours, or is it off the boards?"

"Just conjecture on the part of your father and myself," he told her. "We were tossing around the idea earlier that more than one person might have been involved in Brent's murder. That one person might have done the deed while the other was watching out or keeping guard, so to speak."

"I never thought of that," Wendy said. "But knowing Deedah as I do, I can't picture her actually doing either one of those."

"And Mitzy?"

Wendy did not answer immediately, and her tone was less than confident when she finally spoke up. "As I said before, I just can't picture her letting Brent Ogle rile her up very much. After all, she was the one who intervened in the altercation between Tip Jarvis and Brent. I see her more as a forceful peacemaker."

Ross had an odd smirk on his face. "You just described a rogue. There are plenty of them out there who feel it's their duty to serve up justice on their own."

"Maybe there are," Wendy said, flashing a frown. "But I really don't see Mitzy as that type of vigilante."

The waitress arrived with their food. Her plastic name-plate identified her as Cherry, and her personality fit her name perfectly as she served them like she was delivering lines in a Rosalie Little Theater play. "Your yummy Bluff burger, sir, and your scrumptious Cobb salad, miss. And two iced teas, all fresh from Miz Selena Chalk's kitchen."

"Is she here today?" Wendy said, perking up noticeably.

"Back in the kitchen watching over everything as usual," Cherry said, pointing across the room.

"If you wouldn't mind, would you ask her if she could step out and say hello to us?" Wendy added. "We're two of her best customers."

"Right away, and let me know if you need anything else." And with that, Cherry was off and running.

It did not take long for the Bluff City Bistro's proprietor to appear at their table, though slightly out of breath. The significant girth beneath her formless frock usually did not permit her to do anything but lumber, but she was obviously making an exception, picking up the pace for Wendy and Ross.

"I'm so glad to see you both," she said, giving them a great double-chinned smile and then leaning down to deliver a peck to their cheeks. "I was in my office when you came in."

"How's business, Miz Selena?" Wendy added. "I don't see too many empty tables today."

Selena puffed up her already-formidable chest and made a sweeping gesture. "Thankfully, business has picked up. It's been a gradual thing, of course, but it took some time after those Gin Girls—may they rest in peace despite what they said—wrote that nasty letter to the *Citizen* about my restaurant last year. Of course, not a word of it was true."

"I know," Wendy said, shaking her head. "Dalton Hemmings should never have published it. I don't know what he was thinking." There was a brief pause. "Well, actually, I do. Those ladies all had him under their thumb."

Then Selena gave a little gasp and caught Ross's gaze. "I read about the murder out at the country club in the paper, Mr. Rierson." She lowered her voice to a whisper. "An awful thing, but I have to say, I'm not surprised."

Now it was Ross who perked up. "Oh? Why is that?"

Selena quickly surveyed the tables around her and continued in a low voice. "I hope I'm not stepping on any toes, but that Mr. Ogle was a very rude man. When he came in here, he treated my waitstaff like they were slaves. He even made my dear little Cherry cry once. He threw a fork on the floor in a tantrum and told her it had food spots on it—which by the way could never happen at my restaurant—and he used profanity in telling her that. I'm sure the poor little thing had never heard so many words of that ilk hurled at her that way. And with all the money I know Mr. Ogle must have made as a lawyer, he was the cheapest tipper around. Not even ten percent. More like five. He might as well have left nothing on the table. We all cringed whenever we saw him come in. 'What will he do next?' we were all thinking. So what I'm saying is that I'm not surprised someone did him in, if that was an example of how he treated everybody. But don't read me the wrong way now; murdering someone is a horrible thing to do, no matter what."

Ross nodded but spoke in a professional manner. "Thank you for that information, Miz Selena. We've already started our investigation, and every little bit helps, you know."

Selena gestured at their plates in her best restaurant owner manner. "Well, I'll let you have your lunch in peace. So good to see you both again, of course. You let me or Cherry know immediately if anything's not right, ya hear?"

"Will do," Wendy said with a genuine smile as Selena headed back to her kitchen.

Wendy's phone pinged on the table, and she picked it up and read the text she'd just received.

"Anything of importance?" Ross said, noting the surprised expression on Wendy's face.

"Not sure yet. It's from Carly Ogle. She says she wants to talk to me ASAP at her house."

Ross nodded emphatically. "By all means, hear what she has to say. You'll have to let me know what happens. I know I

intend to question her further. She found her husband's body
even before you did, and there's that odd business about somebody knocking her down in the hallway. We need to find out
who that was, of course. Could be the killer, or someone who
knows who the killer is. You never know where your leads
will come from."

"Do you think there's a chance Carly is holding something back? Am I reading you right?"

Ross took his time, looking a bit uncomfortable. "Anything's possible. Something was definitely strange about her
attitude toward her husband's death. She could have been in
shock, of course, but on the other hand, I got the impression
she just didn't care. Between the two of us, maybe we can
uncover the truth."

CHAPTER 6

As Wendy drove down US 61 South toward Carly Ogle's house, she was filled with conflict. Carly had made no secret of the fact that hers was far from a happy marriage. Her visible alcohol consumption alone pointed to a problem somewhere in her life, and Wendy had long ago concluded that her husband, Brent, was the problem. As far as it was possible to glean from a text in cyberspace, Wendy also detected a plea for help that she could not ignore. It wasn't just the *ASAP* that had done the trick. It went further back than that. It was the way Carly had conducted herself from the moment that locker-room door had opened and she had just stood there like one of the walking dead. Perhaps Carly was going to open up to her in a way that she was very uncomfortable doing with the police. Maybe it was a "trust another female thing."

As Wendy turned onto the long gravel road that led to the plantation-style home that Brent Ogle had built for himself with his considerable fortune and called Brentwood, she was reminded of the character of the man, himself. He had obviously attempted to re-create the iconic Southern mansion with its white columns and many-shuttered windows across the two-story façade. But instead of actually buying and restoring an existing plantation in that style, he had started from the ground up and created something that reflected his personality inside and out—and no one else's. Had he bought the real thing, he would also have inherited a row of mature, graceful live oaks dripping with Spanish moss that formed the typical alley or tunnel so admired by locals and tourists alike. Instead, he had been forced to plant oak saplings on his clearcut acreage, and even though they had grown some since they were put in the ground a couple of decades ago, they were far from the majestic trees that fired up the imagination and gave people an undeniable sense of the past.

Wendy also hoped that Carly might reveal things to her that could possibly enhance the feature she would be doing on women at the RCC. Who better to give her the proper perspective on that than the women who belonged to it?

Minutes later, when Wendy and Carly finally sat down together on the tiger-striped sectional sofa that matched the purple portieres in the gold-carpeted parlor—obviously Brent's idea of commemorating his years at LSU—there was a palpable tension hanging in the air. It was not Wendy's imagination that Carly had not made eye contact with her since Reeny, the maid, had announced her in the doorframe. It also appeared that Carly had been crying—her eyes were pink, the lashes wet and clumped together, as she kept sniffling into a handkerchief.

"What is it, sweetie?" Wendy finally said, since Carly had not even offered a perfunctory "hello."

Carly blew her nose gently and did not answer immediately. She was making quite the production of whatever it was that was upsetting her.

"I got here as soon as I could. I somehow sensed you were in a bad place. Has something else happened since Saturday that I ought to know about?"

Finally, Carly straightened her slumping posture and

sighed deeply. "First things first. My son David's arriving to-morrow from Wisconsin, so I can finally have a memorial service for Brent. But the truth is, I'm not letting it widely be known that we are even having a service at the First Presbyterian Church. I think the turnout will be embarrassing, considering how Brent treated just about everyone. And the coroner's office called to let me know the State Medical Examiner in Jackson is seriously backed up and it'll be a little while yet before they get to Brent's autopsy. I don't see why they needed to do it at all. I didn't want them to. The very idea of cutting people open and rooting around inside makes me ill. But the coroner says that since Brent's death was violent and not due to natural causes, they have to do it in this case. Meanwhile, Brent wanted to be cremated, so I have to even wait on that. I just want to get this over and done with, so I'm going ahead with the memorial service tomorrow. If you don't want to come, you don't have to."

Wendy's eyes widened, and she reached over to rub Carly's arm gently. "Of course I'll come. I'll want to be there for you and meet your son as well. What time is the service?"

"Didn't I say?"

Wendy shook her head. "No. Those tears of yours are interfering with your memory, I'm afraid."

"Probably. Anyway, the service is at seven."

"I'll be there. And I'll try to round up Ross, too."

That seemed to calm Carly down for a few seconds. But that didn't last long. She was soon dabbing at her tears with her handkerchief again. "There's something else I wanted to tell you, though. It's in the way of a confession. Just let me tell it, and then you can tell me what you think I ought to do."

Wendy felt her pulse quicken and her stomach muscles tighten. A part of her wondered if she even wanted to hear what Carly had to say. "I'll give you the best advice I can."

"Let me put you at ease first," Carly said, still sniffling

lightly. "I didn't kill Brent, and I don't know who did. And everything else I told you and Detective Rierson is the truth about someone tackling me, knocking me to the floor, and running away. But I feel guilty about something else, and I just have to get it out."

"I'm right here," Wendy said, tapping her chest lightly a couple of times. "You know you can trust me."

Carly seemed to be agonizing further for a while but finally told her story. "It was just that when you said you were going to the ladies' room, and I told you I wanted to go with you, it wasn't because I had to go to the bathroom at all. You'll recall that I told you I wanted to check in on Brent out on the deck and that I left you at the locker-room door all by yourself."

"Yes. I can't imagine what you're going to say to me next, though."

Carly again avoided eye contact, staring at the handkerchief she'd now put in her lap. "What I'm going to say to you may come as a shock, but my intention was to find Brent so drunk in that hot tub that I could push him under the water and hold him down until he drowned. I can tell you that it flashed into my head once the power went out. It just came to me like some wicked wish and took hold of me and wouldn't let me go. I was still furious with him for that fight he picked with Tip and Connor, and I even thought about telling him that I wanted him out of my life for good. A divorce, finally. And you have no idea how sick of him I was."

"Yes, I think I do have some idea based on what I saw of your husband at the RCC," Wendy said, getting a word in.

Carly nodded and continued her story. "I stayed in the marriage for the sake of our son, David. But he's a grown man now, teaching up in Wisconsin because he wanted to get as far away from his father as he could; and he would ask me from time to time when we were going to get a divorce. He grew up knowing how bad things were between his mother and father. David is so unlike his father, it's not even funny. He's much more like me inside, even looks more like me on the outside. He even started calling himself David when he got out on his own. He was christened Brent David Ogle, Jr., but he detested being called Brent Junior, and his father knew it. Maybe that's another reason Brent was so at war with practically everyone. He couldn't get his own son to give him the sort of respect he required, and I have to tell you, it wasn't David's fault that it turned out that way."

Wendy did not respond further. The revelations within the long monologue had indeed come as a shock to her, and her vocal cords seemed almost paralyzed. Her tongue had become very dry, and she even found it hard to swallow.

"You see why I'm so upset now, don't you?" Carly added. "There I was, seriously considering killing my husband, but someone beat me to the punch. How do you think that makes me feel? If whoever it was that killed him hadn't done it, then I know I would have. I was not thinking straight, I can tell you. It was like I'd been possessed by the Devil. But I was saved from committing murder by someone who wanted to kill him as much as I did. Maybe even more. I can't get that thought out of my head. It was almost a 'take a number' proposition. That's why I didn't bring any of this up to Mr. Rierson. I think it's something he doesn't need to know, since what I was going to do never happened. Still, I feel so guilty—and also grateful to whoever it was that got to him first to keep me out of trouble. That's such a creepy combination, and you were absolutely right when you came in and said you sensed I was in a bad place. It's a very bad place I'm stuck in, and it's really driving me crazy."

Wendy finally managed a response. "I can understand that completely. And I also agree with you that this is something Ross or my father or any of the police don't need to know about. You've got to find a way to stop beating yourself up, though. You'll make yourself sick."

"It's easy to say, but hard to do," Carly added. "It was that gash, Wendy, that gash. The ugliness of it, the brutality behind it."

Wendy was slightly puzzled now. After all, she had shielded Carly from the actual sight of the wound. She had only told her that it was there and not gone into detail describing it. "You're going to have to try as hard as you can to get it out of your head. It should be easier for you than it's been for me since that evening. At least you didn't lay eyes on it."

Wendy's words appeared to have no impact on Carly at all. "But what I was going to do was so wrong, and yet I would have done it and then been stuck with the consequences. I've created this hell for myself, and I can't make it go away. Why . . . did I do it?"

"You've told everything you should have," Wendy said. "It's up to the police to run with that much. But they don't need to know about things you were thinking leading up to the murder, or even afterward, if it doesn't relate to anything you actually saw or heard or did. Thank goodness we can't be put in jail for our worst thoughts, or we'd all be locked up and serving time right now—every single one of us. That's the truth of the matter."

Carly waved her off, still avoiding eye contact. "I appreciate all that, but since you just brought up the matter of the truth, have you ever wanted to kill anyone and gotten to the point where you would actually have done it?"

Wendy exhaled quickly. "No."

"But I *had* gotten to that point. You see the difference, right?"

Wendy mulled things over and decided to take a different approach in order to try to help lift her friend out of her mental state. "If you don't mind my asking, how did things get so bad between you and Brent? Didn't they start out well enough? Weren't you in love with each other at some point?"

"Sure, we were. I thought he was perfect husband material." Carly's tone began taking on a brighter, softer quality, and her eyes took on the distant look of fond memory. "Brent was the heartthrob of Rosalie High School, and I was one of many girls who dreamed of snaring him. We all thought about what beautiful children we could make with him. Then, wonder of wonders, he asked me out. We continued dating then and in college, and then he asked me to marry him right after he graduated and headed to law school."

Carly paused, and there was once again an edge to her voice. "But he began changing once he started practicing law. If you want my opinion, he viewed every case the way he viewed his football games in high school and college. He felt that everyone should cheer him on, the way they did when he was a quarterback. But he forgot that every time he won a huge settlement, somebody else lost, and he wasn't very gracious about it. He rubbed it in and threw his weight around, and I think that's when his so-called 'fan base' began to slip away from him."

"Sorry to hear that."

Carly made a sweeping gesture with a rather glum face. "I'm sure you've noticed all the football photos on the walls. Snapshots of plays, players and coaches on the sidelines, final scoreboards, fans posing with him—why, there's one of the Four-Second Game touchdown in every room of the house. Except the bathrooms. That's so out of character for him because, you know, he always viewed himself as the king of the world on the throne."

The pun lightened the mood, and the two women managed a brief chuckle, even if it seemed a bit out of place. "The bottom line is that Brent was a man who needed to be worshiped constantly, and if it wasn't volunteered, he made people kowtow to him anyway. If he perceived that he wasn't getting his proper due and respect from someone, he went out of his way to punish them for it. There were no exceptions to this, even if Brent's perceptions were wrong."

Wendy needed no further explanation, as Carlos, Hollis, Mitzy, and Deedah all quickly came to mind. Not to mention the greenskeeper, Gerald Mansfield, whom she had never met. But the pair of Tip Jarvis and Connor James continued to remain somewhat of a puzzle to her.

"What was the deal with his golfing partners? Did he really lash out at them because they beat him on the course for once?"

Carly did a face palm while shaking her head. "I'm afraid so. He was that petty. But he would have you believe that those two men envied him. Remember that phrase he used— what was it, oh, yes—*jock sniffers*. Somewhat of a nasty concept, if you ask me. The locker-room language these athletes will come up with."

"I certainly agree with you," Wendy said. "I'd never heard the term before until Brent said it to us."

"Well, it wasn't true that they were, in my opinion. Brent, Tip, and Connor ended up together by default. Their wives, Shelley Jarvis and Louisa James, and I, we all belong to the Rosalie Garden Club, and we're great friends on all the social committees. We dragged our husbands to all the balls and fund-raisers over the years—'dragged' being the operative word—and that's how the three of them got to know each other. Over many, many drinks at many parties, they found out they had golfing in common, and everything just evolved from there. I guess they even thought of it as their 'way out.'"

Wendy pressed on. "What about The Four-Second Game? How did they overcome that since they played for the rival teams?"

"I think they called a truce and put it in the past at one

point. But then Brent dredged it all up again and added that revelation about the officials being paid off. I think that pushed things over the edge."

"Do you think he was telling the truth?"

Carly became emotional again as her voice quavered. "He swore me to secrecy about it all those years. It makes me think he was. But that's another reason I wanted to talk to you. I know for a fact that Claude Ingalls, the clock operator, was living for a long time out at Rosalie Retirement Home. At least that's what Brent told me at some point. I called out there once to confirm it, and I was told that Mr. Ingalls was in the independent wing, not assisted living or memory care. Of course that was a few years back. Should I tell that to the police or not so they can question him about everything, that is, if he's still alive?"

Here, Wendy was quite emphatic. "You don't have to. I'll tell Ross myself, and the police will definitely follow up on the lead. So that will be taken care of, and you can stay out of it completely. As for your desire to drown your husband, that'll just be our little secret. I can readily understand why you needed to get it off your chest, and I hope talking to me has helped in some way."

"I don't know," Carly told her. "Sometimes I think this whole unbelievable thing will do me in."

Wendy took her hand and gave it a gentle squeeze. "I'm glad you turned to me then. But you have to try to forgive yourself."

"I'm telling the truth when I say that I really don't miss Brent at all, but I'm still ashamed that I thought about doing what I was going to do to him for even one split second."

"The best thing is for you to just keep it to yourself, as I said," Wendy added. "No one else needs to know."

"It shouldn't have come to this," Carly said. "It's all my fault. It's been a couple of years since David graduated from college and started his teaching career up in Milwaukee. I should have served Brent divorce papers then and walked away from all this. That was my chance for freedom. There was no love left between us, and I knew it as well as David knew it."

"Why do you think you held on, then?" Wendy continued, her voice as gentle as possible.

Carly threw her hands up in the air and shrugged. "Inertia, I guess. I'd become someone deadened to change. Someone afraid to be on my own again at my age. I don't know. Pick one. It was the mistake of my life. And now, here we are with Brent's body down in Jackson taking a number to be autopsied. Then after that, he'll be cremated. At this memorial service, though, I know I'll feel nothing. Except guilt. That gash . . . and the guilt."

"I'm glad you told me all of this if it's helped you in any way."

Carly managed a weak little smile that didn't last long. "I'm going to try and take your advice about letting go of all this if I can. I hope I'm up to the challenge."

The two women hugged, said goodbye, and Wendy left Brentwood feeling that she had accomplished something in giving good counsel to Carly. It was the least she could do for a bridge-playing friend who had been put through the wringer.

On the drive back to Rosalie with its undulating kudzu-covered ravines on either side of the highway, Wendy revisited the hypothetical secret Carly had divulged so reluctantly to her. Now she knew something about what had gone on that night at the RCC that no one else knew. Well, that wasn't quite right. It was something that might have happened, but no one would ever know about it if she kept Carly's trust. Was it the right thing to keep it from Ross or her father? Did it have a bearing on the actual murder? Carly was clearly an unstable mess because of all she had endured recently—that much was abundantly clear. But why hold that against her? She had weathered the storm of being married to Brent for decades, and that had obviously taken its toll on her.

As Wendy entered Whiteapple Village on the outskirts of Rosalie, she decided that it would definitely be wrong to betray Carly in any manner whatsoever. The evidence clearly pointed to Carlos's pestle as the murder weapon, and that was what Ross and the CID would run with. In fact, Wendy knew that Ross would likely be interrogating Carlos Galbis right about now downtown at the police station. She decided to send him a text to bring him up to date:

just finished with Carly Ogle, went well.

His response arrived about thirty seconds later:

just about to go in and start w/ Carlos Galbis. Ttyl.
kiss, kiss.

Inside the interrogation room with its institutional green walls and TV camera affixed high up in one corner, it was Ross's observation that Carlos Galbis presented a very straight-forward, clean-cut appearance and impression, just as he had the evening of Brent Ogle's murder. Although he was not wearing his customary bartender's tux, he was still impecca-bly dressed in a navy-blue jacket, white shirt, and red tie. To say that the outfit suggested someone who wanted to make a point about being an American and perhaps loyal to its flag was an understatement, and Carlos lost no time in getting around to just that.

"To answer your question about why Mr. Ogle liked to pick on me, you have to understand first, Mr. Rierson, that my father, my Poppo, barely got out of Cuba alive when he was just a boy of fourteen. His father—MiGrando, we called him—was a food broker in Havana at the time of Castro's revolution and takeover from Batista. Those were dangerous times, and life was cheap. So because MiGrando was considered a capitalist and therefore the enemy doing business with America, he was in line for the firing squad. Castro seized his warehouse and his home, but MiGrando, Mamacita, and Poppo got away along with my uncles and aunts and shipped out to New Orleans in the nick of time to start a new life. They were stowaways on a freighter. Then later on, they came up the Mississippi River to Rosalie and MiGrando started a new food brokerage business right here. It did not take long for him to study to become an American citizen. He and Mamacita and Poppo were all grateful to have a country to adopt, and when Poppo married my Mommi and had me and my brothers and sisters, we were all just as proud to be Americans as they were."

Ross was showing off his customary interrogation smile and said, "That's all very stirring, Mr. Galbis, and I'm glad to hear it all worked out for your family, I truly am. But I believe you were going to explain why Brent Ogle bullied you, and I think you've gotten off track a bit."

Carlos sat up even straighter in his chair and brought his hands together. "No, sir. I just wanted to be sure you understood that my family—all of us—are legal immigrants. Mr. Ogle was always implying that we were not—or rather, I was not. It seems to me that the current political climate regarding immigration has made things worse for certain people, and Mr. Ogle upped the ante. He referred to me as a wetback sometimes, as if I'd swum across the Rio Grande, or as someone needing a green card, and he never called me by my given name. I also speak perfect English, being the third generation of the Galbis family to live here in America, but sometimes when he got really drunk, Mr. Ogle would speak to me in some sort of pidgin Spanish. You know—putting *o*'s on the ends of words. Making up things like *drinko* and *quicko*. He was drunk like that the afternoon he was murdered, including all the time he was in the hot tub, of course. That trip out when I took that last drink to him, he was half-asleep when I called his name. Maybe he was about to pass out."

"But he was alive when you left him that last time?"

"Yes," Carlos said emphatically. "And mad as hell that I woke him up, cussing all over the place. I thought for a second he might even throw the drink on me, although he was never one to waste liquor. Still, he was capable of anything."

Ross nodded sympathetically but pressed on. "How did that make you feel when he treated you the way he did all the time?"

There was a flash of anger in Carlos's face. "I won't lie to you, Mr. Rierson. I had to bite my tongue all the time. I didn't dare go and complain to Mr. Voss when he was alive because he and Mr. Ogle were like this." Carlos crossed his fingers and held them above his head. "I have not only been making a good living as the RCC's bartender, but I have a good reputation around Rosalie as well. People will come out there just to try one of my mint juleps, and they keep coming back for more. It keeps me well in the black supporting my wife and three children. Especially the tips. Except nothing much to speak of from the pockets of Mr. Ogle. Ever. He treated us all like his own personal slaves."

"Not surprising from what I've heard," Ross said. "At any rate, we have to deal with the fact that it was your pestle that was used to club Mr. Ogle over the head. There's no way around that. I want you to try and give me the best timeline you can about your whereabouts during the half hour of the blackout. It's in your best interests that you be as accurate as you can, if not regarding the exact minute, then the sequence of events as you remember them."

Carlos took his time, eyeing the ceiling intently before he finally caught Ross's gaze and spoke. "I remember very clearly that when the power went off, I wanted to call my wife, Elena, to see if the power was off at home, too, and if everything was okay with her and the children. But there's a part of the roof over the bar that interferes with this old phone of mine sometimes, as I told you before. So I have to go out to the portico to make calls now and then. That's what I did, and I was able to get through."

"How long were you out there, do you think?"

Carlos considered again. "Maybe five minutes. My wife likes to go on and on, and she even put my oldest boy on so he could tell me he was looking after everybody for me. That Carlos Junior, he is my little prince, and he wanted to tell me all about this book he'd finished reading all by himself. My wife started reading to him when he was very little, and now, he can't get enough of books."

Ross nodded approvingly. "That will serve him well, I'm sure. But moving on—was there anyone else out there under the portico when you arrived, or did anyone else join you during that time?"

"No, I was alone the whole time," Carlos said, sounding very sure of himself. "I do remember seeing phone lights before I went out there, but there was no one around later."

"I'm glad to hear you say that. It'll help me makes some sense of this portico business."

"Pardon?"

"Miz Carly Ogle and Hollis Hornesby have told me that they were also out on the portico before and during part of the blackout but that no one else was there. I have to check into the possibility that someone is not telling me the truth."

The expression on Carlos's face clearly indicated that he had taken offense at Ross's words. "But I am telling you the truth, Mr. Rierson. If they said they were there, then they must have come and gone before I went out there. I am a hardworking, honest man—a family man. Perhaps some would say I had every reason to take my pestle and hit Mr. Ogle over the head with it, but I can assure you, I did not. It would be against my religion to take a human life. I go to Mass regularly here at the Basilica."

"I understand and applaud you for that, but you will concede that you were away from the bar long enough for someone to have sneaked into the great room, taken it, and then used it to murder Mr. Ogle, will you not?"

"That is undoubtedly what happened, Mr. Rierson," Carlos said. "Because I assure you again, I did not do such a thing."

"Did you by any chance notice that the pestle was missing when you returned from your phone call under the portico?"

Carlos sounded supremely confident. "I did not for two reasons. First, it was obviously very dark, and second, I did not expect it to be missing so I did not search for it. Why should I expect such a thing—that someone would be plotting a murder, such an obvious work of the Devil? In any case, everyone in the building knew I used the mortar and pestle frequently to make juleps and mojitos, and they all knew where I kept them both. They were always out in plain sight as the tools of my trade."

"That makes sense, of course," Ross said in that impeccably calm tone he used in his interrogations. "Just as it makes sense that your prints and DNA were all over the bar area, since that's your workstation." Then he switched subjects. "Did you see anyone or hear anything once you had returned to the bar after your call?"

"Yes, I saw Miz Carly and Miz Wendy, and they came up

to me from the locker-room hallway and asked me to follow them. They were both sort of breathless and excited, and I did follow them to Miz Deedah's office, where they told her and the others about Mr. Ogle, and that is the first I knew anything about it."

Ross was making mental notes and said nothing for a while. Slowly but surely, a timeline during the blackout was emerging. Carlos insisted that he had not encountered Hollis Hornesby and Carly Ogle or anyone else out on the portico at any time. Carly had said she had left the portico for Deedah's office shortly after the power outage but that Hollis had stayed out there. Yet the party line seemed to be that Carlos and Hollis had not crossed paths. Were they perhaps in this together somehow as Brent Ogle's favorite targets? Or was he creating a conspiracy theory by overreacting?

So, Ross did a rewind in his head of the timeline: Hollis and Carly had both said on their taped interrogations Saturday evening that they had left Deedah's office before the power outage for some air under the portico—then returned at different times. Ross reasoned upon second consideration that Hollis, Carly, and Carlos were all like the proverbial ships passing in the night, just missing each other in a very tight timeline. Which was the more likely scenario? He did not have enough information at this time to reach a conclusion.

"So you state emphatically once again that you did not hit Mr. Ogle over the head with your pestle?" Ross continued.

Carlos held up his hand and then crossed himself. "I swear to God that I did not, Mr. Rierson."

"In any case, I'm sure you know that we will want you to stay in Rosalie throughout the investigation. Please do not leave for any reason."

"Where would I take my family and go to? Back to Cuba?" Carlos said with great intensity. "Castro may be dead now, but Cuba is still not free. And there were people who never

got out and paid with their lives at the time of the revolution."
Then he covered his chest with the palm of his hand. "Rosalie
is my home now, and it is truly my heart, *mi corazón*."

"All right, then. I have one last thing for you. Miz Carly
states that someone knocked her down in the hallway after
she discovered her husband's body. I am already going on the
assumption that it was not you who did that."

Carlos nodded eagerly. "It was not."

"She also says that she gave a little shriek when that happened and that whoever it was ran away in the direction of
the great room. If you were there at the bar at that time, then
why did you not hear Miz Carly or the footsteps of someone
running across the great room? You saw and heard nothing?"

Carlos frowned, bringing out every line in his face as he
was obviously trying hard to remember. "Well, there was a
period in there that I got enough of a signal to listen to music
on my cell phone to pass the time, and it was plugged into my
ear. I got tired of standing, so I went over to one of the sofas
across the way to lie down for a little while. But I had come
back to the bar when Miz Carly and Miz Wendy came out
from the hallway and told me to follow them to Miz Deedah's
office."

"Well, that fits in very nicely with other testimony, but
again I must ask you not to leave town."

After Carlos had left, Ross stayed in the interrogation
room and thought even further about the timeline during the
blackout. He had come up with a short sentence that he absolutely believed in: *Wendy is my constant.*

No matter what anyone else had said or would say had
happened during that half-hour period, Wendy was the one
person he could rely upon for the unvarnished truth. She had
no reason to lie about anything, nor did she have any hidden
agendas. That was not an advantage he had often enjoyed
during his many investigations. Much of the time, a variety of

suspects presented their own conflicting versions of the truth; and, of course, the guilty party or parties frequently lied to try to confuse things and escape prosecution.

This constant of his—his very own Wendy—just might give Ross the baseline he needed to solve the murder of Brent Ogle in a timely manner.

CHAPTER 7

Carly Ogle had been right when she had suggested to Wendy that there might be a paltry turnout for her husband's memorial service at the First Presbyterian Church. In fact, there could not have been more than twenty-five, maybe thirty people scattered around the historic building with its Calvinist lack of ornamentation, plain white walls, and tall, clear windows that disdained stained glass. But it occurred to Wendy that Carly's had become a self-fulfilling prophecy because she had labored mightily to keep everything somewhat of a secret. Perhaps she simply did not want to deal with tons of people trying to find the words to paint Brent Ogle in the most favorable light. She knew that would be a task for most of them. Or she was not up to standing on her feet, shaking a lot of hands, and smiling obsequiously for an hour or two, pretending that it was the least bit tolerable for her.

In any case, the no-nonsense, iconic Reverend Vernon Foster thankfully had not composed a lengthy, overblown homily to preach from the pulpit. Instead, he had focused on generalities, things that might have applied to anyone who had occupied space during a particular lifetime. These were platitudes with which no one could disagree. And he had ended on a hopeful, though vague, note as well.

"Let us all take this moment to be thankful for life itself as we say goodbye to Brent David Ogle, Sr., of Rosalie, Mississippi."

Sitting in a pew close to the front with Ross on one side of her and her father on the other, Wendy could not help but find those closing words somewhat equivocal, even slightly disrespectful. It was almost like the Reverend Foster were saying, "Thank God we're all still alive, no thanks to Brent Ogle."

Then she caught herself and cringed. This hot tub murder at the RCC was really beginning to do a number on her. It continued to blur the line between the job she was supposed to be doing for pay and the one her father and Ross were doing as part of their job description.

There had been no visitation earlier. Because of the autopsy situation in Jackson, there was no body to view, nor an urn containing ashes on display. Just the brief service. Then, at the Spartan reception in the Fellowship Hall next door— no refreshments other than a pitcher of ice water and plastic glasses had even been provided—Wendy noticed that Carly seemed eager to get things over with as people approached her; she was saying things to them like, "Please don't think you have to stay any longer," and, "Thank you for coming, but I know you have things you need to do today." Taking their cue from her, the sparse crowd dwindled down to practically nothing quickly. In an odd reversal of form, people had come there to comfort Carly, but she had managed to make them feel uncomfortable and drive them away. Funerals were clearly not her forte.

But David Ogle remained by his mother's side the entire time, his face a study in stoicism. Wendy was impressed with

the way he hooked his arm through hers and held her close
to his side, as if trying to infuse her with his own strength.
As Carly had told her at Brentwood, the young man did not
resemble his father at all—neither in looks nor in stature.
Though he was attractive, his features were not sharp and
angular like Brent's had been. His hair was light, not dark.
His was a softer countenance, not unlike his mother's, and he
was also several inches shorter than his more athletic father.
Genes were often more random than people thought, and it
was sometimes possible for offspring to have little in common
with one or both parents. David Ogle appeared to be one such
example, at least where his father was concerned.

Wendy tried at one point to make small talk with him,
as Ross stood nearby. "Your mother tells us you're a teacher.
History, I believe."

"Yes. You can't really succeed in this world unless you
have a sense of history. I mourn for today's generation. Some
of them think the world started the day they were born."

Wendy took the controversial comment in stride and said,
"Have you always wanted to teach?"

David bowed his head slightly. "Always. I never understood why some people didn't share my passion for learning.
But I never wanted to teach down here in the South. It's way
behind in so many ways. Maybe even a century and a half
behind, and sometimes I think that's being too generous."

Carly intervened quickly, forcing a smile. "Now don't get
into all of that, David. The Civil War is over."

"But the lingering effects from it are not. Nor of Jim
Crow. We are all still paying as a country for those sins, and
we will for some time to come. Anyway, I'm just answering
her question, Mom," David said, his face now flushed and full
of intensity. "I'm telling her the truth. This is not the life I
wanted for myself down here. Wisconsin, on the other hand,

is in an alternate universe, and I'm proud to live there. At least there, they've moved into the millennium."

Wendy caught Ross's eye briefly but said nothing further. She was reminded of everything Carly had told her about the strained relationship between David and his father. That Brent had become even more ornery and insensitive because he couldn't seem to make a connection with his own son growing up and even after the boy had reached manhood. Wendy could see for herself quite clearly after the brief exchange she'd had with David how accurate all that had been.

"David would like to stay with me a little longer," Carly said. "But he has to be back in Wisconsin for his job. It's very important to him, of course. It was hard enough for him to get off to come down as it was. Much as I hate to see him go, he's leaving tomorrow."

"I've been telling Mom to sell the house and come up to live with me in Wisconsin," David added. "I'm hoping at some point she'll listen to me and not ramble around the place all by herself. Brentwood was always way bigger than it needed to be. So many rooms, so little time to find a use for them all. It was the ultimate ego trip for my father."

Carly seemed uncomfortable with her son's words. "I told him I'd consider it. I just need some time to think things over. I've been told you should never make major decisions until at least six months to a year after you've lost a loved one, so I'm keeping that in mind as I try to move forward."

"Neither of us liked the house," David continued. "It was all about Dad and nothing else. Thus, the pompous name— Brentwood. I always liked to think of it more as Brentpatch."

The muscles of Carly's face tightened and she leaned against her son. "I think that's quite enough of your airing our dirty laundry in public, David. Don't spoil your visit, please."

"Sorry," he said, catching everyone's gaze in turn. "It's

just that I don't want Mom to be alone now. I have a good life up there in Wisconsin, and I'd like Mom to come and be a part of it, that's all. I don't think I'm asking too much. I'm just thinking of what's best for her."

"I'll work things out my own way in my own time," Carly told him. "Meanwhile, let's let these kind folks be on their way."

Wendy and the two men in her life took their cue and made their manners in short order.

"Please get in touch with me if there is anything I can do for you, Carly," Wendy said there at the end as the two women hugged.

"I promise I'll do just that. And thanks again for coming and for your all your kind concern."

Fifteen minutes later, Wendy, Ross, and Bax were all having nightcaps at a Country Café corner table, the cozy little pub with a classic '50s jukebox just down from Bluff City Bistro on Broad Street that they all sometimes frequented together. Whenever they went in, Bax liked to go over and buy a listen to one of Patsy Cline's classics—sometimes "Crazy," sometimes "Sweet Dreams," or what they were all listening to now—"Walkin' After Midnight."

"Glad you insisted we have a bite before the services and not after, daughter a' mine," Bax said, contentedly sipping his off-duty beer and tapping his foot to the beat of his favorite music. "We'd be starving to death by now. That's the first wake I've ever been to where there wasn't even as much as a dish of mixed nuts to snack on or a paper napkin to wipe the salt off your hands."

"The whole thing was bare-bones and rushed," Ross added, staring down at his scotch and soda.

"I saw it coming, though," Wendy said. "Carly was up-front with me about how unhappy she was in their marriage.

I guess she felt she had to keep up appearances and have some sort of service for social reasons, but as we all witnessed, her heart just wasn't in it. Not by a mile."

"She told me the same thing about her relationship with her husband when I interviewed her Saturday evening," Ross continued. "Offhand, I'd say most Rosalieans weren't going to show up and shed alligator tears for Brent anyway and Miz Ogle knew it. She cut 'em off at the pass and avoided embarrassment. At least that's the way I have it figured. I can't say I blame her if that was the reasoning behind it."

Wendy took a sip of her coffee liqueur and quivered slightly as it slid down her throat with a pleasant burning sensation. "That's one way of looking at it." She glanced first at Ross, then at her father. "How are you men progressing with this case? What bits and pieces can you share with me? If I might, I'd like to say this about it. It seems there are plenty of suspects, but it also seems like none of them are the type of person who would actually do something like club someone over the head with a pestle. In fact, the only person I can think of who might club someone over the head with a pestle is Brent Ogle, himself. Yet I'm more than reasonably sure this wasn't a matter of suicide. Do you guys think I have a point?"

Ross caught himself in the midst of a chuckle but repressed it quickly. "Actually, I think you do, strange as it seems. Carlos Galbis comes off like a hardworking saint to me. Hollis Hornesby seems like a bullied innocent with an artistic but completely mild temperament. His mother is obviously quite qualified to run the RCC and has been cooperative with the department in the extreme. We couldn't have asked for more, the way she let us use her office for questioning. Those golfers are a couple of good ole boys whose worst vice seems to be drinking too much and being a bad judge of character, and that golf pro conducts herself in a very professional manner and doesn't seem to let anything bother her. None of them seem capable of the sort of rage I see in the blunt force trauma that killed Brent Ogle."

"Yet we have a dead body," Bax added. "So somebody is not what they appear to be. There's a façade and a backstory somewhere out there that we're missing or not picking up on."

"Don't worry. We'll turn up the truth eventually," Ross said. "It's just a matter of time."

"Speaking of time," Bax continued, "I called down to Jackson again this morning to check on the status of Brent Ogle's autopsy. They're still backed up like you wouldn't believe down there. The State of Mississippi could stand to give the ME a lot more help than he has now."

Ross swallowed a healthy swig of his scotch and soda and made a macho face as it kicked in. "I don't see what difference it makes, though. The coroner said the COD was clearly blunt force trauma. What else do they expect to find?"

"You never know in murder cases, my boy," Bax said. "The strangest things sometimes turn up. Things you'd never expect. We'll just have to wait and see before we close that part of the case."

Wendy had been hanging on their every word and was now thoroughly intrigued. "You said some strange things have turned up in autopsies, Daddy. Can you give me an example?"

Bax sucked in a bit of air, and his mouth hitched up to one side. "Matter a' fact, I can think of one right off the bat. We had a case once that appeared to be an accident. An older man had walked out onto his front porch, fallen, and hit his head on the front stoop. That had caused a blood clot to form inside his brain and that took him out. But the tox panel in the autopsy later revealed that he had three times the amount of an antidepressant in his bloodstream than his doctor had prescribed for him. That should never have happened, because his home nurse was responsible for his med schedule. It was up to her to see that he got enough but not too much. Turns out the old man's son and the nurse were having an affair and the son couldn't wait to inherit his father's impressive estate and gallivant around the world with her. So he had the nurse overdose the old man, and that's what caused the fall, and you can thank the autopsy for that. Both the son and the nurse are in prison now for premeditated murder. So they didn't get away with anything."

Wendy looked supremely satisfied. She had always been mesmerized by her father's stories from the time she was a little girl. He was surely her Svengali. "I had another thought while we're kicking things around. Has the department done enough so far in regard to backstories?"

"If you mean, have we checked for criminal records among all the suspects, the answer is yes," Bax told her. "No hits on anyone. But the reality is, someone will end up with a record after we put this one to bed."

"I didn't mean that exactly, Daddy. Maybe we should be looking for something else in their background."

"Such as?"

"I don't know." Wendy was alive with speculation. "It's just that something about the term *backstory* is resonating with me for some reason. Isn't that what sleuthing is all about?"

"So your puzzle-solving gene is acting up again, I take it?"

She laughed and gave her father a familiar, affectionate look. "Well, you have to admit, I've solved more than a few puzzles because of it—not to mention The Grand Slam Murders last year."

"That you did. You wowed the entire department. Some of the rookies still talk about you."

Ross spoke up quickly, sounding a bit annoyed. "Yeah, and I have to remind a couple of them with roving eyes now and then that I'm already seeing you. I've overheard some

conversations in the locker room about your hair and your—"
He came to an abrupt halt and trotted out an artificial smile.
"Well, we won't go there."

"Don't be embarrassed. I assure you, I'm flattered," Wendy
told him. "I can handle it if you can."

What was really sticking in Wendy's head as Bax picked
up the tab, however, was that phrase again: *backstory*.

She did not know why quite yet, but her sleuthing skills
were telling her that she needed to pay attention to it; and that
gift of hers would prompt her at the appropriate time to dig
into it with the dedication of a dachshund flushing out a pesky
mole in the backyard.

CHAPTER 8

Just after the RCC was finally released as a crime scene the next day, Wendy sensed it was coming. Had she dreamed about it, or had it just been hovering over her like an unpaid credit card bill piling up interest? And then finally, there it was in reality in Deedah's office, delivered with the solemn essence of a message from one of the Armed Services in wartime.

"I assure you I'm devoted to making a success of our Bridge Bunch just as much as you are," Deedah said, squirming in her seat a bit behind her desk. "But I don't think we should resume playing bridge out here until this case is solved. All eyes in Rosalie are on us."

Wendy had rehearsed what she would say if the subject actually came up at some point: "We don't want to act like we're guilty, do we? Won't that look a bit strange to everyone?"

But she didn't say that when the words came out of Deedah's mouth. Instead, she headed in another direction. "What if it never gets solved? Do we abandon our club altogether? What do we do then?"

Deedah gave her the most skeptical glance she could manage, tapping her ballpoint pen on her desk. "I don't think it's a matter of guilt as much as it is respect. Don't you have more faith in the police department than that? After all, your boyfriend and your father are on the case. And if I recall, you very neatly helped them solve The Grand Slam Murders last year when no one else could."

Wendy perked up noticeably at the mention of her achievement. She never tired of hearing about it all this time later. "You do have a point. I guess I wasn't thinking of it that way. And, yes, I just this minute replayed our earlier conversation in my head, and I didn't sound very concerned about the importance of solving a murder case versus playing a card game, did I?"

Deedah stilled her pen and adopted a more sympathetic tone. "Well, I do understand where you were coming from, but I don't think it would be very appropriate for us to continue our bridge games with what's happened. Even if we're talking about the murder of Brent Ogle, someone I know I've wished would've dropped dead more than a few times. And now, I seem to have gotten my wish. Yet, the whole thing leaves a bad taste in the mouth, doesn't it?"

Wendy's shrug was hesitant. How had everything gotten so complicated? "It is a slippery slope, I'll admit. But in the case of the Bridge Bunch, we're only talking about you and me and your son and Carly. I expect us all to be taken off the board of suspects soon enough."

"I would hope so." There was a lengthy pause, and something about it suggested to Wendy that problematical things were going on inside Deedah's head. "Anyway, I think we should put the Bridge Bunch on hold, knowing that we fully intend to resume playing when everything is finally out in the open and we're comfortable again. I think it's the best course of action right now."

"Are you going to let Carly know, or do you want me to

tell her?" Wendy said. Then she broke into a frown. "You know, I was out there visiting with her recently, and we never even brought up the subject of bridge. She probably doesn't feel like playing it right now anyway. Why would she?"

"Again, I think it's the right instinct for all of us not to play," Deedah said. "I just wanted the two of us to agree to make it official. You let Carly know."

"I will."

At that moment, Wendy also mentally conceded that perhaps her fascination with becoming an accomplished bridge player was a pipe dream and fated never to come to fruition. It seemed to be backfiring on her, over and over again. She could always go back to chess, which she had learned by watching her father and his cronies play while she was growing up, looking over their shoulders. Chess only took one other person to play, and it could even be done by postcard with a partner halfway around the world. She recalled that her father had once played for the better part of a year that way with a professor in Finland of all places. Besides, she had her newspaper feature to create, and that was far more important to the advancement of her career.

"There was another reason I wanted you to see me today," Deedah resumed. "I was thinking about your newspaper article on the women who are running things in Rosalie, and I thought it might be useful for you to meet and interview Gerald Mansfield, our greenskeeper. He could tell you what it's been like for him to work with me and Mitzy Stone, as opposed to the previous regime. That might be another way of illustrating that women can do just as good a job as men can—and sometimes even better. What better way to judge an employer than through their employees?"

All thoughts of bridge vanished as Wendy smiled and said, "I think that's an excellent angle to explore. When and where do we meet?"

"Right now," Deedah told her. "Right this afternoon. Just wander out onto the back deck. Gerald's waiting for you in one of the rocking chairs. I'll text him that you're on the way."

"You have a plan for everything, Deedah. I can't thank you enough," Wendy said, heading out the door with great anticipation.

Having never met a greenskeeper before, Wendy did not know quite what to expect as she emerged from the locker-room hallway out onto the deck. But she was more than surprised by Gerald Mansfield's appearance as he rose from his rocking chair to extend his hand. He was dressed in a coat and tie as if he were going to church, but the suit he was wearing was too big for his young, lean body and the maroon color did not flatter his bony, sunburned face and slicked-back haircut. It flashed into Wendy's head that these were clothes he was not accustomed to wearing and perhaps had even thrown together from a visit to a thrift shop at the last minute to make a favorable impression.

"It's very nice of you to come and visit with me," Gerald said, as Wendy completed the handshake. "Miz Deedah says she thinks I can help you with that newspaper article a' yours. But my goodness, you sure do have pretty hair. What color would you call that there?"

"Strawberry blonde is what I think most people call it."

"Never seen anything like it. It's part red and part blond. I think you got the best a' both."

"Well, thank you very much. I forget all about it until someone like yourself calls my attention to it again."

"Did I say somethin' wrong, Miz Winchester?"

"No, indeed. I was just thinking out loud, I guess. I appreciate your compliment very much."

Wendy took a seat in the rocking chair next to his but was

made somewhat uncomfortable by the fact that the hot tub in which Brent Ogle had been murdered was across the way a bit. "It's really nice to meet you, Mr. Mansfield," she said, taking her notepad and pen out of her purse. "I hope you can help me a lot with this article of mine on the management here at the RCC."

Gerald smiled in a disarmingly boyish way. There was an element of obliviousness in it, too. "I've never been so popular." But he left the remark at that.

"What do you mean?" Wendy said finally.

"The police, they want to talk to me, too. I'm supposed to go down to the station later today and talk to a detective. Miz Deedah thinks I can help you, and the police think I can help them." He pointed to the lapel of his jacket, preening. "I even bought some new clothes, see? I wanna look my best."

Wendy nodded with a forced grin, but she wondered why Ross hadn't texted her about interrogating Gerald Mansfield. Of course, he was under no obligation to do so—even less to share the results of his investigation with her—but he often let her know little bits and pieces nevertheless.

"You'll be talking to Detective Rierson then," Wendy said.

Again, Gerald's face lit up. "Yes. I think that's his name. I'm flattered that they think I can help 'em solve the murder of Mr. Ogle. Of course, I have to say I didn't like him very much. That's no big secret around here. He was always on me about somethin', but I always did the best I could for the country club. Miz Mitzy, now she never had any complaints about me when she came, and I work with her a lot. Still, I don't know anything about the murder."

Wendy decided to put aside her newspaper article mission for a moment. The sleuth in her couldn't help but take the microphone as if she were on a TV field assignment. "You were off the day it happened, weren't you?"

"Yes. I was at home watching TV in my recliner. College

football, mostly. Except when the power went off. Then I had to find where I'd put the candles, you know?"

"Was anyone with you?" Wendy continued. She could picture Ross asking the same questions, but she would get there first.

"No, ma'am," he said. "I live by myself in uh apartment complex. There are some pretty ladies living there, though. I just wish I could get one of 'em to be my girlfriend, ya know?"

"I'm sure you will. Just be patient and the right one will come along," Wendy said, but she could see why he was having trouble with the women. He came off as a bit undereducated and entirely too needy. Confidence was certainly not his middle name, and she knew for a fact that women were not impressed by that.

Then Wendy decided to switch back to her feature article. "Tell me about working with Miz Deedah and Miz Mitzy, if you wouldn't mind."

"It's like night and day since they showed up," Gerald began. At first his demeanor was pleasant, but it began changing as he continued. It was as if a switch had been turned on somewhere inside him. "Mr. Voss, he was always on me to cut the rough down to nothin'. Well, it's not supposed to be that way. That's why they call it the rough. The greens is one thing; the rough, another. But once Miz Deedah and Miz Mitzy came aboard, they pretty much let me do things my way. They're nice ladies, they're a good team, but I can tell you that Mr. Ogle didn't like 'em at all. He made life miserable for 'em and all the rest of us, too." At the end of what had become a rant, Gerald's ruddy countenance had taken on an almost devilish intensity. Where had the innocent boy of a few minutes ago up and gone?

"That seems to be a common sentiment around the RCC," Wendy said. "Mr. Ogle was certainly unpopular."

"No lie." He practically spit out the words, and his brown eyes had a strange glint in them that had not been there before.

The awkward silence that followed, plus the fact that Wendy could still see the hot tub out of the corner of her eye, worked together to push her toward changing her impression of Gerald Mansfield. Her initial perspective of a somewhat unsophisticated young man following orders to be helpful was being replaced by the sensation of a scene being played out for her benefit. It hardly even seemed to be conscious on her part. That island of knowledge she possessed when it came to solving problems was emerging once again for her. The same one that had allowed her at a young age to point to pieces of jigsaw puzzles that always fit without even thinking about it. It was that gift of hers acting up again, and she fully intended to use it.

Words and phrases were flashing before her regarding Gerald Mansfield:

No alibi . . .
New clothes that didn't fit . . .
A loner . . .
Following orders . . .
Part of a good team . . .

Was there something sketch-like and theatrical about all of this? Deedah arranging for her to meet him on the deck near the hot tub? Wendy had not asked for such a meeting. Was there an agenda in the air, or was she just overthinking everything? She recalled how the entire power outage scenario had reminded her again of a stage play where the lights go off and a murder has taken place when they come back on. Was she being overly dramatic about it all just like Hollis Hornesby was about every single moment of his histrionic life?

Then she finally relaxed. If she turned out to be straining

at gnats, she could always compare notes with Ross after he'd finished interrogating Gerald Mansfield. He likely wouldn't share that much with her, but she could bounce some ideas off of him, as she'd done in the past. Talk about your teams.

That last thought about Ross stopped Wendy dead in her tracks. How long was she really going to keep him waiting? She knew she loved him, and that he loved her, but she also knew she had her investigative reporter mission that kept driving her to maintain a degree of independence in her little bungalow out on Lower Kingston Road.

And then talk about your teams, once again. Lyndell Slover was someone who would continue to allow her to grow in the job, not manipulate her as Dalton Hemmings had done. She was determined to make a name for herself, and nothing was going to keep her from her mission. Not even a wedding with all the trimmings that her devoted father had been just bursting to pay for anytime she said the word. Dear, dear Daddy, Captain Baxter Lewis Winchester.

The long, thoughtful silence was finally broken when Gerald said, "Do you think I can really help that police detective, Miz Winchester?"

"Just be yourself," Wendy told him, realizing then and there how much her advice reflected her recent internal monologue.

When the interview came to an unremarkable end shortly thereafter, Wendy found herself wanting to walk in the opposite direction of the hot tub. She had to admit that it creeped her out to be anywhere near it. After all, she could reach the parking lot in the front by following the deck around, which she then chose to do. The significance of that particular maneuver was not lost on her, either.

Perhaps it was because they were just a few days away from Halloween now, but there was an eerie aspect to the fact that

Ross presented the same unspoken concept that had occupied Wendy's thoughts some of the time during her interview with Gerald Mansfield at the RCC. He had done so unprompted.

Team.

There it was again, and it caused Wendy to shudder slightly.

"What's the matter?" Ross said, always attuned to her body language.

They were sitting once again at their favorite Bluff City Bistro front table overlooking the river, having dinner after trudging separately through what had been a long day. Wendy had finished up summarizing her meeting with Gerald Mansfield when Ross had included the magic word in one simple sentence.

"Bax came up with the idea of this murder possibly being the work of a *team*," he had said. But Wendy had imagined that he had raised his voice when he said it. In fact, he had not. But she felt obligated to elaborate, putting down her fork and temporarily abandoning her Greek salad.

"Funny," she said. "I've been tossing that idea around, too. But I think I'm making myself dizzy with all the possible combinations. Some of them seem impossible, and others seem insulting to these people I've come to know." She paused. "Or think I know."

"That's the rub, isn't it?" Ross said, picking up a French fry with his fingers and making short work of it. "My experience in law enforcement tells me that what you think you know about certain people is often completely wrong, and the truth is often shocking. The most appealing faces can be masks for hiding something truly ugly."

"Then you don't think I'm crazy for spending time on this, I take it?"

"No, I don't. Bax and I have been doing the same thing. That, and working on the timeline during the blackout.

That's the real stinker here. One or more of the suspects have to be lying to us about where they were—at least part of the time. We have a dead body but no incriminating prints or DNA around the hot tub thanks to all the humidity, steam, and water, except that of the deceased. Meanwhile, the RCC is swimming in prints and DNA elsewhere, and none of it is the least bit incriminating. All these people, including yourself, were all over the place leaving traces of themselves, but it doesn't help us much. I'd give anything if the RCC had had surveillance cameras anywhere, even in the parking lot. But there's not a one of them. I think you should suggest that to Miz Hornesby next time you see her."

Wendy resumed spearing some of her salad with her fork and said, "I'd be surprised if she hasn't already authorized something like that herself, but I'll bring it up."

Ross took another bite of his Bluff burger and fell into a "cow chewing its cud" mode. Finally, he spoke up. "The other thing that Bax and I have been talking about is that wrap-around covered deck. I made an overall diagram, and the fact is that the deck would have made it possible for someone—anyone—to go outside and get to the hot tub and Brent Ogle without going through the building. And they would hardly have gotten wet doing it. Everyone I interrogated Saturday night was as dry as they could be."

"It wasn't raining the whole time we were there, either," Wendy pointed out. "We had lulls. There were gaps on the radar, and I'm sure some of us would have headed home had the murder not happened. But it's interesting that you and Daddy and I seem to be on the same page again. When I finished up my interview with Gerald Mansfield, I deliberately went back to the car walking under the deck in the opposite direction from the hot tub. I'm just uncomfortable getting anywhere near it. It seems like a shrine of evil to me."

"I can't blame you," Ross said. "And I agree with you

about the gaps. Bax and I think the power outage obviously threw everyone off their game." Ross shook his head in silence. "Except it's my belief that it inspired someone—maybe more than one person—to go into action. Of course, at some point they would have had to get hold of that pestle inside the building. The covered deck angle can only get us so far. There are two components to this thing that we can't overlook. First, you get the weapon. Then you find a way to use the weapon and get to the victim without being observed. We've nixed the idea that this could have been premeditated because of the randomness of the power outage. But I do think at least one person lost it and acted out, and the rest is history and part of my job to solve."

Wendy did her own version of thoughtful chewing for a while. "So can you give me your impression of Gerald Mansfield? I kept getting the strange feeling that something was off."

"Inconclusive, I'd say. He clearly didn't like Brent Ogle, but that seems to have come with the territory among all the suspects. Bax says he can't believe how much Brent had changed over the years. Seems he went from conquering hero to the Devil, himself, in one lifetime. I wouldn't say that Gerald Mansfield shed any new light on our investigation, though."

"Even though he has no alibi?"

"That may be," Ross said. "But there is no evidence that Gerald Mansfield was there that Saturday. No one saw him anywhere at any time. There were some prints of his in Miz Deedah's and Miz Mitzy's offices, but when I asked him about that, he said that he sometimes went into their offices to tell them something or other. Or they wanted him to come in for a meeting. That seems reasonable. At any rate, as with the rest of you, there was nothing incriminating of his around the crime scene."

Wendy looked up from her salad, taken a bit by surprise. "Haven't you taken me off the list yet?"

"Your father and I have, of course. You know you're in the clear. I'll try not to phrase things that way in the future."

Wendy took a sip of her Rosalie muscadine wine and absolved him with a smile. "So who are you interrogating next? Or are you through?"

"Not hardly." Ross's eyes bugged out for an instant. "Tomorrow, I've got Tip Jarvis down at the station first thing in the morning and Connor James a little later for their second sessions. They do fit the concept of the team effort that we've been tossing around. Every time I look at the diagram, I can't help but notice how close the men's locker room is to the bar, and how easy it would have been for one of them to sneak down the hallway and steal the pestle at the right moment while the other stood guard. Then they could have had the same arrangement when the murder was committed—one actually doing it while the other was a lookout."

"Yes, that's one of the team combinations I've considered that doesn't give me a sense of betrayal," Wendy said, looking slightly sheepish. "Mainly since they're not part of the Bridge Bunch, and they hung around with Brent Ogle for whatever reasons. I think they exercised very poor judgment in doing so. That said, I don't know much about either of them."

"Well, I do intend to find out as much as I can tomorrow. The key thing will be to see if they can keep their stories straight. What you find a lot when two or more people are involved in an investigation is that there will be the inevitable discrepancies that tip you off. Sometimes it helps, sometimes not. But both of these guys are definitely persons of interest, considering that brawl they got into with Brent Ogle. Men coming to blows sends up a red flag for sure."

Wendy played with a look of disgust. "Men and their testosterone. Will the nonsense never stop?"

"I keep mine under control," Ross said without hesitation, while giving her a wink. "I save it for special moments with my lady."

"No complaints. You do a great job."

He took a generous swig of his wine, and the stare he gave her was full of affection. "Thanks. I just hope I can do a great job with this case. We need a real break of some kind to stop this wandering around in the darkness, slowly feeling our way. Sometimes, you know, you can have too many suspects, and that really does confuse the situation a lot."

Ross had chosen not to make a night of it at Wendy's bungalow because of the early day he had on his agenda with Tip Jarvis and Connor James, so the two of them had kissed and hugged under the lacework balcony of the Bluff City Bistro and then headed toward their cars. Once she got home, however, Wendy couldn't seem to get the concept of *teams* out of her mind. She decided it was actually time to sit down at the kitchen table and prioritize the combinations she had been entertaining in her head. Perhaps that would clarify things a bit.

She took out a piece of paper and began to print in all caps. The heading she wrote was to indicate the combinations that had come to mind first. Under it, in caps and lowercase, she began her list, but she only got one pair done before she found herself staring incredulously at what she had just written:

POSSIBLE TEAMS
Tip Jarvis and Connor James

She began to feel distinctly uncomfortable as she actually tried to put pen to paper where other couplings were concerned. She realized immediately that she was too close to the situation to be as objective as police detectives such as Ross had to be. Of course it wasn't her job to solve this crime, but the sleuthing side of her had made its successful debut last year and was showing no signs of becoming a wallflower at the dance anytime soon.

Deedah and Mitzy had made her mental cut as well, but it made her cringe. She had come to know them both in a meaningful way, although it was Mitzy who had actually mentioned the concept of "teamwork" to her during their interview. And working with Deedah had been as pleasurable an experience as it was ongoing with Lyndell Slover. It was difficult to imagine Deedah in any murderous combination.

Except . . . perhaps where her wildly theatrical son, Hollis, was concerned. And even that seemed somewhat of a stretch. A mother and son committing such a brutal crime together on the spur of the moment? Stranger things had been known to happen, but for the time being, it seemed unlikely and continued to be distasteful for Wendy to even consider.

Including Carly Ogle in any combination made Wendy feel like a criminal, herself. She had never in her entire life witnessed such genuine catharsis as she had when Carly had confessed the vile and base thoughts she had had about her husband in their conversation out at Brentwood. That was to her credit, though. She did not have to reveal such wretched things to anyone. Besides herself, Wendy had decided that Carly definitely did not belong on any list and was instead in dire need of empathy and professional grief counseling.

What about Carlos Galbis in some combination? He had always seemed like such a gentle and polite man to her. She enjoyed his cocktail skills and his cheerful manner. Ironic, then, wasn't it, that he had the easiest access of anyone to the murder weapon. Not only that, but he had actually made the

the short walk down the locker-room hallway more than once that Saturday to serve Brent Ogle his drinks. His motive, along with all of the others,' was well established. But Wendy knew from casual conversations with Carlos over the past few months that his main focus was on supporting his family. He could hardly do so from prison or with a death sentence hanging over him, so Wendy's instinct was to cross him off her list.

Ross had seemed mostly dismissive of Gerald Mansfield. But there was Wendy's lingering impression that he was following orders of some kind. On the surface, Deedah's orders, of course. It was Deedah who had inserted him into the mix in the first place, bringing up the concept of "someone from outside" possibly being a factor in Brent Ogle's murder. Wendy did not care for the fact that that had brought her back to Deedah again. She must maintain her objectivity at all costs, if for no other reason than she was in the midst of a feature on women like Deedah running things in Rosalie. Would a woman that prominent, intelligent, and accomplished risk it all to get Brent Ogle out of the way for good? To be sure, the man had threatened to withdraw his significant funding of the RCC on his last day on earth, and that would have been a big deal had he followed through.

So, where was all this fevered conjecture getting her as a sleuth? She felt like she was running around in circles, unable to bear down and be objective enough to get the job done.

Wendy sighed and then crumpled her fledgling list into a ball, throwing it into the small trash can off to one side of the refrigerator. Then, she returned to the idea of the entire murderous scenario reminding her of a stage play. Perhaps spontaneously generated by the power outage but nonetheless striking someone's visceral emotions as surely as lightning had struck transformers all over Rosalie and plunged the city into darkness.

The challenge was to determine who among those assembled at the RCC that fateful evening was telling the truth and who was playing the villainous part of a lifetime, rehearsed or unrehearsed.

CHAPTER 9

Ross had to admit that Tip Jarvis had a beautiful set of white teeth. He had actually come across a dentist or two who did not and had ended up being walking advertisements for turning people off and going to the competition as a result. But though Tip obviously did not watch his weight, he surely paid attention to his flossing and dental cleanings. All that aside, Ross was intent on finding out as much as he could about what lay behind the man's flawless smile and overly obsequious manner in his answers so far in the interrogation room.

"If you don't mind," Ross said, continuing his line of questioning, "I'd now like to revisit this tussle you had with Brent Ogle last Saturday afternoon. You came to blows, and you told me previously that you just lost it because of his cockiness. It appears you wanted to strangle the guy, and I have to say, that doesn't look good for you as we continue this investigation."

Tip maintained his smile, but there was less confidence in his tone. "As I told you, he just got on my nerves. Without the booze I'd had, I probably would have let it go. Brent could be very irritating at times. Uh, let me revise that. He was irritating nearly all the time. You just had to retrain your brain not to notice. You had to think of other things and other people while you were around him."

"Well, it seems to me that you were thinking about him exclusively when you went after him. It took Miz Stone to pull you off of him. If she hadn't, what do you think would have happened?"

Finally, Tip's smile diminished significantly, as he appeared annoyed. "Why are we discussing something that didn't happen, though? I thought law enforcement was about collecting evidence and getting the facts. You already know that I did not strangle Brent, and I assure you I did not club him with that pestle. Do you have any evidence against me to suggest that?"

"I'd prefer to ask the questions, Mr. Jarvis."

Tip was now in the midst of a sour expression, and his transformation from vacuous smiley face was now complete. "Go ahead, then."

Ross made a grim slash of his mouth and caught the man's gaze intently. "I'd like to present a scenario to you. You and Mr. James were just right down the hallway in the men's locker room and also not very far away from the bar where Carlos Galbis's mortar and pestle were very accessible. You are using each other for an alibi as to your activities during the blackout. But is there something you're not telling me?"

"Like what? We've both already told you that we went into the locker room to play gin until there was a letup in the storm outside. Then when we couldn't do that after the power outage, we just scrolled on our phones. It was beyond boring. And anyway, once we started to get into our running gin game—the best three outta five for starters, by the way—any bad, over-the-top feelings for Brent had dissipated. He was drunk as usual. Not that I'm saying that me and Connor didn't get drunk with him a lot. I'm not the pot calling the kettle black here."

Ross broke his gaze and looked up at the camera in the corner of the room for a moment. Without a two-way mirror, his small-town police department had to rely upon it to review their interrogations at length. "I think what I really want to know is this. Did you believe Mr. Ogle's story that his father had paid off the officials in The Four-Second Game? I know about the RHS and St. Mark's rivalry and how intense it's gotten from time to time."

"So you think after thirty years, I'd be carrying around enough pimply, juvenile bad sportsmanship to want to kill Brent Ogle whether he was telling the truth or not?" Tip said, looking incredulous.

"Since you posed the question so conveniently for me, I'd like for you to go ahead and answer it."

"No. Plain and simple. No. I have a successful career, a nice wife, and two kids in college now. That's what's important to me, not some overrated football play from the days of my youth. Like I said, Brent just got on my nerves a little too much, and I'll admit to not acting very much like an adult about it."

"But you didn't tell me whether you thought Brent Ogle was telling the truth or not."

Tip looked surprised. "Didn't I?"

"No, you didn't."

"Well, for the record, *I* didn't."

Ross noted the emphasis. "Meaning?"

"Meaning that I think Connor did believe Brent was telling the truth and that the man was bragging about it, too. Brent's picture is in the dictionary under the word *bragging*, so I can understand Connor thinking that way. You can ask him about it if you want a better explanation."

"I assure you I will do just that," Ross said. "So let me get this straight once again. There was never a time in the locker room that you and Connor were separated. You were always together, and you always knew where the other one was. You're sticking to that story."

Tip was about to answer and then hesitated. "Well . . ." He seemed reluctant to continue.

"Well, what?"

"Now that I think about it, there was one brief period of time. You know, when nature calls. I took a leak when we first got to the locker room, because liquor goes right through me. But after the power outage, Connor said he needed to go; so there was a time when I was still sitting on the changing bench with my phone and Connor made his way to one of the stalls or the urinals. You'll understand that we didn't discuss which number before he left." The last remark returned a hint of a smile to Tip's face.

"How long do you think Mr. James was gone?"

"I'm not sure. I was paying attention to the weather radar movement on my phone. It looked like there was a good gap on the way, and that we might be able to get away soon. Connor was gone maybe a few minutes. I did hear flushing, and then he joined me again."

"I suppose Mr. James will confirm this for me."

"I don't see why he wouldn't. I don't think either of us brought it up the first time because, well, who talks about going to the bathroom? It seems kinda beside the point, doesn't it?"

Ross offered up an understanding grin. "Ordinarily, you'd be correct. But not where murder is concerned. In this case, the fixtures in the locker room are close to the door and the hallway. A small window of time is all that would have been necessary for a crime to be committed. I've seen it over and over again in my work."

Tip was now in full-frown mode. "You're not telling me you think Connor may have sneaked off and killed Brent, are you? He's not the type any more than I am. We have our moral limits. Brent, on the other hand, did not."

"That's why I'm interrogating both of you again. Who knows what little detail we might turn up? For instance, you've just admitted to me that neither one of you bothered to tell me that you *did* have a period of time in which you were apart. The first time around, you both insisted that you were always together."

A hint of anger crept into Tip's voice. "Hey, that was no conspiracy or anything like that. As I said, who thinks about reporting trips to the bathroom? It just slipped my mind and Connor's, too."

Ross changed the subject quickly. "Is there anything else you may have forgotten to tell me? I'm not saying this in an accusatory manner. Just search your brain as thoroughly as you can."

Tip took a while and said, "I can't think of anything else at the moment. If I should come up with something, I'll let you know."

"Please do. Thank you for coming in today. We'll be in touch if we need you further. Meanwhile, don't leave Rosalie."

In the beginning of his interrogation with Connor James, Ross kept wondering why the man looked so much older than his contemporary Tip Jarvis. After all, Tip carried around a noticeable paunch, while Connor's belly was flat. Then, it hit him. It was the hair. Connor had very little to speak of, while Tip's crew cut gave him a younger appearance. It somehow seemed unfair, since Tip obviously wasn't paying much attention to his diet; but his genes were working in his favor when it came to hair follicles.

Connor also started out as cooperative as Tip had been, though not nearly as smiley faced. Ross also noticed the man seemed to enunciate his words carefully, emphasizing certain syllables here and there. Then he remembered from his previous interview that Connor was a pediatrician. Perhaps talking to children all the time when they weren't feeling well had engendered a rhythm or technique of sorts. It had to be to his advantage to sound reassuring to the little ones and not frighten them.

"I'd like to touch upon something that your friend, Tip, told me earlier this morning," Ross was saying. "He suggested to me that you *did* believe Brent Ogle when he claimed his father had paid off the officials in The Four-Second Game. Could you comment on that, please?"

Connor looked surprised. "He said that?"

"He did."

The slightly patronizing speech pattern Conner had been using disappeared. "I wouldn't go as far as to say I actually believed Brent. It's just that I react in a different way to things than Tip does. I mean, he has a certain mentality, and I have one of my own."

"And what would the difference be?"

Connor cracked a hint of a smile. "I mean, he's a dentist. He sees a cavity and goes for it. He takes that drill and grinds away after he's numbed his patients with the needle, and that gets the job done."

"I don't quite see how that's relevant," Ross said, looking sideways. "Please enlighten me."

"It's just that I can't be that direct, dealing with kids the way I do. And their worried parents. I have to take my patients dead serious, even if what they're saying makes no sense. I can't make any false assumptions based on the way a child sees and feels the world. So, there was a part of me that took Brent seriously when he threw his weight around with that story."

It took Ross a while to process Connor's answer. Something about it seemed overly rehearsed and perhaps a bit too touchy-feely. "All right, then. Let's go on the assumption that Brent was telling the truth. Did you have the same visceral reaction that Tip did? Did the story stir you up and make you want to go for the jugular? Or the neck, like Tip did?"

"A little. But not exactly like Tip. He's always been a guy that acts out when he needs to. I . . . I sorta keep things in. If you want to know where that's gotten me, I have an ulcer to show for it. It's under control with medication now, but at least I know why I have it."

"Glad it's under control," Ross said. "My late father had one, and it was hell for him to manage."

"Sorry to hear that."

Ross nodded gratefully and then moved on. "Do you ever find yourself wanting to explode because of the way you keep things in?"

Connor's frown indicated he understood the implications of the question. "What are you getting at?"

Ross leaned back in his chair as if he were about to tell a joke. "Just something that occurred to me. I see the results of road rage a lot in my work. You know how people can get in traffic. They let things build up and build up until their frustrations explode and get the better of them. Sometimes with fatal results." He let that lie there for a while, and Connor did not seem to want to respond.

Finally, Connor said, "I've never been guilty of road rage. As I said, I keep things bottled up inside."

"Duly noted, once again," Ross continued. "Which brings me to this. Tip also told me that the two of you were mistaken when you both said you were always together during the blackout. He mentioned that you took a bathroom break for several minutes. During that time, you would have been apart from each other."

Connor looked astounded. "And? Do you think I wanted Tip to go with me? I'm a grown man."

"The point is," Ross said, straightening his posture, "that

you had a window of opportunity during that time to retrieve the pestle and pay Brent Ogle a very nasty little visit."

Connor's cultivated pediatric demeanor had now completely vanished. "That's nonsense. I did no such thing. I'd have to be in the middle of one helluva rage to do something like that."

"Yes. I would agree that whoever did this had to be in . . . as you say, one helluva rage or not in their right mind. Blunt force trauma to the head is never pretty."

"I could never do something like that," Connor said, shaking his head. "I make my living healing little children. I took an oath to do no harm. That also applies to my life outside the doctor's office. I think you need to look elsewhere for the culprit in this case. Tip and I both are not the man you're looking for."

"Or not the team I'm looking for?"

"If you want to put it that way."

"We have no evidence that either of you are," Ross told him. "But we have to keep at it with our questions. Somebody killed Brent Ogle, and I'm sure you appreciate the fact that the altercation both of you had with him requires that we investigate further. We wouldn't be doing our job if we didn't."

"I do understand that," Connor said. "And for what it's worth, I abhor what happened to Brent. He was somewhat of a conceited scoundrel, but our wives brought us together socially, and we seemed to have found the lowest common denominator for hanging out—drinking. Oh, and golfing. There wasn't much more to it than that. We weren't really friends where it counts. I wouldn't say we'd go out of our way to risk our investments or anything like that for him."

"That's pretty straightforward. But I'll tell you what I told Tip. We may need you to come in again as the investigation proceeds. And stay in town until we get this thing solved."

Connor said that he would and then left with a polite goodbye. Ross again leaned back in his chair and did a quick mental review. He had to admit that the "team" of Tip Jarvis and Connor James suddenly seemed far less viable as suspects. There was plenty to merit that impression now. They were both professional men with full lives, and the risk either of them would have taken to commit murder did not line up with Ross's knowledge of human behavior. True, they were the closest to the crime scene and the bar, but Ross felt that the psychology seemed all wrong. Now wasn't that a hoot and a half? Of course, if either or both of the pair were not telling the truth, all bets were off. All along, they had been backing each other up, but now that he had gotten to know them a little better, Ross had concluded that either they were very clever liars, or they were innocent. And he was willing to bet that when Bax reviewed the tapes with him, his mentor would come to the same conclusion.

Wendy was thrilled when Lyndell had popped into her cubicle ten minutes or so earlier and offered to take her to lunch. It was the first time she had done something like that since replacing Dalton Hemmings. There had been plenty of meetings in the editor's office, during which Lyndell had more than once dangled the promise of "getting a bite together soon."

Now it was finally happening, and when Wendy was asked to pick a place that served shrimp and grits—something Lyndell said she had just been dying to try since forever—The Toast of Rosalie fit the bill perfectly. Seafood was their specialty, and the place was a bit pricey. But since Lyndell was treating, Wendy saw no reason not to go all out to impress her boss.

The Toast of Rosalie was one of those restaurants whose strength was the cuisine, not the ambience. If Rosalieans wanted a little bit of both, they frequented the Bluff City Bistro or The House on the Hill, an eighteenth-century tavern that had been repurposed several times before its successful incarnation as a Southern comfort food establishment.

The Toast of Rosalie made no bones about its purpose in life. There were no fussy potted ferns and palms, fancy paintings on the walls, or stained-glass windows for show. Just a ceiling with exposed ductwork and a hardwood floor that had seen better days; and most of all, knowledgeable career waiters who knew which fresh fish had just been flown up from the Gulf and which specials of the day were to die for.

Meanwhile, there was always their version of shrimp and grits every time out—laden with sweet julienned bell pepper, chopped onion, mushrooms, a bit of andouille sausage, a base of cheesy grits, and, of course, those oversized shrimp on top, grilled to perfection. It was a lot of food to eat, and Wendy could not recall a time when she had not asked for a doggy bag.

"I gather your feature is going well," Lyndell was saying after their older, distinguished-looking waiter with salt-and-pepper hair had taken their order and headed off with menus in hand. "I haven't heard you complaining about anything. I have to tell you—I do appreciate that quality in a reporter. Let them figure it out for themselves, I always say."

Wendy nodded while quickly squeezing lemon into her ice water and then making a little whirlpool with her spoon. "I've gotten loads of cooperation from everyone so far."

She swallowed a sip and then caught Lyndell's eye. "But I wanted to tell you how perfect your timing was with this lunch meeting, so to speak. I do have some concerns about how we make this article work in a positive way, instead of making it look like we're ganging up on a dead man. I don't think we want to go there with our readers. I've been thinking it over, and I realized that no matter how unpopular Brent Ogle was with everyone out at the RCC and even around town, the fact remains that he was brutally murdered. So, I have to find just the right slant, you know. Both Deedah Hornesby and Mitzy Stone minced no words about how much better things were now that William Voss and Brent Ogle weren't running things. Do you see the slippery slope I'm suggesting to you?"

"Yes, I do," Lyndell said, cocking her head to one side. "We can't be disrespectful or appear to be blatantly judging. Your assignment is going to be a bit more difficult than I thought at first."

"It's also occurred to me that our article showcasing women in power positions and having unusual jobs in Rosalie might be a little easier to read after Brent Ogle's murderer is caught and his motivation is revealed."

"Or *her* motivation."

Wendy sounded and felt a bit sheepish. "Of course. You're absolutely right. It's no foregone conclusion that the murderer was a man. I guess there's still the idea out there that men do certain things better while women do certain other things better, and ne'er the twain shall meet. I should know better, and I'll try to keep an eye on these knee-jerk reactions."

She took a deep breath and continued. "The point I wanted to make about our article coming out after the case is solved is that everyone would be talking about why Brent Ogle got murdered. There's no way the reasons will be uplifting, I'm quite sure. That way, if we do have any comparisons to make between the old male regime and the new female regime, people will understand it all a bit better, and they won't think we're piling on."

"That was a bit long-winded," Lyndell said. "But you finally got there. Still, we'll want to be careful not to get into outright sensationalism with any of this. It's easy to do."

The remark brought a wry grin to Wendy's face. For the first time since Lyndell had taken over the editorial reins, she had made a statement that reminded Wendy of something Dalton Hemmings might say. But it was all good. She never wanted to be guilty of veering into tabloid journalism and the lowest common denominator that it attracted. So she was quite comfortable with the reminder. Perhaps it sounded different coming from a woman. Or someone she respected. Either one or both.

"Who will you be interviewing next?" Lyndell continued.

"I thought I might visit Hollis Hornesby at his art gallery. As a matter of fact, we're meeting later this afternoon," Wendy said. "With his mother being a major focus of the feature, I wanted to get his point of view. Of course, he also happens to be a suspect in the case."

"Try not to do too much double duty, though. Unless you want to give up the newspaper business and actually join the police department."

Wendy laughed brightly. "Now you sound exactly like my father. He's lobbying all the time."

"An interesting man, I've heard. I've been meaning to meet him in person and just haven't worked it into my schedule yet," Lyndell said.

"That can be arranged. I'll tell him to drop by sometime. The newspaper editor and the Chief of Police should definitely be on speaking terms."

"Oh, we've spoken over the phone a couple of times. I confess I liked the sound of his voice."

Wendy couldn't help but read between the lines. It had been nearly a dozen years since she and her father had lost Valerie Lyons Winchester—wife, mother, and artist specializing in primitive acrylics—to pneumonia; but Wendy had never pressed her Captain Bax about the issue of further companionship. The matchmaker in her was instantly intrigued, however.

When the plates of shrimp and grits finally arrived, Lyndell lit up like a little girl at a Disney princess–themed birthday party. Then, when she got her first taste, she looked like she just might rocket out of her chair up to the ceiling. Wendy remembered her own exaggerated reaction the first time she'd tasted the dish.

"Ohh!" she exclaimed, making dainty circles in the air with her fork. "This is every bit as delicious as I thought it would be."

"Isn't it? If I could afford it, I'd probably eat here every day for lunch and shoot my budget to pieces."

Lyndell shrunk down to normal size and looked at her sideways. "Is that by any chance a request for a raise?"

"No, thanks," Wendy said, chuckling. "Just had one when I got this investigative reporter job last year. On the other hand, if you're offering . . ."

"We'll see after I've been here a tad bit longer," Lyndell told her, but her tone was friendly and promising.

After that, the conversation morphed into small talk and additional raves about the food—the newspaper business being put aside for a spell. It was time spent well delegated, and the bond between editor and reporter had clearly grown even stronger by the time the dishes had been cleared. Wendy sensed that that had been Lyndell's mission in the first place.

"I'm too full of good food and good conversation to order dessert," Lyndell said, giving Wendy a fond glance. "Unless you have something light as a feather to recommend."

"Afraid there's no such creature like that here on the menu," Wendy said. "Everything sweet they whip up is beyond ooey-gooey and heavy. Good for the taste buds, but not good for the figure."

"Thanks for the heads-up," Lyndell said, getting the waiter's attention for the bill with a delicate wave of her hand.

"A sedentary job like this can sometimes lead a woman astray if she doesn't watch it, but sometimes I just say to hell with the discipline and treat myself."

Out of the corner of her eye on the way out, Wendy caught sight of Gerald Mansfield as she trailed behind her boss. She managed a mini-swivel of sorts to confirm that he really was the man she'd just spotted. He caught her maneuver, smiled, and waved at her, and she nodded back politely. All that time, he had been seated at a table in the distance with a clear line of sight to her own table. But she had been too preoccupied with Lyndell and their conversation to notice, not to mention that Lyndell had been blocking her view much of the time.

For some reason, she found the fact that he was there at all, possibly observing her throughout her meal, a bit peculiar. Was it just a coincidence? Surely, it had to be. How could he have known that she would be at The Toast of Rosalie today? Her sleuthing mode had kicked into high gear once again. After all, he was quite some distance away from the RCC to be taking such a leisurely lunch break, although she had to admit she had no idea how long he had been sitting there. Perhaps the man treated himself to something upscale to eat every once in a while. Perhaps there was nothing more to it than that. Practically everyone in Rosalie, it seemed, was crazy for The Toast of Rosalie's shrimp and grits. Why should Gerald Mansfield be any different?

At any rate, Wendy let these meanderings linger in her head as Lyndell crisply led the way out the door and down the street to her car. Wendy had told Ross that she thought there was something not quite right about Gerald Mansfield during that rocking chair interview she had conducted with him out on the deck. Ross had seemed to dismiss her impression and said he'd found his own interrogation of the man mostly unremarkable. Perhaps she had been overly influenced by the appearance of the hot tub nearby—that, and the memories of

Brent Ogle's blunt force trauma to the head. Who wouldn't
have found all that loathsome to deal with?

Then a phrase reappeared on the front burner of her brain:
following orders. That had been a perception of Gerald that
she'd had that first time. Was he still doing that? And, if so,
for whom?

CHAPTER 10

Hollis Hornesby's art gallery—preciously named Hollow Horne—occupied one of the many brick and lacework buildings scattered around downtown Rosalie, this one on Locust Street. Unlike the other brick and black lacework structures, however, Hollow Horne's balcony and delicate columns had been painted white for as long as anyone could remember, and that gave them a distinctive flair. Several Rosalieans had written letters to the *Citizen* expressing their delight that the long-vacant store had been repurposed for such an upscale, cultural mission. It remained to be seen, however, how those same Rosalieans actually embraced the art pieces inside with their pocketbooks. It was too early to tell if they would end up placing Hollis's one-note French Quarter studies on the walls of their homes and businesses.

"Welcome to Hollow Horne," Hollis said in that dramatic fashion of his as Wendy came through the glass-paneled front door. He then executed a fanciful twirl with a wide gesture and wineglass in hand. "These are my earnest offerings to the world, reflecting images of my vivid life down in the French Quarter for all those many years. You're more than welcome to browse to your little heart's content. My Mardi Gras section is to the right, and my French Quarter Street section is to your left. Is this your first visit to my little shop?"

"It is," Wendy told him, noting that several lighted votive candles on the checkout counter were filling the room with a strong vanilla fragrance. "Please don't hold that against me, either. I've been so busy with my work that I just haven't been able to work it into my schedule."

"I wouldn't dream of holding such a grudge. It's beyond juvenile. Being devoted to work is something I completely understand. If I could just get Mother to slow down a bit out at the RCC, though. She's so driven to make everything perfect. Nothing ever will be in this world, you know, but Mother keeps holding out hope that it will happen for her if she just tries hard enough."

"I can be somewhat of a perfectionist, myself," Wendy said.

Hollis starting talking out of the side of his mouth, and his eyes shifted to one side. "Mother's been looking for a real project she could sink her teeth into ever since Father died. She liked it well enough, but being an accountant really didn't do it for her. Now, though, she's totally hooked on running the RCC. Pretty much nothing stands in her way. She's her own little caftan-wearing bulldozer."

"Do you mind if we sit?" Wendy said, bringing out her notepad and pen from her purse.

Hollis looked as if he might faint and fanned himself. "Please, please forgive me. Where are my manners? There's a table right over there against the wall. Oh, and would you like some of this wine I've been drinking? It's just one of our drier Rosalie muscadines. I'm not a big fan of the sweet ones. They cloy on my palate. Or I also have some sparkling water or cider chilling in the mini-fridge in the back room if you'd prefer that."

"Nothing for me, thanks," Wendy said, as they seated themselves and settled in. "I've just had an enormous lunch with my editor at The Toast of Rosalie. I may never eat or drink anything again."

"Let me guess. Shrimp and grits?"

"What else?" Then Wendy began making notes. "Give me just a minute to get caught up."

Hollis waited patiently for her to finish and then said, "Was there anything in particular you wanted to know about Mother and the RCC?"

"Yes. The changes Deedah has been making. They seem to have been well received by everyone except Brent Ogle, of course. Would you confirm that that's an accurate statement?"

Hollis did not answer immediately, but Wendy could tell he was enthralled with the question by the sly expression on his face. "Perfectly accurate," he began finally. "And I've been so pumped about the Bridge Bunch because I've loved the game since Mother taught it to me when I was in high school. Then I found a bunch of guys in the dorm at Tulane who swore by it, too. But then . . . but then . . ."

Wendy noted the downturn in his tone and on his face as he came to a halt. "But then what?"

"Would you believe I couldn't find three other people down in New Orleans who liked to play? All those years, I went without it. Not just cold turkey but Ice Age turkey practically. And then suddenly, you and Mother came to my rescue, and I was playing again. Not only that, but you and I had won that first rubber before things came to a screeching halt with all that macho foolishness Brent Ogle stirred up. Of course, he was always doing things like that." Hollis gave Wendy a desperate glance, and his nostrils flared for a few seconds. "Please tell me you're not going along with Mother on suspending play until this grievous murder is solved. Pretty please with brown sugar on it."

"Oh, that," Wendy said, somewhat surprised that he had

gone there. "I have to confess I wasn't convinced we should stop playing, either. I told her I thought that maybe it might make us look guilty. But your mother prevailed in our discussion. At least for the time being."

"And you don't think you can change her mind?"

Wendy shook her head slowly but said nothing.

"Foot."

Wendy was amused by his response. She had expected something more dramatic and colorful, perhaps something even profane, followed by Hollis draining his wineglass. "At any rate, we've gotten off the subject a little bit. Tell me a little more about your mother's mission at the RCC from your point of view."

"She and I have discussed it at length, of course, and Mother doesn't want to compete socially with the garden clubs. She knows she couldn't do that, as established as they all are. But she feels the RCC is too much of a 'jock place' and certain people are uncomfortable with that. It's not exactly my cup of tea, either." He paused and managed a coy smile. "I take that back. I do love to stay in shape with my swimming. I'll miss it grievously during the winter months ahead. But the point is, Mother doesn't see any harm in softening the place's sharp, masculine edges. As you probably know, Brent Ogle was dead set against everything Mother was trying to do. I've developed a pretty tough skin over the years because of my being . . . different and all, but nothing riles me up quicker than someone attacking my mother in any shape, form, or fashion. Where family is concerned, I can be fierce."

Wendy was surprised by Hollis's intensity near the end of his lengthy speech. She flashed back to the discussion she and Ross had had about the "rage" reflected in the act of someone clubbing Brent Ogle with that pestle. Were mother and son both capable of such rage on behalf of each other? She found herself shuddering noticeably at the notion of Deedah, particularly, being that vicious and out of control. It did not suit her persona at all.

"What's the matter?" Hollis said, picking up on her discomfort.

"It's nothing, really," she told him, recovering quickly. "Just a weird little chill that went up my spine."

He leaned in, again talking out of the side of his mouth. "There's a rumor Halloween's coming up soon." He paused and then said, "Boo!"

They both chuckled, and after a decent time, Wendy said in a serious tone, "Unfortunately, the RCC has become its own House of Horrors lately. It's really put our image behind the eight ball."

"Mother insisted that Brent Ogle had already turned it into a hostile place during all the time he and Mr. Voss ran things," Hollis said. "And then right there at the end he threatened to take his ball and run away so nobody could play anymore. It would have broken Mother's heart had he lived to do that."

"But he didn't. Someone saw to that."

Now it was Hollis's turn to reflect discomfort. "Yes . . . they did. I . . . I can't pretend that I'm not glad it happened, though."

Wendy didn't hesitate. "I think everyone is being honest about that—just as you are. No reason to say otherwise."

Suddenly, Hollis took a deep breath that seemed to consume all the air in the room. For a second, Wendy thought something might be wrong with him physically. "Are you all right? How much of that wine have you had?"

There was another, smaller intake of air. "Maybe one glass too much. But it's not that. It's just that there's something . . ." He pressed his lips together and maintained the pose for a

while. Had his teeth been showing, it would have amounted
to a genuine grimace.

Wendy softened her voice as much as she could. "What is
it? Tell me what's on your mind."

Hollis tried his best to relax his facial muscles, but he
couldn't seem to do it. Tension oozed from his every con-
torted feature. "There's something I haven't told anyone. Not
even Mother. And I certainly didn't tell Mr. Rierson when
he interviewed me Saturday. I'm actually supposed to see him
tomorrow. He just called me before you came in and told me
he wants to question me again. I'm sure that implies that I'm
a more serious suspect now, doesn't it?"

Wendy continued to try to soothe him. "Not necessarily.
It's probably the same thing he's doing with everyone. It's his
job to explore all the possibilities. Don't read things into it
that may not be there."

"Maybe you're right, but this thing I haven't told anyone about is sorta complicated," Hollis continued, his voice
strained and thin. "I just think I ought to tell you first and see
if you think I should go ahead and tell Mr. Rierson."

Déjà vu was practically pushing Wendy out of her chair.
Was this going to be Carly Ogle all over again? Wendy was
beginning to feel like a priest on the other side of the confes-
sional. Something about her personality seemed to be having
that effect on people these days.

"Go ahead then," she said. "I think if you don't tell someone, you might explode, judging by the way you're acting
right now."

Hollis put both his hands on the table, palms down, and
leaned toward her with a suggestion of tears welling up. "I
haven't mentioned this because I thought it might incriminate
me. You see, there was a short time on Saturday that I was
alone out there under the portico after Carly Ogle had left.

I don't know what got into me, but I decided I was going to run back to that hot tub and confront Brent Ogle about those threats he'd made to my mother. Even in the dark with just the light from my phone. I wanted to tell him off for that and for the way he'd been treating me since I came back from New Orleans and started coming out to use the RCC pool. I've been bullied all my life, and I decided it was time for me to finally stand up for myself—and my mother, of course." He paused for a breath.

"So are you telling me that you followed through on that?"

"I intended to. But . . ."

"Go on. You've gotten this far."

"I . . . started following the deck around to the hot tub. But when I was halfway there, I had second thoughts and sat down in one of the rockers to think it through again. Finally, I decided to forge ahead. I even called out Mr. Ogle's name when I got close enough, but he didn't answer me. I called out again. Same thing—no response. And then when I got closer, I could see why he didn't answer me. I shined my phone down on him and saw that awful gash on the top of his head and his eyes so blank, and I just knew he had to be dead looking like that. And then I panicked. I was so horrified that I didn't even think to go back the way I came. My brain just wasn't functioning. Instead, I just bolted through the hallway door, and on the way, I ran into someone and knocked them down and then I ran off as fast as I could toward Mother's office."

Wendy nodded eagerly. "That was Carly Ogle you knocked down. She had no idea who it was. She said she couldn't even tell if it was a man or a woman."

"I can believe it. Everything happened so fast in the darkness that there wasn't time for me to make head nor tail of anything, either. My adrenaline felt like a bathtub overflowing. Or at least it seemed that way to me. So I didn't have the least bit of trouble expressing shock when you and Miz Ogle came in a little bit later and gave everyone the bad news that I already knew about."

Wendy finished writing something and then looked up. "So it was *your* footsteps both Carly and I heard."

"I admit it. That was me. Those were my fear-laden sandals you heard making tracks. But can you see why I didn't want to bring this up to Mr. Rierson on Saturday? It puts me right at the crime scene at around the right time with a motive and an opportunity. Except I didn't have that pestle in my hand, I swear, and I didn't club Mr. Ogle with it. But would anyone believe that I didn't have it with me? Now, there's my dilemma. What should I do?"

"You must trust me when I tell you that Mr. Rierson needs to hear all of this when you meet with him," Wendy said, stretching forward a bit to put a hand over his. "Don't leave anything out. Tell him that you told me all of this, too. And tell him why you were reluctant to reveal it the first time around. Being honest about everything now is going to help you in the long run. I find your story believable, and I don't see you as the type of person who would commit that sort of violent act, even if you'd had enough of Brent Ogle's threats and mistreatment."

Hollis grimaced briefly. "If only I had stayed out under the portico the whole time, or left when Miz Ogle did."

"Don't play *what if*? It won't get you anywhere. What counts now is the truth. If you want to eliminate yourself as a suspect, you must tell Mr. Rierson everything you've told me. There was no DNA of any kind in or around the hot tub, except Brent Ogle's. You coming forward like this was exactly the right thing to do."

There was a distinct sigh of relief from Hollis. "Thanks. My instinct was to keep everything hidden from the second it happened. But then, I ran over somebody in my panic—Miz

Ogle, you've said—and that meant that it would be no longer possible to keep everything hidden. After all, somebody had to be there in the hallway to collide with her. I've been terrified all this time that someone would put two and two together and come up with Hollis Hornesby of Hollow Horne. I've hardly slept, and Mother has been bugging me about going to the doctor and saying things to me like, 'You look downright pekid. I know you never eat anything to speak of, so it's no wonder you have no immune system.'"

"She's your mother. She can't help it."

Hollis rolled his eyes, not once but twice. "It gets old. Mother is the most controlling person in the world. In that respect, she's a lot like Mr. Ogle was about running things." Then he realized what he had just said and briefly covered his mouth with his hand. "I don't think that came out the way I wanted it to. I didn't mean to say that. It doesn't make Mother look too good, does it? You're here to zero in on all the positives, aren't you?"

"Yes. But don't worry. I wouldn't even think of using that particular comment of yours."

"Even if they always say *in vino veritas*?"

"Yes. Even if they always say that."

Hollis went silent for a while, the creases across his forehead growing deeper. He made a fist of his right hand and nestled it under his chin, supporting it with his elbow on the table. It made him come off like some sort of hippie oracle. "I don't know why I should be feeling so guilty about discovering the body the way I did. I wasn't going to do anything but chew him out. And I guess I felt that I could pull it off because he'd be there in the hot tub with hardly any clothes on and I'd be hovering above him and have the upper hand. All I wanted to do was to strike a blow for every kid that's been bullied at recess, or on a school bus, or just anywhere at all growing up. I wanted to tell Brent Ogle once and for all that I wasn't afraid of him and that he could deep-six all his snarky remarks about me. But I never got the chance."

Wendy nearly mimicked his sad expression as she spoke up. "You're absolutely right about one thing. There's no reason for you to feel guilty about what you wanted to do. No harm would have come to Brent Ogle if he'd gotten a good calling out for once. It was long overdue. Now you, on the other hand, might have been splashed with a lot of hot water, at the very least."

Her comment lightened the mood immediately, and they both managed to laugh for a few seconds.

"So you definitely think it's the right thing to do for me to level with Mr. Rierson, then," Hollis said.

"I promise you it will help clear things up. In order for him or anyone else working on the case to solve it, they'll need to settle on who didn't do it before they can pin down who did. Unless someone just steps up and conveniently confesses."

Hollis still looked somewhat worried. "But my telling him this won't prove I didn't do it."

"Are you lying to me about it, any or all of it?"

"No," Hollis said emphatically. "I'm telling you exactly what happened that evening and why."

"And I believe you."

"Will Mr. Rierson?"

"I think he will. There's still no DNA linking you to the pestle. Or anyone else, for that matter. The water in the hot tub took care of that. And you'll clear up who knocked down Carly Ogle in the hallway. Was that person a man or a woman? Was that person the killer or just at the wrong place at the wrong time?"

"I see your point," Hollis said, looking more comfortable. "Maybe I can get some decent sleep tonight after this."

"I'm betting you will."

Eventually, the conversation settled into a son's admiration for his mother, even before she'd taken over the RCC— material Wendy would have to evaluate and then integrate carefully to avoid making her feature sound too maudlin and not objective enough. And then Hollis made one last pitch for his paintings.

"If nothing else, they are madly colorful," he was saying as the two of them browsed the Mardi Gras section depicting tons of multi-colored beads flying through the air off gigantic, fanciful floats.

"It wouldn't be Mardi Gras without purple, green, and gold trinkets, and all sorts of doubloons, not to mention every other color under the rainbow decorating the floats and in the costumes," Wendy said. "But you know what? I'm going to have to take a rain check right now on buying any new paintings for my house. You may not know this, but my late mother, Valerie, was also an acrylic artist. While you were down in New Orleans all those years, she specialized in Rosalie scenery, particularly studies of the Mississippi River. Some were by moonlight, some by sunlight, and I have lots of her work on my walls in my little bungalow."

Hollis sounded almost apologetic. "No, I didn't know that. I'm so sorry to hear she's not painting anymore. But I'd love to see your mother's work sometime."

"Next time I have some people over, I'll invite you and Deedah, and you can check everything out."

"That would be fabulous," he told her. And then he finally drained the last of his wine with a flourish and put his free hand on her shoulder. "If what I've told you today—and I promise to tell Mr. Rierson the same thing—if it helps get this thing solved soon, then hallelujah. I am so itching to play bridge like you wouldn't believe. And if there's any way you and I can be partners again, let's arrange it. I think we had something almost psychic going between us."

"Aha," Wendy said, shooting him a playful smile. "Metaphysical bridge is the only kind worth playing."

Hollis bowed low. "I hear you loud and clear, O wise one."

Wendy's brain seemed nearly as full as her stomach had been after her lunch with Lyndell. On the way back to her car, she kept thinking about the way Carly and Hollis had volunteered information they could easily have kept to themselves. Had they done that of their own accord, or had there been something of an organized effort about it all? Would there soon be others coming her way and marching to that same tune?

On the one hand, she remained convinced that she had done the right thing by advising Carly not to tell Ross about her wicked thoughts regarding her husband once the RCC had been plunged into darkness. On the other hand, she felt that Ross needed to know what Hollis had actually done. That was the difference. Something swirling around inside somebody's head versus something that had actually taken place that evening. Thoughts versus action. She allowed herself a hint of a grin as she remembered she had just used the word *metaphysical* before saying goodbye to Hollis at his gallery. Murder, however, was not the sort of thing that lent itself to anything other than hard-core evidence and cause of death.

And then, right after she had slid into the front seat of her Impala and shut the door, it struck her. She was going on the unquestioned assumption that both Carly and Hollis had been telling her the truth. As far as she was concerned, they were. It felt right to her in her gut. She really had no reason not to believe either of them.

Suddenly, however, she found herself playing Devil's advocate. What if they both weren't leveling with her? Or what if one was telling the truth and the other wasn't? And how would she know which one was which? Darn it all. Where was the metaphysical when you really needed it?

She must get with Ross and discuss all this with him, especially since she had promised to let him know about anything she discovered while doing the research and interviews for her feature article. She turned on the ignition as a reflex action and adjusted her rearview mirror. Somehow, it had gotten slightly askew, perhaps when she'd touched up her lip gloss last time.

Then, as she slowly pulled out of her spot, she caught a glimpse of a man quickly dashing across the street and getting into a car in the block ahead of her. He pulled out into traffic and effortlessly blended in. Something about him was very familiar, but she decided to concentrate on her driving, as there was a car coming up behind her and she didn't want to risk a fender bender. At the next traffic light, she caught the red light and forced herself to focus for a moment or two until it changed to green. It didn't take long at all for the recognition to come.

It was Gerald Mansfield she'd seen. She was almost positive of it. Her sleuthing skills would not allow her to dismiss this second encounter from a distance within such a short period of time as merely a random occurrence or coincidence that she should ignore. She now must consider the possibility that he was following her or hanging around for whatever purpose, although even if that was what he was really doing, he wasn't very good at it. She'd spotted him both times. It was something else she needed to discuss with Ross the next time they got together.

CHAPTER 11

When Wendy had finally returned to her cubicle at the *Citizen*, she texted Ross about getting together that evening to compare notes on Hollis Hornesby and bring up her concerns about Gerald Mansfield. But apparently, Ross was having none of it.

meeting claude ingalls at retirement home; not sure how long it'll take.

she texted back.

when did that come up?
today; called out there to confirm he's still with us.
he's the clock operator, right?
right; but no idea when I'll be thru; going late.
need to talk about hollis hornesby & gerald mansfield.
why mansfield?
trust me; important we talk.
okay; i'll text u when i'm thru w/ ingalls; what about hollis h.?
stuff out of left field.
a breakthrough?

don't know; but you'll want to interrogate him.
okay; ttyl

Wendy put down her cell and frowned. She'd temporarily forgotten about Claude Ingalls, one of the men Brent Ogle had insisted his father had paid off to rig The Four-Second Game, if any of them could manage it. That revelation had created a physical confrontation among Brent and his golfing buddies, but it was still unclear whether he had been telling the truth or whether either Tip Jarvis or Connor James had actually believed him.

Then she made an executive decision. Perhaps she should attend to some alligators in her cubicle and then head out later to the Rosalie Public Library to research The Four-Second Game so she could be prepared for whatever Ross chose to share with her of his conversation with Claude Ingalls.

And then that led to another bit of tantalizing conjecture on her part. All those years that Brent Ogle had made a general nuisance of himself to people—not only at the RCC but all over town—no one had seen fit to knock him off. There were certainly plenty who had had provocation, but they apparently had made their peace with it. But suddenly, within a couple of hours of Brent's drunken boast that The Four-Second Game had truly been rigged, he had met a brutal end. Perhaps Ross had come to the same conclusion, but it seemed to Wendy that it was more than likely that *someone had taken Brent Ogle deadly serious*. Someone had believed him and decided he needed to be punished for it then and there. With that pestle in one angry, vengeful blow.

What if his death had had nothing to do with bullying or disrespecting people or threatening to withhold funds from the RCC? Suppose it had been about the results of The Four-Second Game all those decades ago and nothing else? In that case, it appeared once again that Tip Jarvis and Connor James would move to the head of the list of suspects, although Ross had stated that they had been interrogated twice and nothing conclusive had come of it.

Wendy felt she was driving herself crazy. All these angles were weighing heavily on her mind—some of them at cross-purposes: Hollis discovering the body and telling no one about it; Carly confessing she had had murderous thoughts about her husband; Deedah wanting to micro-manage everything at the RCC; Carlos with the easiest access to the pestle and the hot tub, the only one who had that convenient a combination; Mitzy Stone claiming that she and Deedah made a great team, but to what was she actually referring?; and now Gerald Mansfield creeping around town to keep an eye on her and for what purpose?

And then, her new idea that the only thing that mattered in this case was that someone had decided to take Brent Ogle out after learning the truth about The Four-Second Game. But was it the truth? Had someone actually believed a lie and been led down the path to violent murder because of it?

Not to mention that her favorite new phrase was tantalizing her.

Backstory.

It was time to finish out her afternoon and then head to the library. Ha! Shades of her term paper days at Mizzou.

Ross never talked much to anyone about the way he'd lost his parents twelve years ago. Not even to Wendy and Bax. Of course, they both knew that Donald and Jocelyn Rierson had died in a terrible head-on collision one foggy January night as they were heading to their small country home about ten miles south of Rosalie off US Highway 61. Ross had been a freshman at Ole Miss when his grandmother Dot Rierson had called him up with the bad news, her voice anything but composed. After that, he had gone to live with his grandparents in

Rolling Fork in the Delta until his graduation, then returned to Rosalie to join the Rosalie CID. But he had never seen that country home of his youth again because his grandparents had had to sell it off to afford to continue sending him to Ole Miss. The life insurance his parents had left him was minimal.

It was a traumatic period of time for him to endure, to say the least, but he had come through it with a determination to make a good life for himself, infused with the kind of love his parents had always given him. Wendy, of course, was a big part of his long-term plan, if she would just settle securely into her newspaper job and say yes to him.

Yet, as he approached the parking lot of the Rosalie Retirement Home, which sat atop the highest of the bluffs just north of the city, he found himself growing increasingly nostalgic. Claude Ingalls had reached a ripe old age, and Ross couldn't help but wish it were his parents he was visiting and that they had had the chance to live that long. But he pulled himself together as he locked the car with the remote and headed toward the front entrance of the facility. Charm, however, was not its strong point. It looked a great deal like a pedestrian brick and mortar motel, even though Ross knew the staff inside was more than qualified to look after its many aged patients.

So he headed in with a snap to his step and promptly signed his name in the ledger. The efficient receptionist, a pleasant-looking man with severely thinning blond hair whose silver nameplate on the counter identified him as Morris Loring, picked up the phone and notified the assisted living wing of the visitor waiting in the foyer to see Claude Ingalls.

"She'll be right out to get you and take you to Mr. Ingalls," Morris told him, putting down the receiver.

"She?"

"Nurse Louise Hawkins. She's in charge of that wing."

"I see."

After only a couple of minutes or so, Nurse Hawkins emerged from one of the corridors and shook Ross's hand warmly. She was an older woman who exuded empathy but obviously had not missed many meals. Hers was a somewhat fleshy face, but the laugh lines imprinted on it surely gave her patients an additional dimension of comfort as she tended to their needs. As a result, "jolly old girl" were the words that were most often used to describe her.

"As I told you over the phone," she began, "this would be the best time to come for a visit. He's just had his dinner, which always puts him in a happy mood. He'll be good for another hour or so, and then he'll want to watch a little television and then go right off to bed."

Ross deferred to the notes in his head. "How long has it been since he was transferred from the independent living wing to assisted living?"

"Sometime last year, I believe," Nurse Hawkins told him. "The night security guard found him at three in the morning a couple of times waiting in the hallway outside the dining room thinking it was time for breakfast. As a result, his doctor thought it was time to keep an eye on him a little bit better. A sense of time is often the first thing to go in these patients. So he was moved to assisted living. But if you ask me, he's still all there. Now mind you, that's just my opinion, not the doctor's. I've seen them go downhill fast from independent to assisted to memory care, though. At any rate, I wanted to tell you to get to the purpose of your visit quickly. Don't beat around the bush, because he does tire easily."

Ross said he understood and followed Nurse Hawkins down a corridor or two until they had reached a door with the brass numbers 113 fastened to it. Just outside it on the wall to the right was a shelf with an arrangement of leaves in the colors of autumn—bright golds and oranges and reds.

"Those are silk, not real," Nurse Hawkins said. "Mr. Ingalls's daughter, Patsy, changes 'em out during the year and especially if there's a holiday coming up like Thanksgiving or Christmas or Easter. We find it cheers the patients up when family members do these little displays on the shelves."

"How nice. They're very pretty."

Nurse Hawkins knocked on the door twice and cried out, "Mr. Ingalls, are you decent? Your visitor, Detective Rierson, is here to talk to you."

"Y'all come on in," came the thin-voiced reply from the other side.

Nurse Hawkins opened the door and gestured for Ross to go on through. "Here he is just to see you, Mr. Ingalls. Now you push the button if you need me for anything, y'hear?"

"Thank you, Miz Hawkins. Hello there, Detective," Claude said from his vantage point in his recliner facing the flat-screen TV on a wall that was otherwise cluttered with what looked like family photos. Then he gestured to Ross with a big smile. "Won't you have you a seat? I'll turn off this program I'm not much innerested in anyway. One of them infomercials trying to sell me somethin' or other. But I'm not sure I know what it is. My daughter Patsy is all the time gettin' after me for buyin' things I see on the TV and then when I get 'em, I cain't even use 'em."

As Nurse Hawkins closed the door behind her and Claude aimed his remote at the set, Ross headed over to an armchair that definitely was in need of a new upholstery job. When he sat down, his rear end made contact with some ornery springs somewhere beneath the cushion and it was difficult to find a comfortable position.

"Sorry 'bout that," Claude said, watching Ross's struggles. "My daughter Patsy brought that old buttsprung thing in here a while back, but it's worse'n useless, if y'ask me."

Ross offered up a game smile. "Don't worry about it, Mr. Ingalls."

"You call me Claude, now."

"Of course . . . Claude."

Ross appreciated the cheerful tone of his voice, even if it was thin. Thinner still was the man himself. Not yet gaunt, but getting there, his bony physique was emphasized further by the oversized guayabera shirt he wore. If his daughter had bought it for him, she had not chosen well. The pale-yellow color matched his sallow complexion, and the entire ensemble made him look faded and washed out. To complete the sickly impression, there was the faint odor of Vicks VapoRub hanging in the air.

"I have to tell ya, Mr. Rierson, that I'm flattered you wanna talk to an old codger like me 'bout anything," Claude said, while Ross continued to shift his weight to make peace with the armchair. "Now you said over the phone you wanted to ask me 'bout The Four-Second Game? Wazzat it? After all these years? Seems like some folks just can't seem to get over it."

Ross decided to give up fussing with the armchair and concentrate on his task at hand. "Yes. That seems to be the case. I'm sure it's been a while since anyone has brought that up to you, right?"

"True 'nuff. But I can still remember it all like it'z yesttidy. Course, I can't remember what day of the week it is, but that I can remember."

"Glad to hear it," Ross said. Now, do you mind if I go ahead and record our conversation, sir?"

Claude shook his nearly bald head. "Nossir, I don't. But I have to tell ya, I don't know what good it'll do."

"You just let me worry about that, okay?" Ross said, bringing out his best interrogation smile.

"Alrighty, then. Ask me whatever ya want."

Ross clicked on the recorder and said, "If I remember correctly, there was an accusation by the St. Mark's fans that you tinkered with the game clock to give RHS another shot at the end zone that evening. It was a matter of an extra second instead of the game ending on the previous play where Brent Ogle's pass was broken up. The St. Mark's people thought the game was over."

Claude's voice suddenly grew a bit stronger. "Yep. They did accuse me a' that. There were some places I coudd'n show my face 'cause a' all that, ya know. In fact, some woman did throw iced tea in my face at a restaurant, and since I'm a gentleman, I won't repeat the words she yelled at me."

"But I believe you denied those clock accusations to everyone, didn't you?"

Claude grinned. "Yep, I did."

"Claude, are you aware that Brent Ogle was murdered last Saturday out at the Rosalie Country Club?"

"I was not," he said, jerking his head back with a frown. "Are ya tellin' me the truth 'bout that? Who'd do such of a thing?"

"I am telling you the truth, and we don't know who did it yet. But we're investigating the possibility that something Mr. Ogle said to a whole roomful of people Saturday afternoon may have led to his death."

Claude couldn't seem to stop shaking his head. "What on earth's this crazy world comin' to?"

"I know what you're saying," Ross told him. "But I'd like to run what he said by you and get your reaction. He claimed that his father paid off all the officials that worked that game to do anything they could to make sure RHS won, and he included you, the clock operator. His wife says she thinks Brent was telling the truth by the fact he made her swear that particular revelation to secrecy. So, did he pay you money to affect the outcome or not?"

Claude seemed almost gleeful now and lowered his voice almost to a whisper. "I know I denied it way back then, but the truth is that Brent's daddy, he did put uh wheelbarrow fulla money in my bank account. And I made sure that clock didn't run out after Brent's pass was broke up in the end zone. Yep, I surely did what they said I did. I wanted to earn that money, though."

"Wow!" Ross said, his face a study in disbelief. "So Brent didn't really win that game legit."

"Nosirree. That game shoudda ended on the play before. But I seen to it that it didn't."

Ross exhaled and then thought for a moment. "Do you mind my asking how much money you were paid?"

"Am I gonna get in trouble if I tell ya?"

"Not at this late date," Ross said. "And you don't have to tell me if you don't want to. The fact that you've admitted you were paid and actually influenced the outcome of the game is more than enough for me, and that won't get you into any trouble, either. Thirty years have passed, and an entire generation has grown up during that time. That's a great deal of distance to put between all the controversy that The Four-Second Game generated and today. I really don't think that many people would care anymore."

Claude motioned for Ross to lean closer. "Okay, then. I'm trustin' ya that I won't get in trouble."

"Believe me, you won't."

Finally, Claude was out with it. "Brent's daddy, he paid me close to . . . one billion dollars in pennies."

Startled, Ross could only manage a weak, "What?"

"Well, almost a billion. It was short a few pennies, but it was the same as he paid the others. We all got that much money apiece. But to bring mine up to a billion exactly, I went in to one a' them convenience stores where they have the little dish that says: 'LEAVE A PENNY, TAKE A PENNY,' and I took three pennies. Thataway, I had exactly a billion dollars in pennies."

Ross shut off the recorder and said, "I see."

"We all hit the lottery," Claude continued with a vapid grin on his face. "Ridin' in high clover."

"I'm sure you were."

"That was why I hadda deny all them accusations. I didd'n want nobody lookin' into my finances and all like that. I was afraid they'd come and take my money away from me, ya know? They'd ask where did it come from, and I'd have to up and tell the truth then."

Ross nodded pleasantly, realizing that the interview had come crashing down around him. Nurse Hawkins had advised him not to tire the man out, but reality and Claude Ingalls had definitely parted company. After all, he had been admitted to assisted living sometime last year for being spotted in the hallway in the middle of the night waiting for the dining room to open for breakfast. And now there were exactly one billion reasons to keep him in assisted living and monitor him closely in case he needed memory care at some point after that.

"It was nice chatting with you, Claude," Ross said, more than relieved to get up out of the armchair from Hell. "I'm going to leave you to your TV shows now."

"Didda help you any?"

"Yes, you did, sir. I came to a definite conclusion."

"Well, you can come back anytime you want. I'll be right here in my recliner," Claude said, his grin even wider than before. "Maybe you and me, we could watch a football game together or somethin'."

"I appreciate the invitation. You have a good night, now."

After Ross had signed out at the front desk and headed toward his car, he decided that the visit with Claude Ingalls had not been a complete waste of time. There was one conclusion that Ross thought nearly impossible to escape. There was someone in the RCC that Saturday afternoon who thought

Brent Ogle was telling enough of the truth to murder him in a fit of rage, even if no one would ever know all of the story. That was all there was to it.

Then, once he was settled in the front seat of his car, he shot Wendy a text:

thru with Claude Ingalls; a bust.
scrolling thru microfiche at library.
ur place or mine later?
I'll drop by yours; still need to tell u about Gerald Mansfield.
okay, I'll be waiting; take care.
u 2.

Wendy sat at the library microfiche table, dizzy from all the scrolling she had done of the *Citizen*'s account of the 1990 high school football season. She had yet to get to The Four-Second Game, but she plowed ahead knowing her goal was not far away. Finally, there it was, complete with the sports page headline in bold caps:

MIRACLE FOR THE DEVILS: LAST SECOND WIN

Beneath that were two photos side by side: one of Brent Ogle celebrating in the end zone with his teammates, and another of the grim look on Coach P. J. Doughty's face as he stood on the sideline when the game was finally over. Wendy scanned the copy quickly, noting that the reporter had included a lengthy quote from Coach Doughty afterward:

We thought we had it won. Our guy, Mike Besser, broke up that last pass play like he was coached to do. Our guys on the sideline started jumping up and down because we knew we had it. But then I looked up at

the scoreboard clock, and somehow there was still one
second left on it. Now, how is there still one second left
when there was only four seconds before Brent Ogle's
toss into the end zone? You can't get off two plays in
four seconds.

Wendy couldn't help but commiserate with the man.
The look of devastation on his craggy face in the picture was
overwhelming. She scrolled ahead somewhat and eventually
landed on an article announcing Coach Doughty's dismissal
at the end of the season. The tone of the piece was disingenu-
ous, stating that the man had decided to step down for "health
reasons" and "was grateful for the opportunity to coach the
St. Mark's Saints all these years." There was also another statement that "he, his wife, and his daughter were going to miss
Rosalie and that it was a unique place to live."

Wendy went back to the actual coverage of The Four-
Second Game and studied the picture of Coach Doughty
again. It came to her immediately that she had seen the photo
before. But where? She scrolled back, but this time in her
brain. Of course—at Brentwood. It had to have been among
the many shots of football games that Brent Ogle had obviously hung on the walls of his eponymous home as the spoils
of his athletic career. Imagine that. A photo to remind The
Baddest Devil of Them All to gloat over another man's lack of
success. It was hardly a stretch to picture Brent doing something like that and enjoying it fully.

Wendy spent the rest of her time making notes and pen-
ning a couple of questions that she intended to review with
Ross when they got together. This whole business of The
Four-Second Game was less than edifying, no matter what
Ross had or had not discovered at the retirement home. Not
only that, it continued to be her firm belief that Brent "play-

ing around with it" so wickedly had led to someone's uncontrollable rage and then his brutal murder.

Ross's bachelor apartment in his Whiteapple Village complex was somewhat minimalist. True, it had all the basic requirements of modern life—a kitchenette, a living room/dining room combination, a master bedroom, a guest room, and one full bath. But it was hardly what anyone would call luxurious, and it was haphazardly decorated in a style that only an oblivious man dedicated to his career could improvise. There was no artwork on the walls, just photos of scenes from his police work. The furniture style was random—wicker here, upholstered pieces there—and though Ross was not color-blind, the overall impression was that he definitely had to be with the clashing palette scattered everywhere. Orange doodads on the shelves, for instance, did not go with black whatnots, except at Halloween, which incidentally was fast approaching. Nor did royal-blue drapes go with brown shag carpet. The entire place desperately needed an interior decorator's touch, but that was obviously not something that was on Ross's front burner.

"So, Claude Ingalls was a dead end in my estimation," Ross was saying to Wendy as the two of them sat at his small dining room table having a cup of coffee together. "He's gone over the hill a bit, and I wouldn't trust a thing he says now at his age." Ross revealed the rest of his conversation out at the retirement home, and Wendy could no nothing but shrug.

"It's remarkable that he's even still alive," she said. "But I think your point is well taken."

"What did your stint at the library turn up?"

"The full account of The Four-Second Game in real time, of course. And a heartbreaking picture of Coach Doughty after the loss. The way he was hanging his head, you would've thought somebody close to him had died. When I was out at Brentwood visiting with Carly Ogle earlier this week, I noticed that the same picture was one of many Brent had hung up all over the place. I think you'd have to call it rubbing it in . . . forever."

"At the very least. What else did you find?"

Wendy put down her coffee mug and glanced at her notes. "I wrote down this question, and I think maybe it falls under the category of backstory."

"Shoot."

"I wrote: *What happened to Coach Doughty and his family? Where did they go? Does anyone know that?*"

Ross thought for a moment and said, "I guess you weren't able to find anything about it, then."

"No. When you think about it, there's no reason for the *Citizen* to have followed them. Apparently, they left town, and that was that."

"Maybe your daddy knows something," Ross said. "That was his era."

"I could ask him. Or you could at work tomorrow."

"Write me a little note from your pad to remind me." He took another sip of his coffee, as she printed the message for him on a piece of paper and handed it over. Then he said, "Now, what's this business you couldn't wait to tell me about Gerald Mansfield?"

Wendy went into details about the afternoon's twin sightings, and they both let that sit for a short while. "My sleuthing skills tell me that we're not talking about a coincidence here," she said finally. "It all just goes against my instincts. The guy is an odd duck, and I've thought so from the first time I laid eyes on him."

"Do you think you're in any danger?"

"I have to admit I hadn't looked at it that way," she told

him. "It was more that I thought his behavior might have some bearing on the case. And then it also occurred to me that if he were spying on me for some reason, who was behind it? I just don't figure Gerald Mansfield for the type who strikes out on his own. He regularly takes orders out there at the RCC to keep the course looking like it should, and so I was leaning toward the idea that he might be taking orders from someone else in this instance, too."

"He works closely with Deedah Hornesby and Mitzy Stone all the time," Ross said. "Miz Stone made a big deal out of how well the two of them ran things out there when I interrogated her."

"Teamwork," Wendy said, almost under her breath.

"Yes, there's that idea again that Bax came up with. That more than one person might have been involved in Brent Ogle's murder."

Wendy put the palm of her hand on her forehead as if she were testing it for a fever. "We just seem to be going round and round, don't we? Is there ever gonna be a breakthrough in this case?"

"Patience, sweetie, patience. There are cases that go on for years, and some that simply go cold and are never solved." He finished off his coffee and added, "Do you want me to put a tail on Gerald Mansfield for you? I can ask Ronald Pike to do it tomorrow and see where the guy goes. But don't get your hopes up. Mansfield may end up staying at the RCC all day long working. It's a bit unwarranted for us to walk up to him and ask him to explain why he was eating at The Toast of Rosalie and what he was doing getting into his car later on. At least, not at this point. Frankly, it would come off as police harassment. Let's just see what a little concerted surveillance turns up first, okay?"

Wendy was smiling, fully accepting his observations.

"Sounds like a solid plan to me. It's not like me to be this paranoid, of course. Do you think I might be getting there, though?"

"I seriously doubt it. You have the proverbial sound mind. In any case, I wouldn't let anything happen to you, of course."

She blew him a kiss, and he caught it. "I know you wouldn't."

"All the same, I appreciate you telling me about Mansfield. It's been my experience that you never know what will break a case open." He paused and looked her straight in the eye. "Now, are you not gonna tell me anything about this 'outta left field stuff' regarding Hollis Hornesby? You know you promised to share anything you turned up with the department."

"So I did," she said. "I don't know if it's what you've been looking for, but at the art gallery, Hollis said he followed the deck around from the portico all the way to the hot tub and discovered Brent Ogle's body and that he got so panicky that he rushed into the hallway, and he was the one that knocked Carly Ogle down."

"Was he now?" Ross said, sounding not as surprised as Wendy thought he would.

"You think he's not telling the truth?"

Ross shook his head emphatically. "I didn't say that. If he is, though, it really doesn't clear things up all that much. He'd be admitting only to discovering a dead body. He should have come forward in the first place and told us that, though. I'm taking a dim view of his withholding it from us."

"He said that he was afraid it might incriminate him if he mentioned it," Wendy added.

"He was right, of course. It does put him in the right place at the right time. Or the wrong place at the wrong time, however you wanna look at it."

"Then he asked me if he should come clean with you."

Ross was smiling now. "Let me take a wild guess here. You told him to do just that, right?"

"Well, you have to admit it's something you didn't know before. If he's leveling with you, at least you would know who the man in the hallway was. If I recall, you said to me at one point that whoever knocked Carly Ogle down wasn't necessarily the person who killed her husband."

"You have a good memory," Ross told her. "I did indeed say that. Hollis is coming in tomorrow and we'll see if there's anything more he's not letting us know about."

"Then I did good?"

"You know you did," he said, leaning over and planting a little kiss on her lips. "Now we'll just have to see what tomorrow brings."

CHAPTER 12

Ross was sitting in Bax's office the next morning, having just summarized for his boss the brainstorming session that he and Wendy had conducted energetically the evening before.

"I'm not surprised you didn't get anything out of Claude Ingalls," Bax said. "It was worth the old college try, though. He was no spring chicken back when he was working as the clock operator for all those high school games. It seems we're back where we started. Was Brent Ogle telling the truth or not? But I do agree with both you and my daughter that it really doesn't matter that much now. Somebody believed him, and at that point his fate was likely sealed. I think that's the basic assumption we have to go on without a doubt."

"Do you think it's worth putting someone on a surveillance detail on the other matter?" Ross said next. "Maybe Pike could do it if we're not too busy."

"It's okay by me unless things get hectic around here, as you say. Wendy's my only daughter, and I'd rather be safe than sorry in case Mr. Mansfield really is up to something no good. Human behavior never fails to surprise me, of course. You tell Pike to go ahead and then report back to me."

Ross gave him a thumbs-up and then said, "There was

something that came up as a result of Wendy's doing her research at the library. She—or rather both of us—wondered if perhaps you knew where Coach Doughty and his family went after he was let go thirty years ago."

Bax leaned forward and folded his hands on the desk. "Let me see now." There was a significant pause. "I seem to recall that he moved to somewhere in Alabama. Maybe Mobile. Or was it Montgomery? I'm not sure. What I heard was strictly by the grapevine, not firsthand—a contact on the school board that was particularly fond of him mentioned it to me once."

"Do you remember who that was?"

Bax nodded eagerly. "I do, as a matter a' fact. It was Earnie Grayson. His family and mine went way back. Unfortunately, Earnie is no longer with us. I went to his services a good ten years ago, so he's not around to confirm what I just said about the coach moving to Alabama."

"Is there anyone else who might know where he went?"

"You're talking about thirty years ago," Bax said. "I also believe the rest of Earnie Grayson's family has moved away from here, too. Why the sudden interest in where the coach went?"

Ross threw out his best smile. "You know Wendy—how determined she is once she's gotten something into her head. She's latched on to this idea of the importance of backstory that we all discussed, thinking it might be of significance where this case is concerned."

Bax leaned back and laughed. "That daughter a' mine is something else, isn't she? Every day I think she gets closer and closer to giving up reporting for good and signing up to be a cop alongside me."

"You don't think that's a bit of wishful thinking? She says she's never been happier being a part of the newspaper business—now that she's working with Miz Slover instead of Dalton Hemmings."

"Good ole, bad ole Dalton. Prob'ly is wishful thinking on my part about Wendy," Bax said. "But you can't blame a father for hoping. Anyhow, you go tell Pike to give it a shot on Gerald Mansfield's whereabouts, and we'll see what's what. If Pike says there's anything that looks suspicious going on, we'll bring Mansfield in for another interrogation. We can always tell him that it's an official matter regarding the investigation."

Ross rose from his chair and said, "Never a dull day when you're involved with Wendy Winchester."

"You said a mouthful, son."

"I'll text her about the surveillance detail right now."

It was about five minutes after Wendy received Ross's text that her doorbell rang, and she felt a spurt of adrenaline beneath her sternum as she was sitting at the kitchen table with her coffee, scrolling along on her phone screen. Her brain returned immediately to the session she and Ross had had the evening before. Could that possibly be Gerald Mansfield at her door for a purpose unknown? There was that fledgling paranoia kicking in again.

She rose from her chair, thinking she was acting positively silly but still tentatively approaching her small foyer. But all apprehension vanished immediately when she caught sight of Merleece Maxique through the glass pane, holding up something round and aluminum covered with her right hand.

"What in the world?" Wendy said, giving her friend a peck on the cheek and welcoming her in.

"Good mornin'. I thought I'd surprise you with this applesauce pie. Maybe I shoudda called ahead, but I took a chance anyway that you still here and not at work yet," Merleece said. "I make two a' these last night, and I know you like 'em since you make me give you the recipe."

Wendy took the pie with delight and gestured toward the

kitchen. "Come on. Let's have us some coffee together and chat like girlfriends. I've always got some time to spare for my Merleece."

"You not gone be late for work?"

"That's one of the nice things about my new editor," Wendy said. "We do punch in and out like we've always had to, but as long as we get the work done, Lyndell's not all that much of stickler about a few minutes here and there."

"I heard that," Merleece said, raising her index finger in the air. "Miz Crystal the same way. She never waitin' at the door pointin' to her watch. I tell ya, I coudedn'n put up with that if she did. No way."

Once they were settled at the table with their mugs in hand, the visit began in earnest. "It threw me a bit when I saw you out on the porch," Wendy said. "I thought, 'We're in between your cleaning days. Or have I lost track of time?' I've been known to do that once in a while."

Merleece arched her brows. "You know, I could come in erry week instead of two weeks if you want, Strawberry. Miz Crystal coudd'n stop me if I put my foot down and I tell her I want to come. I got her wrapped round my little finger."

"Things still about the same at Old Concord Manor?"

Merleece leaned in with a sassy wink. "You know they never gone change. But I tell ya, Strawberry, Miz Crystal pitch a fit to end all fits the other day."

"What happened?"

Merleece could not suppress a hearty laugh. "When I come to work one mornin', she was moanin' and groanin' all over the place and coverin' up her face with her hands like an actress in the movies. I near 'bout thought somebody had up and died. But no, that wudd'n it."

"Was she sick?"

"Not hardly. She sit me down at the table just like we doin' right now and say to me, 'I stepped in it.' And I say back to her, 'What you step in?' I know she wudd'n talkin' 'bout that silly poodle she got. I do know that dog definitely housebroken."

"This is gonna be good, I can tell," Wendy said, unable to restrain her glee.

"You got no idea," Merleece told her, taking a big sip of her coffee before she continued. "Anyways, Miz Crystal say she got a phone call from Miz Helen Hope Williamson earlier that mornin' 'bout some committee they both sit on for the Rosalie Garden Club. Don't know which one, but they havin' some kinda trouble on it. I only know Miz Crystal then tell Miz Helen Hope loud as all git-out what a nuisance it is to work with some other lady on the committee. I believe it was a Miz Dickey or somethin' like that. You know who that is?"

Wendy got a quick word in. "That would be Miz Ilona Dickey. I know that family well."

"Anyways, Miz Crystal say she start goin' on and on to Miz Helen Hope 'bout how tacky and picky Miz Dickey is and all like that—"

"Miz Crystal is a fine one to talk about being tacky," Wendy managed as Merleece took a quick breath. "She's always at the outer limits of taste, if you ask me. Money doesn't automatically give you good fashion sense."

"I know that's right," Merleece said as both women smiled broadly. "So what it all boil down to is Miz Helen Hope finally get a word in and tell Miz Crystal that Miz Dickey and her be close first cousins. I can still hear Miz Crystal carryin' on like she in a Little Theater play with her arms goin' in all directions at once: 'Oh, what am I gonna do now, Merleece? I've offended one of the social goddesses of Rosalie.' So, I say to Miz Crystal, 'It cain't be that bad.' "

"This is just too funny," Wendy said. "Miz Helen Hope really will bite your head off for the least little faux pas or if you sneeze wrong around her."

"So then Miz Crystal go on and on: 'Oh, no? Can't be that bad, you say? Miz Helen Hope, she hung up on me. She slammed that receiver down. Now, what am I gonna do, Merleece? Tell me what to do.'"

"And what did you tell her?"

"I tell her to calm down first and that she gone ruin her makeup and have to start her day all over again drawin' on her face. The sun gone rise the next day, believe it or not, I say. Strawberry, these ladies have nothin' to do but fuss and fight all the time, but they get over theyselves erry time that I remember. All that time I was workin' for Miz Liddie Rose at Don Jose's Retreat, I see it happen over and over. They all make up in the end, usually over they drinks. Many, many drinks, I have to say."

"Too many to count, right? I remember talking to Daddy once about all the drinking that goes on here in Rosalie, and we both agreed that as small as this town is, it had to be the alcohol consumption capital of the country, bar none."

"Ay-men to that." Merleece sipped her coffee in smiling silence, as if she were enjoying the glow of an imaginary crackling fire in front of her. "But they is a lesson here. You gotta keep that mouth shut in Rosalie when you start runnin' folks down. Look to the right, look to the left, and you best look behind you, too. You never know who related to who and who might be listenin'. They last names might be different, but that don't mean they not blood kin somewhere along the line. A place like Rosalie can really get you in trouble when gossip get back to the right person. Seem like errybody related to errybody else—no matter what color they skin is or what church they go to. It can go a ways back, too. So I always tell Hyram and anybody else I know up in this town to do the smart thing and zip it if you know what good for you."

"Wise advice," Wendy said.

"You best b'lieve it is." There was a lull during which

Wendy checked something on her phone with a few strokes of her fingertip. Then, Merleece changed the subject abruptly. "Have they caught whoever kill Mr. Brent Ogle yet?"

"Nope. The investigation's still ongoing, and they don't seem to have made much progress. It's more like they're going round and round in circles."

"Now you tell me the truth. You don't think somebody gone get away with it, do you?"

Wendy could think of nothing to do but shrug with a helpless expression on her face. "Daddy's told me more than once that some crimes never do get solved. They go cold, and the culprit's never caught."

Merleece shivered and made an unpleasant face. "I don't like to think about that too much, Strawberry. I mean, the notion that somebody runnin' round free here in Rosalie who actually did kill somebody else. You cain't let the Devil get away with the Devil's work."

Wendy checked the time on her phone again and gasped softly. "Well, I do have to get on down to my little cubicle at the *Citizen* sooner or later. But I tell you what I'm gonna do before I leave. I'll cut me a slice of your pie and nibble on it all day long. That'll make me one happy reporter."

"I guess I knew you coudd'n resist it too long, Strawberry," Merleece said, finishing off her coffee.

They both rose from the table, and then Wendy said, "This was just so much fun. You don't have to come over here just on your cleaning days, you know. You can drop by anytime so we can chat and catch up, especially if Miz Crystal gets to be too much to handle at the Manor. I know she can be off the wall at times."

"I know that's right. But we still Strawberry and Merleece, and nothin' ever gone come between us."

"Sisterhood, here's to it," Wendy said as the two women

hugged it out. "I need more of this. Let's go ahead and meet for lunch today at Simply Soul and order some a' those greens we both like so much."

"Don't forget the corn bread, sister."

"Can you manage Miz Crystal and get the time off?"

Merleece laughed as if she didn't have a care in the world. "You just watch me, Strawberry. I just need to know what time."

"Let's be conventional and say high noon."

"I got it covered."

Ross's approach with Hollis Hornesby in the interrogation room was different than it had been before. It had been Ross's experience that when a suspect held back something important that subsequently came to light, it frequently resulted in cracking a case wide open. Ross didn't necessarily think that Hollis had committed the murder yet, but he was not inclined to give him the benefit of the doubt as much. It was time to press ahead and press hard.

"So tell me again why you thought you should withhold your little trip to the hot tub from us?" Ross was saying. "That doesn't look very good for you right now, I have to tell you."

Hollis looked very uncomfortable, and Ross could see beads of sweat across his forehead. "Like I told Miz Winchester, it was a combination of things. Shock when I realized what had happened to Mr. Ogle, and then fear that I might be accused of doing it if I revealed that I was there at all. Can't you understand that? Listen to what you just said to me."

"I can understand it, but nevertheless, you are a piece of the puzzle," Ross told him. "Now that we know you were there around the time of the murder, can you tell us what time it was when you discovered the body? I can understand why you were reluctant to reveal that before, but if you did notice the time on your cell phone, tell us now. It will help us with our timeline."

Hollis's tone had an "eager to please" edge to it. "Yes . . . yes, I did notice. It was 6:29. Yes . . . I know that's it. For some reason, I remember thinking, 'Oh, it's nearly 6:30.' Isn't that odd? Now, why would I think something like that when I'd just discovered a dead body?"

"I can think of at least one reason," Ross said. "You could have been in shock, as you said. The brain doesn't necessarily function logically at times like that. It does the best it can but often fails miserably."

Hollis seemed to be jumping at Ross's conclusion. "I'm sure you're right. I know you are. Why else would I have run into the hallway the way I did and knocked Miz Ogle over?"

Ross leaned forward, his trademark smile nowhere to be found. "Fortunately, she wasn't hurt. Just startled. So when you decided to sneak back to the hot tub, your intentions were only to chew out Brent Ogle? Nothing else?"

"I swear," Hollis said, raising his right hand. "At that point, I'd gotten so riled up about the things he'd said to my mother about funding the RCC that I was determined to tell him off. He had it coming, and I was just sick and tired of being abused by him, myself. If he had problems with me, it wasn't because of anything I'd done or said to him. If you want my take, he just hated me because I existed. There are people like that, you know."

"So when you found him, his head was leaning back on the edge of the hot tub and somebody had already clubbed him with that pestle?"

"Yes. Although I didn't know what had caused that gash at the time. In any case, I did not have that pestle in my hand. After that, it was all so hurried, and my brain went to mush, as you know."

Ross went silent but continued to catch Hollis's gaze. His experience was telling him that Hollis was not someone who was capable of murder and that he was telling the truth about his ill-advised excursion to the hot tub. If nothing else, however, the timeline for the murder was being narrowed down—the window of opportunity that had existed that evening for foul play was definitely shrinking.

Ross told Hollis once again not to leave town and then dismissed him. Then, he began making notes:

1. *the killer clubs Brent Ogle with pestle, runs away*
2. *Carly Ogle discovers the body first, heads back to locker room to get Wendy*
3. *Hollis Hornesby discovers the body right after that, panics, runs into hallway, knocks Carly Ogle down, who is returning to locker, and then runs to Deedah's office*
4. *Wendy and Carly go back to hot tub together to see body*
5. *Wendy and Carly return to Deedah's office to report the death to the others*

Ross turned a page in his notepad and started printing again: *Murder had to take place no later than 6:29; allowing at least a minute between time Carly and Hollis discovered body, murder had to take place before 6:28. Power lost at 6:13. Allowing at least a couple of minutes for someone to get pestle and get to hot tub—murder took place between 6:15 and 6:28. No more than a thirteen-minute window. Why can't we narrow this down more? Get together with Bax and the map I made of RCC. Revisit this based on Hollis's testimony.*

Bax called Ross into his office around five-thirty and told him to take a seat. "Pike was just in here, and I just finished going over all his surveillance material. Very interesting stuff."

Ross leaned forward in his chair expectantly. "And?"

"It appears my daughter's instincts are still sharp and first-rate. No way was her initial impression incorrect that Gerald Mansfield's various activities were not a matter of coincidence."

"What happened today? Come on, give," Ross said, the alarm clearly registering in his voice. "You've got me on the edge of my seat."

Bax looked down at the notes Pike had made and started speaking with a certain disinterest. "Nothing in the morning going on. Mansfield showed up at the RCC around 8:30, and Pike says it was a snooze fest for the next three hours. But then, Mansfield got into his car around 11:35, and Pike followed him to the *Citizen*'s parking lot. For the next fifteen or twenty minutes, Pike says Mansfield just sat in his car in one of the spots, waiting around. Then around 11:55, Wendy came out of the building and went to her car. Pike says Mansfield waited long enough to follow her in his car, but not too obviously, and then Pike followed them both. Wendy met up with someone—a black woman—at Simply Soul for lunch, it looks like, a little after twelve, but Mansfield didn't go in. Seems he parked his car down the street a ways and waited for her to come out of the restaurant, which was around 12:45 with the same woman. The two embraced. Wendy then returned to the *Citizen,* and Mansfield followed her back. After she went into the building again, he left in his car and returned to the RCC, where Pike says he remained until five o'clock. Pike followed him straight home after that. And that, my friend, is the end of the report."

Bax finally looked up from Pike's notes and cocked his head. "So then, what do we make of all this, son?"

"I don't know, but it's enough to bring him in for questioning. I'm creeped out by all of this, and Wendy is absolutely right. Something is going on, and we need to find out what it is."

"You bring him in tomorrow, then," Bax added. "Meanwhile, I think I'll call up that daughter a' mine and see if she was at all aware of Mansfield's activities, since she knew about Pike's detail."

"Not much gets past our Wendy, as you know." Then Ross summarized his interrogation with Hollis earlier in the day. "If he was telling the truth, maybe it gives us a better chance to narrow this thing down. Wendy and Carly are the only ones we know for sure who didn't do this, at least based on their testimony taken together. They have each other's backs. Still, we ought to be further along than that at this point."

"That's the way it goes sometimes," Bax said. "It backs up and backs up on you, and then, all of a sudden, something unexpected happens and the dam bursts. You wonder why you didn't see through the confusion and dead ends and red herrings to the solution all along."

CHAPTER 13

It did not surprise Wendy in the least when her father called and told her the results of Pike's detail, even though she had made no effort to be more conscious of her surroundings than usual all day. She had not caught a glimpse of Mansfield in her rearview mirror at any time—perhaps a tribute to his own skills at tailing someone more than anything else. Yet she felt a profound sense of relief now that everyone had arrived at the same conclusion: there was a story behind all of this, and perhaps it would help them all solve the case.

She and Ross had decided not to do anything together on this particular evening, although they had come up with a fun twist for a Halloween outing the evening after. They would get a reservation at The Toast of Rosalie and have dinner in costume just for the hell of it. But they would not coordinate their characters—they would just take potluck and see what kind of pairing turned up. To their way of thinking, that was the adult way to celebrate the holiday. No over-the-hill trick-or-treating, no trying too hard at somebody's costume party; just a cocktail or two and a good steak or seafood dish for the main course.

In fact, Wendy had already made her choice and even

rented her costume from Rosalie Painted Faces and Fantasies, the town's shop of choice when it came to Mardi Gras and Spring Tours balls, parades, and cocktail parties. She would show up for their dinner date explaining herself to Ross as Titania, Queen of the Fairies, from Shakespeare's *A Midsummer Night's Dream*. She had had plenty of "fairy princess" outfits—always a favorite of little girls everywhere—from which to choose. The one she had rented was silver and white with sequins glittering all over, and it came with a bejeweled wand and tiara for accessories. Indeed, the little girl in Wendy immediately came out to play after she had tried it on and taken a gander at herself from all angles in the three-sided mirror. She could easily picture herself lighting up The Toast of Rosalie with quite the sparkling display, and she also envisioned that Ross would have to go some distance to match it in form and figure.

It was after a light and simple supper of a toasted cheese sandwich with a small bowl of tomato soup that she sat back at the kitchen table and began turning things over in her head about Brent Ogle's murder once again. That sleuthing gift of hers was bothering her again. Not in a bad way, of course. It was more a nagging feeling that she had that just wouldn't go away. That she had overlooked something that she shouldn't have. In fact, she even had the distinct impression that she might have overlooked more than one thing that she should reconsider.

For a moment, she thought about getting up and doing the dishes, but then dismissed the idea. They could wait. They weren't going anywhere. She had something on her mind, and she didn't want to let go of it. As she focused with greater intensity, she decided that her recent session with Merleece might have triggered something. She laughed out loud for a second or two. What was it about Merleece's applesauce pie that always refreshed her mental acuity? She had nibbled on it all day until she'd finished it off. Was it the sugar? No, she knew quite well the difference between a sugar high and a high tide of brains. Merleece had put her on the trail of something that she could not ignore.

Finally, the notion presented itself as if it were taking a bow with a bouquet of flowers after a grand theatrical performance:

Who all was related in Rosalie? Or something similar to that.

Names were no protection. Cousins had different names. Sisters took on different names than they were born with after they married. One, two, three generations could grow up with these name changes that disguised people's relatedness over time. You had to be careful what you said about people in polite society because it could come back to bite you in the butt when you least expected it. Sometimes the price paid would be very dear, indeed.

That mental exercise led to another question that she had asked herself after doing research at the library:

What had happened to Coach Doughty's family?

And then, it hit her. She realized she had made an assumption about something that might not necessarily be true. She had pored over all those football pictures at the library, and she remembered clearly that one shot in particular had seemed so familiar to her. It was the one of Coach Doughty on the sidelines all down in the face with slumping posture after losing a game he thought he had won, beating his archrival for the first time in many years. But that one extra second had defeated him and then had even cost him his job.

Yes, I saw that picture on the wall at Brentwood, Wendy had concluded then. *Brent Ogle rubbing it in,* had been her knee-jerk assumption. It would have been so typical of him.

Now, however, she was having very troubling second thoughts. All those pictures she had seen at Brentwood had been about Brent Ogle and no one else. His many victories,

his countless celebrations in the end zones and on the sidelines, his spectacular plays—some called by the coaches, some
he had improvised in the form of scrambling and rolling out
of the pocket—but every one of them resulting in success.
They were all a celebration of his prowess as the athlete who
had come to be known as The Baddest Devil of Them All.
Had she really seen a picture of Coach Doughty in defeat
on Brent Ogle's walls? Had her brain just been a bit lazy and
taken the path of least resistance to reach that conclusion?

If she had not seen the picture at Brentwood, then why
was the shot so familiar to her and where else could she have
seen it?

Of course.

There was only one other place she could have seen it. On
Mitzy Stone's apartment walls. There had been lots of sports
pictures on her walls, and now Wendy was positive that there
had been one of Coach Doughty hanging there as well.

Part of the puzzle was beginning to fall into place for her.
Was this the answer? To find out, she must set up another
interview with Mitzy as soon as possible—tomorrow, if she
could. Perhaps Mitzy was the only person who could answer
the question: *what had happened to Coach Doughty's family after
they left Rosalie?*

Halloween Day in Rosalie dawned with a bite to it. The
temperature was hovering a few degrees above freezing,
and there was frost on all the manicured lawns everywhere.
Although the sun was predicted to come out and warm
everything up into the high fifties, it would still be trick-or-
treating weather, getting every child in every neighborhood
primed for the privilege of being something or somebody different and being rewarded for it as well. That was the undeniable attraction of Halloween and the spell it cast, even for
some adults who took the opportunity to let off some steam

and revert to the more carefree days of their youth when they had been allowed to eat ridiculous amounts of candy without being scolded.

As Ross prepared to interrogate Gerald Mansfield down at the station, his mind briefly wandered to the costume he had chosen for his dinner date later with Wendy. Although he had no idea who or what she had chosen to be, he was certain she would be delighted to sit across the table from the venerable White Knight from Lewis Carroll's *Through the Looking-Glass*.

Ha! Who was he kidding? He wanted to be her knight in shining armor, literary reference aside. Thank goodness, the costume he had rented only *appeared* to be made of metal. Instead, it was just white cloth with a bit of cardboard reinforcement sewn inside to give it a more substantial look from a distance. At least he would not be clanking around the restaurant or feeling like he was packed unmercifully inside a sardine can all evening.

Once the interrogation began, however, he tossed aside all thoughts of the end of the day and bore down, dispensing with his customary smile.

"We know you've been following Wendy Winchester around the last few days, in case you were wondering why we called you in today," Ross began. "We need to know what you're up to in case this has a bearing on Brent Ogle's murder. If you know what's good for you, you'll level with us. This is serious business, you know. Make it easy on yourself if you're holding something back that we ought to know."

Gerald looked incredulous, his jaw dropping immediately. "Mr. Ogle's murder? How did we get onto that? You've gotta be kidding."

"I assure you, I am not. We had a tail on you yesterday, and we know you headed for Miz Winchester's place of business around lunchtime. Then, you followed her to Simply Soul, but you didn't go in to eat apparently. You just stayed in your car the whole time Miz Winchester was in there. That's very peculiar behavior in my book."

"I . . . I wasn't hungry."

"Then why did you follow her at all? We also know you were at The Toast of Rosalie the other day while she was having lunch there with her editor. And she spotted you getting into your car a little later after she'd finished visiting Hollis Hornesby's art gallery."

Gerald added a hint of an attitude as he answered. "I *was* hungry that day. That's all. I like their food a lot. Most everybody in Rosalie does. And I waved to Miz Winchester when I saw her, and she waved back. You ask her if that's not what happened. It was just a friendly gesture between the two of us is all. What was I s'pose to do—ignore her?"

"She told us about all of that. But you haven't answered my questions to my satisfaction, Mr. Mansfield. What is all this really about? Are you taking orders from someone to spy on Miz Winchester? Does this have anything at all to do with Brent Ogle's murder?"

"So you're back to his murder again? And takin' orders? From who? That's ridiculous. Where'd you come up with that stuff?"

"Then explain it to me, please, so I can understand."

Gerald became increasingly flustered. "I . . . uh . . . there's nothin' to tell."

"This is not the time to play games with me, Mr. Mansfield."

"I'm . . . not," he said, avoiding eye contact.

Ross raised his voice to up the ante. "Last chance to come clean. Tell us what's been going on. I can sit here all afternoon with you until you tell me the truth. I got nothing but time on my hands."

Suddenly, something in Gerald Mansfield's demeanor seemed to snap. He slumped in his chair, and if possible, his already-sunburned face grew even more flushed. "I haven't done nothin' wrong. Nobody put me up to what I been do-ing; I swear it. It's all been on me."

"So what exactly have you been doing?"

"I been . . . I have . . . it's just that I have this . . . well, I have this crush on Miz Winchester. I have since she inter-viewed me the other day at the RCC. The only thing any-body put me up to was when Miz Deedah asked me to meet with Miz Winchester and see if I could help her with her newspaper article about her and Miz Mitzy and what they were doin' at the RCC. That's all there was to it; I swear."

Ross made no attempt to disguise his displeasure. "So you were stalking her, is that it?"

There was now genuine panic in Gerald's eyes. "Stalkin'? No, sir. I wouldn't call it that. I just . . . I just wanted to see her, that's all. She's so pretty. Her hair, specially. Kinda red and kinda blond. The first time I saw it . . . uh, she . . . it just knocked me out, ya know?"

Ross continued his intensity, determined to shut Gerald Mansfield down for good. "I'm well aware of the color of her hair. Let me put it to you this way, then. You prob'ly don't know it, but I'm seeing Miz Winchester socially, as they say. She's my girlfriend. She's spoken for, bud. She's off-limits. So I don't appreciate what you've been doing, no matter what you call it. You will cease and desist immediately; do you understand me?"

"Yessir. I do. And I didn't know she was your girlfriend," he said, swallowing hard. "If I had, I'da never've done it."

"Well, now you know. And I expect you to act accord-ingly. You will not follow Miz Winchester around Rosalie or anywhere else under any circumstances. What you've been doing could definitely be considered stalking, whether you think so or not. Do you know what a restraining order is?"

Gerald exhaled noisily. "I . . . I think so. It's where you can't go nowhere near somebody by law."

"That's the gist of it. Now, you don't wanna have me issue one against you on Miz Winchester's behalf, do you?"

"No, sir, I don't. I promise, it won't happen no more."

"See to it that it doesn't. Now, is there anything else you want to tell me that would have any bearing on Mr. Ogle's murder?"

"No, I don't know nothin' about it. I wasn't even there when it happened, I swear to you."

Ross stood up and emphatically gestured toward the door and the stoic guard standing beside it. "Then I think we're done here. Just remember what I told you about Miz Winchester, and that way, you'll stay outta trouble."

"Yessir. I got the message."

Mitzy Stone's office just off the pro shop was even smaller than Deedah's was next door. The main difference was that it had a window to let in some light and air, unlike Deedah's dark, stuffy closet of a room that had to be depressing and sleep inducing to occupy. Mitzy's workspace also had the fresh scent of unsold merchandise—mainly from the brand-new golf bags made of nylon, canvas, and leather that were prominently displayed in the nearby shop. Mitzy was more than welcoming to Wendy as the two of them settled in across her desk; but Wendy couldn't help but wonder how long the friendly feelings would last when the questioning began.

"You said over the phone there was this new development in the murder case you wanted to discuss with me?" Mitzy said, beating her to the punch. "I don't know why you've come to me, but I'm intrigued."

Wendy thought on her feet to find just the right words to ease into what would likely become a testy situation. "It's not exactly a development. It's more me revisiting something that I hope you can help me with for the sake of the article."

Mitzy maintained her smile. "And what's that?"

"I was doing some research on The Four-Second Game at the library, scrolling through the microfiche, when I came upon this picture of Coach Doughty on the sidelines after the defeat," Wendy said. "And then, if I'm not mistaken, I remembered that when I came to your apartment to interview you recently, you had that very same picture of him on the wall."

Mitzy's face fell immediately, and Wendy knew then that her hunch had been right. "What do you want to know, Wendy?"

"Can you tell me what happened to Coach Doughty and his family?" Wendy let that sit there for a while, as Mitzy kept her eyes downcast, obviously lost in thought.

Finally, she broke the silence, her voice soft and steady. "Coach Doughty was my grandfather. I am his granddaughter—his only grandchild."

Wendy did not speak immediately. She felt that the revelation demanded a certain degree of respect, a period of silence before gathering her thoughts. Then, she answered in the same quiet tone that Mitzy had used. "I would not have had a clue about any of this, of course, except for that picture in your apartment. I just go with my hunches. What else can you tell me?"

Mitzy was now making direct eye contact as she continued. "Grandpop didn't want to leave Rosalie. My mother told me he and my grandmother loved it here. They made lots of friends, and my mother did, too. But his Achilles' heel was not being able to beat RHS, as you know. So, he was let go for that and that alone, although the school made up some story about Grandpop having health issues. The only one he had, though, was probably being a little too fond of bourbon, his liquor of choice. Then he found another coaching job in Montgomery, Alabama, but things were never the same for him. He started drinking more heavily, and he was eventually fired from that job, too. As for my mother, she was uprooted at the age of sixteen when she had to leave Rosalie, and it broke her heart. She had to leave all her friends and classmates behind, and she was never the same, either. That was all before I was born, of course, and—"

Wendy decided to cut in. "You don't have to go into all these details if you don't want to. If it stresses you out too much, I mean."

"No, it's okay. I need to talk about it, and I'd rather do it with you than anybody else. Deedah and I both like your assignment for the paper, and we trust you." Mitzy was somehow able to keep the emotion out of her voice as she continued. "Anyway, things went from bad to worse for Grandpop. Mother says she and my grandmother didn't see it coming, but Grandpop took his own life—an overdose of sleeping pills. He left a note saying he thought of himself as a failure and was sorry he hadn't done a better job of supporting them. They were devastated, of course, but somehow they were able to pick up the pieces. My mother fell in love with my father, Jason Stone, over there in Alabama, and then I came along after things had settled down a bit. That was twenty-seven years ago, but I grew up knowing what had happened to Grandpop here in Rosalie."

Mitzy let out a sigh, seeming to have found a stopping point in her family story, so Wendy picked up the slack. It was clearly taking a lot out of Mitzy to revisit such unpleasant memories.

"How did you end up in Rosalie, if you don't mind my asking?"

Here, Mitzy leaned back, briefly gazed at the ceiling, and sighed again. "On purpose, if you want to know the truth.

I was determined to come to Rosalie if I could manage it,
even though I'd never lived here before, and then I planned
to make a success of myself as a golf pro. No one really had
to know why I'd come here, but I would know, and that's all
that really counted. Where Grandpop had failed, so to speak, I
would succeed in honor of his memory. I was working down
at the Red Stick Country Club in Baton Rouge when I heard
about the opening. So I sent my résumé to Deedah, and she
hired me. It was lucky for me that the opening hadn't occurred
under Mr. Voss, from what I've heard. No way would he and
Brent Ogle have given me this job. Not those two sexist so-
and-sos. And that's the politest thing I can say about them."

Wendy steeled herself. The hard questions lay ahead. "You
know I have to ask. How did it make you feel when you ran
up against Brent Ogle here at the RCC? Did you even think
about the possibility that you might run into him if you took
the job?"

"No, I honestly didn't even think about that," Mitzy said.
"He could have moved away or even died, for all I knew. But
I have to tell you, I had to keep my head on straight when that
particular reality kicked in, and he showed up bigger than life
and right up in my face to boot. I kept telling myself, 'Don't
lose it. Just do your job, Mitzy; do your job. Don't pay attention to what that Neanderthal says or does.'"

Then came Wendy's curveball. "Did you believe Brent
Ogle when he said his father had paid the officials to cheat?
Particularly that part about the clock operator?"

"I don't know. . . . Uh, I knew Brent was good and
drunk. What else was new? I thought he might just be being
obnoxious to his friends. I mean, there was a remote possibility he might be telling the truth, but it was all ancient history.
Whether Brent Ogle's father paid off the refs or not, none of
it was going to bring my grandpop back or change what happened to his family. And that includes me."

Wendy saw that Mitzy was beginning to tear up, and fell back once again on what Ross had told her more than once about detective work. There was an art to it that came from evaluating human behavior and recognizing certain tells in body language and speech. It seemed to Wendy—at least for the moment—that Mitzy lacked the component of rage to bludgeon a man to death, even though she had good reason and the strength to do so. She also appeared to have made peace with her family story; and more than that, she exuded pride in her accomplishments at the RCC.

Then, as if reading Wendy's mind, Mitzy added, "I did not kill Brent Ogle. What would that gain me? I'd be found out eventually, and he would win in the end. I'd be in prison, instead of enjoying my position here as the first female pro at the RCC. My grandpop would be proud of me for returning to Rosalie and doing what I've done. He would not be proud—no one in my family would be proud—if I'd actually committed murder."

"Do you keep in touch with your family?" Wendy said, trying to lighten the mood a bit.

"My grandmother is gone now, but I Skype with Mother and Dad now and then. I mostly spend holidays with them over there in Alabama, but sooner or later I'm gonna host them over here when I can get a bigger place. I've been saving up for that, you know."

Wendy started turning things over quickly in her head, and it was causing her to frown.

"What's the matter?" Mitzy said. "Did I say something that puzzles you?"

"It's just that I'm running out of suspects that I can believe actually killed Brent Ogle. Everyone just seems incapable of doing such a thing. Something just doesn't add up."

Mitzy cracked an awkward smile. "But it's not up to you to solve this case, is it?"

"No," Wendy told her. "It's just this thing I've got—this puzzle-solving thing in my head that I've had since I was a little girl. My daddy keeps after me to put it to good use by joining the police force, but I don't want to carry a gun around. It's not my style. I've always wanted to be an investigative reporter the same way you wanted to be a golf pro, and now we're both living out our dreams."

"I completely understand where you're coming from." Mitzy took a few moments and seemed lost in thought again. "Do you think I should tell Detective Rierson about my relationship to Coach Doughty, or do you think it matters at this point?"

Wendy's smile turned into a prolonged chuckle. "That seems to be the story of my life these days. People coming to me and revealing their secrets and then I end up advising them what to do with those secrets where this murder case is concerned. I'm beginning to feel like some sort of graven image that people shouldn't be worshiping. I'm sure I don't have all the answers, though I try my best."

Mitzy offered up an uncomfortable grunt. "In my opinion, you just described there at the end what Brent Ogle expected of everyone—to worship and praise him constantly and never stand in his way. The man never grew up. He was trapped forever in his football glory days. He couldn't do without the crowd roaring for him, and there was hell to pay when people didn't play that role for him."

"That's a sad epitaph. But to answer your question about telling Mr. Rierson, I can pass along what you've told me and let him take it from there. You'll hear from him if he wants to question you further. Anyway, I'm glad you told me all that about your family. I think it will greatly enhance the article on you and Deedah that I'm doing. That is, if you don't object to my revealing who you really are. You're right about it being a success story. Here you are in Rosalie making a name for yourself after what happened to your grandfather. It speaks to my theme of strong women accomplishing things. So, what do you think? Do you object to my telling your backstory?"

Mitzy took her time. "Do I have to answer that right away?"

"No, I don't suppose so. I'm nowhere near having my feature put together yet."

"Then remind me when you are. I'll give you my decision then. I kept all of this about my grandfather on the down low for a reason. I wanted the privacy. I needed the privacy. Can you understand that?"

"Yes, of course I can." Then feeling a heightened camaraderie with Mitzy, Wendy decided to push ahead and go for it. "Strictly off the record, who do you think killed Brent Ogle?"

Mitzy seemed hesitant but finally said, "Strictly off the record? You won't repeat this to anyone?"

"You have my word."

Almost as a reflex action, Mitzy lowered her voice, although there was no one near to eavesdrop. "I'm leaning toward Gerald Mansfield. His job was on the line, and Brent Ogle was bound and determined to get him fired. I'm told he and Mr. Voss had been working on it for some time. I think Gerald felt threatened enough to take the risk of committing murder. Now, don't get me wrong. I like Gerald. He's easy to work with and has never given me a minute's trouble. But he's a little on the dim side. I don't think he even finished high school. Maybe in a moment of desperation he thought that was the only way he could keep his job. Of course, he didn't have to go to those lengths, if he actually did it."

Wendy was surprised by Mitzy's accusation but tried valiantly not to show it. It seemed a bit meandering and equivocal. She also knew that Gerald Mansfield was someone capable of stalking, but she did not see him as a murderer; and there was still no proof that he had even been at the RCC on that fateful evening. Mitzy's opinion had not been of much help.

"You think I'm off base, don't you?" Mitzy said, interpreting Wendy's facial expression correctly. "I hesitated to tell you, but you asked. In fact, you drew all of this out of me, and I have to admit, I never expected anyone to discover my secret. Unless I chose to tell them, that is."

"I really don't know what I expected you to say in answer to my question. I'm not sure why I even asked you. But I know I just mentioned to you that I've run out of believable suspects for Brent Ogle's murder. As a result, I don't think Gerald Mansfield fits the bill, but that's just my opinion."

"Not everyone is as up-front with who they are as Brent Ogle was. With him, you didn't have to guess about anything. You knew he was bad news through and through, and you just tried your best to stay out of his way. But there are people who can hide behind masks and fool you. That way, they can preempt you from realizing the truth about them. I prefer people who are at least up-front with their problems and prejudices. At least you know what you're dealing with and have time to develop a strategy," Mitzy added.

Develop a strategy.

Where else had Wendy heard that phrase? After a few moments, it came to her. *Deedah Hornesby.* She had used exactly those words in referring to putting up with Brent Ogle.

Meanwhile, Mitzy's unsolicited observations were resonating immediately and strongly with Wendy. There it was again: *preempt.* The word she had trotted out for her mini-bridge lesson before the first session of the Bridge Bunch had begun. It now seemed like light-years ago, though it was only a week. She had explained to her fellow bridge players—and quite well, she thought—the tactic of interfering with your opponents' ability to perceive the deal clearly, to lessen their

ability to communicate with each other and reach a successful contract and conclusion. It was an artificial but patently
aggressive move. And it often worked in the game of bridge.
But this was a game of sorts, too—a game of life and death.

And then, one of Mitzy's last sentences was branded upon
Wendy's brain: *That way, they can preempt you from realizing the
truth about them.* She knew she needed to file that away for
safekeeping. The reality had to be that the person who had
actually committed the murder had executed such a maneuver
to perfection and therefore thrown everyone off their game.

What had been continuing to be extremely difficult for
Wendy to dismiss was her perception that no one among the
suspects seemed capable of killing Brent Ogle, though all had
their well-known reasons. That much was out in the open.
Perhaps difficult to dismiss, but it could not possibly be a correct assumption now; and Mitzy had just volunteered a helpful reminder that greatly clarified things.

There was a *preemptive* murderer among them. A very
clever one, who had covered his or her tracks with an elaborate illusion about what they were or were not capable of
doing, hiding their true moral compass from view. From
that new perspective, then, everyone was back on the list
of suspects. Every single one of the innocent-appearing,
professional-acting, artistic, cathartic, church-going, secret-
confessing, or even some combination of those, was a possibility again—even Mitzy herself, despite her calm and collected
presentation. At least one of them had audaciously and oppor-
tunistically prevailed in murder via sleight of hand and word
in a narrow time frame in the darkness. It simply could not be
otherwise because Brent Ogle had not committed suicide—
that much, thankfully, was certain.

They all had continued to come forth to Wendy or her
proxy in law enforcement, Ross; one by one, revealing this

and that, sometimes solicited, sometimes not. But one of them had made the ultimate mistake in engaging Wendy's gift of puzzle solving. Eventually, she would fit all of the right pieces together, and the perpetrator—the raging bludgeoner masquerading as a guileless soul—would be revealed, caught, and made to pay.

CHAPTER 14

Wendy stood before her full-length bedroom mirror primping in her fairy princess costume a half an hour before Ross was scheduled to pick her up for their Halloween dinner date at The Toast of Rosalie. She decided to allow herself a conceit: no more fascinating adult fairy princess had ever waved a wand and granted a wish. This was going to be so much fun tonight as the other diners looked on and whispered among themselves about the "fascinating" couple in costume who had dared to throw caution to the wind and appear in public that way. Were they coming from or going to a Halloween party? Were they husband and wife, or something else to each other?

Husband and wife.

The phrase had crossed Wendy's mind more than a few times over the past year since Ross had tried to propose to her by offering up that little black box with the engagement ring inside. But she had not let him open it, saying that she just did not think she was ready for the whole nine yards yet. That they would continue seeing each other as they had been and that she would know when the time was right to stage the wedding with all the trimmings that her father had been pressing her for, and not so subtly at that.

"Ross is a fine man and one of my most meticulous detectives. If I'd had a son, I'd want him to be just like he is," Bax would remind her from time to time.

And she would always respond practically the same way. "Daddy, I do love Ross, and we are seeing each other seriously. But we're not rushing into things, either. Just let us work it out our own way in good time."

Wendy had felt it far more important to take the past year to become truly comfortable in her new position as the *Citizen's* first full-time investigative reporter, and her relationship with Lyndell Slover was making that as seamless as could be expected. So, was it time to reconsider Ross's proposal of marriage and give in to his agenda of starting a family?

Perhaps. Perhaps not. Ross had made it clear in their most private moments together that he wanted children. At least two, maybe three. There, Wendy was not quite so sanguine. She had liked being an only child, enjoying the exclusive attention Bax and Valerie Winchester had lavished upon her. Did she want that same experience for a son or daughter of her own? Or did she want to try her hand at bringing up siblings?

Then she considered the genetic makeup of any children she and Ross made. They would be fair and Nordic looking, what with her strawberry-blonde and his dirty-blond locks, barring a throwback to some unknown ancestor. They would be "sunblockers," and wouldn't tan well as a result. She found herself chuckling out loud. The phrase *burn, baby, burn* popped up next.

But enough of surface appearance. What sort of intellect would they have? Probably sharp, given the sleuthing skills she and Ross both used to maximum effect. Maybe they'd even be artistic as her mother, Valerie Lyons Winchester, had been. Then she frowned. When it came to the roulette wheel of genetics, who knew anything? Because anything could show up or dominate—she hoped nothing negative.

She stared intently at her reflection in the mirror. "Look at how I'm dressed while I'm going on like this," she said out loud as if she were auditioning for a play or a part in a movie. "This proves I am nowhere near ready for motherhood yet," she added, sticking her tongue out at herself. "You, Wendy Winchester, do not merely wave a magic wand a couple of times to become a good mother, no matter how many children you have or what they inherit."

Then, she reverted to her internal monologue. Was it possible she was suffering from that old male bugaboo? *Fear of commitment.* She let that sink in for a while. Could it be one of those ironic reversals where Ross was the one who'd made the ultimate romantic leap while she remained stubbornly protective of her independent streak as a woman?

Her smartphone's ringtone instantly brought her out of her intellectual reverie. She walked over and saw that it was Ross calling.

"Hi, sweetie," she said. "I was just thinking about you." She did not, however, qualify that any further.

"Listen, something's come up," he told her, sounding rushed. "I'm gonna change the reservation to seven-thirty. We've got what may be a break in the murder case, and I'm gonna have to interrogate someone who's come forward. I'm at the station right now with Bax, in fact. This could be the breakthrough we've been looking for, and we have to act on it quickly."

Wendy instantly forgot all about Ross moving the reservation and pressed on. "Are you at liberty to say which suspect?"

"Not any of our suspects," he told her. "Someone new."

"Ross, you have me on the edge of my seat. Can't you tell me anything? Don't tell me there's a witness to this thing. Come on, now, you can leak just a little to me like Daddy always does. You know he doesn't mind."

There was brief silence, and then Ross said, "Okay, we

don't know yet about the witness part, but I'll go ahead and tell you that it involves Carlos Galbis. Seems he had someone on the side, so to speak, that called us up and says she has some information to share with us that she thinks we ought to know about."

Wendy had to blink a couple of times. "Someone on the side? You mean as in a mistress?"

"Yes, she told us that much over the phone in so many words. Listen, sweetie, I've gotta run. Our person on the side just walked into the station dressed to kill. I'll get back in touch as soon as I can. In the meantime, don't you dare spoil your appetite by nibbling on anything. I'll talk to you later."

After Wendy had said goodbye and put the phone down, she sat on the edge of the bed with her chiffon fairy princess gown making all sorts of rustling noises and began shaking her head in silence. Carlos Galbis with a mistress? She could not envision such an improbable thing. Quiet, family-oriented, religious Carlos having an affair? In her conversations with him at the RCC, he had never impressed her as the type of man who would even consider doing something like that. He was so the opposite of macho and spoke so glowingly of his wife and children all the time.

Who on earth was this woman who claimed to be close enough to Carlos to come forward with information about him concerning the murder case? Would she be telling the truth, or did she have an agenda of some kind? Had she even been paid to besmirch his name and reputation? It all seemed so theatrical, so film noir-ish, like someone playing a part or following orders. For not the first time, Wendy was tossing that phrase around in her head: *following orders*. She'd had that exact same impression of Gerald Mansfield at first, even though he'd insisted to Ross that he'd been stalking her on his own and that no one else had been behind it.

Wendy temporarily shut down her speculations and

headed over to the kitchen, despite Ross's playful suggestion that she not spoil her appetite. She opened the fridge and took out a small block of Monterey Jack that she had wrapped in cellophane after sampling it a few times. A little bit of cheese and maybe a small glass of wine would hold her for now. Being the sleuth she was, however, she realized that she was far more interested in what Ross pulled out of this mystery mistress than the dinner they were going to order and eat a bit later in the evening. Even the excitement of their doing that in costume was taking a back seat.

Ross was staring across the table in the interrogation room with Bax sitting next to him. This woman, who had identified herself as Berry Passman, reminded him of a certain "exotic dancer" he'd paid good money to see at a Memphis strip club in his wild and woolly college days. As he recalled, her name had been Vanilla Swirl and he and some frat buddies had gone up to Beale Street one Saturday evening to "eat, drink, and be merry," more or less. In fact, it had been just before the beginning of Christmas holidays that they'd set out on their macho mission, and Ross had ended up contributing more than a few singles to the growing collection hanging out of Vanilla Swirl's G-string.

But Berry Passman was not scantily clad. Her clothes were expensive while still managing to show off her spectacular figure, and her makeup was not overly applied. It was mainly something about the way Berry held her mouth in an inviting little pout that brought back Ross's "gentlemen's club" memories. And the hair—the straight, dark hair—which was pulled back away from her face toward the crown, where it was tied in a ponytail that hung all the way down to her waist. All of which seemed to suggest that wild horseplay was there for the taking. It flashed into Ross's head that whatever else Carlos Galbis was, he was only human.

"So before we get to this information you have for us, how did you and Mr. Galbis meet?" Ross was saying after they'd gotten the preliminaries out of the way. Namely, that she had moved to Rosalie about six months ago from Jackson to live with her cousin for a while until she found new work, that the gentlemen's club she had been working for had gone out of business, and that she was through for good with that line of work.

For his part upon hearing that last part, Ross had had to struggle mightily from pumping his fist and saying, "I knew I recognized the type," out loud. But he had managed to restrain himself and continue his questioning in a dignified, professional manner.

"I met Carlos at the country club, of course," she told Ross. "My cousin had told me what delicious mint juleps they had out there, and so I went just to try one. I do have a fondness for well-made cocktails. And when I got there, here was Carlos, and then he started mixing one up for me. He looked so cute in his little tux, and I was fascinated with the way he worked that mortar and pestle thing, or whatever you call it. I guess it was the grinding motion that really got me interested, if you catch my drift. So I started flirting with him. He flirted back, and then one thing led to another, you see. Not right then, but soon after. I mean, no one was forcing his hand, believe me."

"So you were having an affair with him, then."

"Duh. I would not know what I know if I hadn't been."

Ross glanced at Bax briefly and then continued. "Did you not see the ring on his finger, or did that not matter?"

Berry flashed on him. "I did not come all the way down here to be judged, Detective. I came here to tell you something you need to know for your investigation. And besides, we are not seeing each other anymore. Carlos . . . well, he broke it off with me a few days ago."

"He did, did he? And did he tell you why?"

The anger Berry had just conjured up did not dissipate in the least. "He said it was because of that Mr. Ogle's murder. He said something about life being too precious and too short and keeping in mind what really mattered." Her voice suddenly went all high-pitched and mocking with a greatly exaggerated facial expression to match. "That his precious family was the only thing that really counted, and he had let them down—and what was he thinking even getting involved with me in the first place? That sort of old-fashioned, corny thing. But we all know the answer to that, don't we? You men are all alike. You only want one thing, and when you get tired of it with someone, you walk away."

Ross and Bax again exchanged furtive looks. "Not all of us," Ross said after taking a deep breath.

Berry shot him a disgusted glance but said nothing further.

"All right, then. Let's get to this information you came down here to give us, Miz Passman," Ross continued.

She took a few moments to compose herself and then said, "As I told you before, I know this because of our . . . well, our pillow talk. People tell other people things they would never mention after they've gotten a little, you know. And no wisecracks, please. You really need to hear this."

Ross managed a grin. "We're listening."

"Anyway, there were a few times when we got together that he would rant and rave about that Mr. Ogle. He told me his life would be perfect if it weren't for that man—the way he ran Carlos down and humiliated him, and all Carlos could do was sit there and take it because of his job. And there was this one time I remember that Carlos said to me something like, 'I swear, if I could find a way to do it, I'd kill him. Under the right circumstances, I know I would.'"

Berry took the time to throw out her impressive chest

and then added, "And here's the payoff. I distinctly remember Carlos ending with, 'I'd like to bash his head in.' "

Bax and Ross waited for something more out of her mouth, but there was only silence.

"Is that it?" Ross said finally.

"Isn't that enough? Didn't the lights go out and didn't someone hit that Mr. Ogle over the head with that pestle thing? That's what Carlos told me, anyway, and it was in the paper, too."

"All of what you say is true," Ross said. "So you wanted us to know that Carlos was frustrated and angered by Mr. Ogle. We already knew that. Mr. Galbis told us that himself. He also told us that he did not kill Mr. Ogle by bashing him over the head with the pestle."

"And you believed him? Of course he'd say that, wouldn't he? How many killers actually come up to you and confess?"

Ross tilted his head to one side quizzically. "You'd be surprised when push comes to shove."

Berry's hostility seemed to have morphed into sarcasm. "Well, excuse me for doing my civic duty and volunteering something I bet you didn't know. I coudda kept my trap shut and maybe let Carlos get away with murder, then."

"I assure you, your visit has not been wasted, Miz Passman. We'll call Mr. Galbis in again and get his side of the story."

Now Berry's anger was back with a renewed fervor. "His side? There's only one side. We had an affair, and he told me what he told me. If you want my opinion, I think he did it, and if someone had treated me the way Carlos said that man had treated him, I'd 'a bashed his head in, too. So, make of it all what you will."

"That's our job, Miz Passman. That's our job."

★ ★ ★

"So what do we make of Miz Passman and her impassioned testimony?" Ross said, turning to Bax after she had walked out of the room in somewhat of a huff.

Bax, who had been totally silent throughout the interrogation, suddenly erupted with erudite observations. "The way I see it, it's likely one of two things. We have on our hands either a Hell Hath No Fury scenario or an Occam's Razor scenario. The first is obviously that Miz Passman is a woman scorned and will stop at nothing to muddy the waters and hope that Carlos suffers dire consequences as a result. That was the first thing that came to mind while she was rattling on and on about her motivation for coming forth. I assume that occurred to you, too?"

"It did," Ross said, nodding agreeably. "I may have even gone a bit too far with the wedding ring bit."

"Don't worry about it. You didn't hurt her feelings, and she gave it right back to you with that comment about you judging her."

"So she did." Ross gave Bax a sideways glance. "As for the Occam's Razor comment . . . uh, I think I recall what that's about. But go ahead and refresh my memory anyway."

"Gladly. I'm sure it'll all come back to you quickly enough. Occam's Razor is a philosophical principle that says that all other things being equal, if there are more than two explanations for an occurrence, the one requiring the least speculation is usually the better one. Another way of putting it is that the simplest explanation is often the right one."

Ross considered for a while, his face clouding over, and said, "So as that would apply to Carlos Galbis, we would go back to our very first hypothesis when he was our prime suspect because he had easy access to the weapon, motive, and opportunity. Carlos was the one who did it would be our simplest solution, despite his denials. And now we have this further testimony that he had actually uttered the words *bash his head in* where Brent Ogle was concerned."

"If Miz Passman can be believed. She could have put the words in his mouth. It's strictly a 'he said, she said' proposition when you come right down to it," Bax told him. "Remember that the Hell Hath No Fury scenario has not been dismissed yet. In fact, I think it's very much in play."

"So, what if we have a combination of both of those scenarios at work here, Bax? What then?"

Bax put his hands on the table with a firm thud, and the effect was to add gravitas to his words. "Well, it seems to me that our job is no tougher than it's always been from the get-go. All these suspects milling around the RCC with motivation and opportunity, but nothing more than circumstantial evidence at best to put this thing to bed."

"Just look at you. Something out of a fairy tale. You look beautiful," Ross said after he showed up at Wendy's door in his police uniform, holding a hang-up bag. But before she had a chance to respond to his outpouring, he quickly explained himself. "I've got my costume in here. I hadn't changed into it yet when your daddy called me about the last-minute interrogation. So just let me do a quick change, and we'll be ready to head on out."

She gestured toward her bedroom and said, "I thank you for your kind words, sir. Be my guest. I can't wait to see what you've come up with."

Minutes later, he emerged to her cute little shriek, followed by light applause. "I love it. My white knight."

"Exactly," he said, taking a bow. "Here to whisk you away to some good vittles." He glanced at his watch. "And by my calculations, we have just enough time to make our reservation."

During the drive from Wendy's bungalow to The Toast

of Rosalie, Ross brought her up to date on the interrogation of Berry Passman with her father and his mentor by his side.

"About what went on here tonight with this Miz Passman. You know Wendy will get it out of one of us sooner or later," Bax had told him just before he had headed out to the parking lot to pick Wendy up. "In all the many years I've leaked things to that daughter a' mine, she's never betrayed my trust."

So Ross was completely comfortable with painting a detailed picture of Miz Berry Passman and her relentless pursuit of the role Carlos Galbis may have played in the murder case, all the while keeping a careful eye on the road.

"How did she really strike you?" Wendy said after he had finished.

"As vengeful, mainly. That was the overwhelming impression that I got the second she opened her mouth. I'm thinking this may not amount to very much in the end. But we've got Carlos Galbis coming in tomorrow for another round of questioning, of course. We'll see if he changes his story at all."

"Occam's Razor," Wendy said as Ross masterfully handled the curves of Lower Kingston Road. Then she repeated the words, this time more slowly. "I happen to remember it quite well from Philosophy One-oh-one at Mizzou. I kept thinking to myself during that particular lecture, 'Will something like that ever actually come up during my lifetime?' And now, here it is, big as life, staring me in the face. But even if it's true that Carlos Galbis as the murderer fits the definition of Occam's Razor, you still have no proof of anything, unless he just up and confesses. Do you think this so-called revelation by this Passman woman would be enough to do the trick?"

"Right now, I'm leaning toward 'no,' because it still goes against the grain of who I think Carlos really is. I can't match any of that up with the man who says he goes to Mass every week and loves his family with every ounce of his strength. It's a misfit in every sense of the word."

Wendy knew that that was her cue to tell Ross about her meeting with Mitzy and her surprising backstory and then introduce to him the concept of someone preempting who they really were and what they had actually done. When she had finished with it all, Ross sounded overwhelmed. It had even caused him to slow down a bit.

"Wow! That's a lot to take in all at once, especially on the heels of Berry Passman turning up with her story."

"They all can't be lying to us, though," Wendy said. "That would imply that they are all guilty." Wendy paused for a moment. "Is that even possible? That they all had a role in this?"

"That would take some extraordinary planning," Ross told her. "Who would be capable of masterminding something like that?" He managed a shrug. "Perhaps the director of the RCC? Not to cast aspersions on your bridge club cohort."

"I'm afraid you did just that. Why Deedah Hornesby?"

"Well, her profile doesn't fit Occam's Razor. Miz Deedah as the culprit is far from the simplest solution. She'd have to take a number in line behind some of the others," Ross began, his eyes shifting as if he were reviewing every suspect in turn.

"Besides, Bax and I have discussed multiple people being involved when he brought up the idea to me a while back of at least two people teaming up together to pull this thing off. No matter what, though, who could count on the power outage? I can never get past that part. Who could rely upon an act of nature like that? And even though they all had a motive to take out Brent Ogle, it goes against my experience that they would all have agreed to participate in such a risky criminal activity. I'm more inclined to give some weight to your intriguing idea about just one of them being devious enough to throw us off the scent. Preempting, as you say. I like the idea. Maybe I should take up bridge after all. Do you think your little group would agree to admit a novice like me? Or would they be afraid I'd chase the skeletons out of their closets?"

Wendy pointed to the steering wheel as they hit a pothole and the laws of physics disturbed everything inside the car. "Very funny. Pay attention to the road. As for the bridge club, if I have anything to say about it, you're golden. After all, I'm one of the founders of the Bridge Bunch. We haven't actually made up any rules yet for membership. Deedah and I should probably do that soon. But mostly, I think we'll fall back on the tried and true—that the only thing you need to get in is the desire to play . . . and socialize a bit. At this point, all we're really looking for is more warm bodies."

"I'll let you know if I'm truly interested in joining," Ross said. "Because I do think I fit the definition of *warm*."

"I can vouch for that," she said, patting his leg a couple of times. Then she withdrew her hand quickly so that he could give all his attention to his driving. "But back to the idea of the murder being planned and lots of people being in on it. Suppose there really was a ringleader, and suppose people were to play different roles in such a plan. Perhaps all that planning could have taken place in advance at a different place and time, and all the power outage did was make it easier to execute. I've had the strange sense all along that something about the murder had a theatrical flair to it."

"Are you pointing a finger at Hollis Hornesby by any chance?"

"No, I didn't mean theatrical in that way," she said. "Although I have to admit, Hollis seems to be playing a role every time he opens his mouth. I think he missed his calling. He should have been an actor instead of an artist. I was just suggesting that this murder may not have depended upon the power outage to work. That would remove your objection that no one could count on something like that. As I mentioned, perhaps the darkness made everything a little easier."

"Let's file that away for later, shall we?"

They had finally arrived at the Toast of Rosalie lot, which offered valet parking. When the young, uniformed valet who looked like he was trying to grow a mustache handed Ross his ticket, he actually stepped back and applauded their costumes.

"Excellent," he told them. "If we had a competition going on in the dining room tonight, you two would easily win the prize because everyone else just came as themselves so far."

"Thanks," Ross said, as Wendy waved her wand at him with a smile.

"M'lady," the valet said in return with a bow of his head.

"I know you're bound to be hungry," Ross said, as they entered the restaurant quickly to get in out of the chilly Halloween night air. "I'm starving, even though I've been given a lot of food for thought tonight."

"We both have, so that means we're in this together."

In the midst of savoring their shrimp and grits with glasses of champagne, along with the continuous smiles their costumes were eliciting from diners as they either entered or left, Wendy remembered something she had been meaning to discuss with Ross but kept forgetting.

"I was having a conversation with Lyndell not long ago," she said, "and I read between the lines. She wants to meet Daddy soon, and I think in more than a professional capacity."

Ross swallowed a sip of champagne and then gave her a quizzical glance. "You mean they haven't met already? The editor of the *Citizen* and the Chief of Police? How did that happen?"

"I don't know, but it turns out they haven't. So I was thinking about having a little to-do at the bungalow sometime soon. Maybe just the four of us. Don't you think that'd work?"

Ross's skepticism was showing as he pointed a finger at her. "Depends on what you're trying to accomplish. Sounds like you wanna be a matchmaker. Has Bax told you he's even in the market?"

"I honestly don't think he knows what he wants when it comes to women. He's told me from time to time that he'll never get over losing Momma and that she was the one and only love of his life, but he hasn't said that much lately on the subject. I mean, what could it hurt to introduce him to an available woman who's expressed a little interest in him? It would just be a simple dinner with witnesses. If they don't click, they don't click."

Ross seemed genuinely amused now. "I love the way you put that—'witnesses.' Well, I have only one thing to say. I'm glad I'm already sold on you, because you're pretty persuasive about justifying the things you do. Hey, it's fine with me if you want to throw this small dinner party." Then he leaned back and laughed out loud. "I'll be there as Bax's wingman." He pointed to her wand, which she'd put down to the right of her plate. "But just remember, you can't wave that thing and make them fall in love."

"O ye of little faith," she said, batting her lashes at him.

CHAPTER 15

To say that Carlos Galbis had the frightened look of a wild animal trapped in a corner was an understatement. Unlike during his earlier interrogations, he now seemed filled with a certain nervous energy, unable to look either Ross or Bax in the eye as he took a seat across from them the next morning at the station.

This time, it was Bax who took the lead in the questioning. "Mr. Galbis, we thank you for coming in so promptly today. But we need to ask you some questions about information given to us last night by a Miz Berry Passman. Do you acknowledge that you know her?"

Carlos shifted his weight and continued to avoid eye contact, speaking hesitantly. "Yes . . . I . . . I know her."

"In what capacity?"

There was a prolonged silence.

"Mr. Galbis," Bax continued. "Please answer the question. You do yourself a great disservice by prolonging this. Your best strategy would be to tell us the truth and let us take it from there."

Finally, he spoke up, continuing to look down into his lap. "I'm ashamed to say that . . . I was having an affair with her."

"That's what she told us in no uncertain terms. But that's not what primarily concerns us now—"

Carlos interrupted with great urgency in his voice. "Things aren't the same, though. You need to know that I have gone to confession and told my priest everything that happened. I am no longer seeing Berry. But please . . . please don't tell my wife about this. She would fall to pieces, and I could not bear the thought of the pain I know that would cause her."

"We have no intention of doing that," Bax told him. "That is not in our job description. It's up to you and your conscience. But as I was about to say, we are concerned with something Miz Passman told us that you said at some point during your affair with her. She revealed to us that you said you wished you could bash Mr. Ogle's head in. Do you remember ever saying something like that to her? Or was she making that up?"

The distress on Carlos's face became even more pronounced. "I . . . I may have. I can't remember everything I said to her. Pillow talk of any kind is what it is. But . . . but she really meant nothing to me. I realize that now. She came on to me so strong and made herself so available, and then the next thing I knew, we were . . . well, you know how these things go."

Bax drew himself up with a determined glint in his eye. "Actually, I don't, Mr. Galbis. I was always faithful to my wife in the precious years we had together. But that's not the point here. This isn't about me. You've told us previously that Mr. Ogle humiliated you time after time. He never left you a decent tip. He treated you like you were his slave. We believed you then and we will believe you now if you say that you hardly wished him well, human nature being what it is. You had that in common with practically everyone else out at the RCC. The question is, though—did you follow through on your desire to bash his head in? You understand why we have to ask you this."

"I've told you before, I did not do such an evil thing. It's one thing to stray from your marriage. That is sinful enough, especially when it means the world to you. But to murder someone in cold blood—there is no absolution for that. You will carry that with you to Hell, itself. Can't you see what Berry—uh, Miz Passman—is up to here? I did the right thing, finally came to my senses and broke up with her. Meanwhile, she took off her high heel and threw it at me when I told her we couldn't see each other anymore—that it was definitely over. I'm thankful she missed because she was aiming for my head. That could easily have ended up being the murder weapon for her. I might not even be here, talking to you, if she'd had better aim."

"She didn't mention that."

"No, why would she? Of course she wouldn't mention anything that put her in a bad light. This was all about getting back at me any way she could, but I set myself up for this."

"Good point." Bax then turned to Ross and said, "Do you have anything you'd like to ask Mr. Galbis, Detective?"

"Yes, I do," Ross said, leaning in with authority as he did so well. "The impression I got from our previous interrogations with you, Mr. Galbis, was that you were a devoted family man and churchgoer. There was a sincerity to your statements that I could not deny, and I still believe that that is who you truly are. But tell me why you think you strayed. I'm not trying to be your priest, but it will help me believe in you again. It might make all the difference in our investigation."

Carlos was shaking his head and again avoiding eye contact. "You won't believe me if I tell you. I mean, I hear myself saying it in my head, and I'm not sure I'd believe it, either."

"Try me."

"It was *him*," Carlos said with great intensity.

"Who?"

"Mr. Ogle. It was him."

"How so?"

Carlos raised his voice again, speaking with added emotion. "He brought out the worst in people. He was the Devil, himself. He made me feel like I was less than a man with the way he treated me, with the way he talked to me and about me. He snatched little bits and pieces of my manhood as time went on. Maybe that was why when Berry came after me the way she did, I let the worst part of me, the weakest part of me, take over. Maybe I thought I needed to prove something to myself. It seems so immature now, like something an insecure high school punk might do. And I told my priest that I knew that I was ultimately to blame. I chose to do what I did. I knew I needed to be absolved. But still . . . there was something about Mr. Ogle that made you doubt yourself. I know I should have been stronger than that, but I admit that I wasn't. Sometimes, the flesh is all too weak."

Ross said nothing while he briefly glanced at Bax, who looked as if he approved of what Carlos had just told them.

"But you both need to know," Carlos continued, "that I never acted on any impulse I ever had to do away with Mr. Ogle. If I said I wanted to bash his head in, it was an unfortunate choice of words, as it turns out. But that was all it was—just angry words in the heat of the moment. I did not pick up my own pestle that is a cherished tool of my trade and use it to murder Mr. Ogle." There was a pause during which Carlos finally made sustained eye contact with the officers. "You aren't gonna arrest me now, are you?"

"We have no actual evidence that you committed the crime," Ross told him. "We only know that you were at the crime scene delivering drinks and putting up with Mr. Ogle's usual abuse all afternoon and into the evening. We also know that someone showed up there with the pestle, clubbed Mr. Ogle with it, and then threw it into the hot tub where all prints and DNA were conveniently compromised. As a result,

Mr. Galbis, you are free to go. But as we told you before, please do not leave town in case any sort of solid evidence does show up."

Carlos thanked them and then scurried away, as if by lingering even slightly he might incur further questioning and bring additional shame upon himself.

"It's my educated guess that Carlos fits the Hell Hath No Fury scenario and not Occam's Razor," Bax was saying as the two men began evaluating their most recent interrogation. "Miz Passman was clearly out for blood. I consider that her performance here with us today was a hatchet job."

Ross nodded, but there remained an unmistakable look of frustration on his face. "No matter what happens, though, it seems we always get back to a lack of solid evidence, thanks to that blasted hot tub. It turned out to be the perfect device to erase all helpful clues. Did someone plan that in advance or was this a spur-of-the-moment thing? Without a confession— and not the kind Carlos made at the Basilica—I'm afraid we're stymied again."

"At the moment, yes, but that doesn't mean that something won't show up that turns the case around," Bax told him, tapping his finger on the table for emphasis. "I've seen it happen time and time again in this bid'ness. Just when you think you have no hope of solving the case, there's the break you were looking for."

Ross looked anything but convinced. "Well, we thought this Miz Passman might be just that, but as far as I can tell, it's a bust. My faith in Carlos has been slightly restored again."

"I'm inclined to agree with you, but no one is off the hook until we find the solution to this."

Back at his desk, Ross worked off some nervous energy of his own by tidying up a bit while thinking about the preemptive concept that Wendy had explained to him the evening before. Had Carlos actually done something like that to take the pressure and suspicion off himself—painting a picture of himself as too good to be true? When Ross had initially interrogated the man, he could have sworn that Carlos would have been incapable of cheating on his wife. Yet incredibly, that had happened, and his lover had come forth and ascribed to him some very base and visceral feelings. Carlos, himself, had admitted that he had allowed the worst part of him, the weakest part of him, to influence his decision to have an affair. In the heat of the moment and having at last had more than enough, had he also allowed the worst within him to bludgeon Brent Ogle to death?

Yes, the Hell Hath No Fury concept made the most sense in all of this, which involved giving Carlos the benefit of the doubt. But Occam's Razor was still out there, stubbornly hanging around as the outlier.

At the same time that Ross and Bax had been questioning Carlos, Wendy had been busy at her cubicle reluctantly putting together the first draft of her feature on the women who were now running the RCC. Lyndell had told her earlier that morning that she wanted to schedule the article for the upcoming Wednesday edition, if at all possible. That was the day of the week offering all the restaurant, grocery, laundry item coupons and penny savers that made it the most widely read as a result—even edging out the larger Sunday edition with its many wedding write-ups and colorful comics by just a tad bit.

"Do you think you can get it polished by then?" Lyndell had asked her in the editorial office.

Wendy had told her that she thought she could. Yet she had her concerns, even though she had not brought them up to Lyndell then and there. It made her shudder to think so, but what if, by some unthinkable chance, either Deedah or Mitzy were exposed as Brent Ogle's murderer by then? And if that did not happen by Wednesday, how would her feature look in retrospect if either was exposed at a later date?

In fact, Wendy had not gotten any further than the first paragraph before she left the cursor blinking and decided that it might be in the *Citizen*'s best interests to postpone the feature a little longer just to be on the safe side. Resolutely, she headed toward Lyndell's office, mentally rehearsing how she was going to handle the situation without seeming to go against her boss's wishes in somewhat paranoid fashion.

"I have to admit I hadn't thought of that angle," Lyndell told her after Wendy had expressed her concerns in a straightforward manner. "But how long do you suggest we postpone this? We have no way of knowing how long it will take the Rosalie CID to solve this."

"Yes, that's true."

The déjà vu that beset Wendy was easily explained. Deedah had used the same argument to suggest that the next meeting of the Bridge Bunch be postponed until Brent Ogle's murder was solved. Now the shoe was on the other foot and Wendy was using the same argument for postponement with Lyndell. But the two scenarios were entirely different. One involved putting off playing a social card game; the other involved the possibility of the *Citizen* having a great deal of egg on its face at some point. Furthermore, Wendy saw clearly that her reputation as a journalist might be severely damaged by taking the chance that she might end up having praised the virtues of a murderer beforehand.

Lyndell maintained her composure as usual and said, "Do you really think either of these women committed this crime? From what I've heard of them from you, it seems so unlikely."

"I wish I could give you a definitive answer. I wish I could guarantee you that neither of them did it and that our path was clear to go into detail about their accomplishments at the RCC. But I can't actually do that."

Lyndell sat back in her chair, and for the very first time since she had taken over as editor, she appeared to be displeased with something that Wendy had said to her. "Tell me the truth now, have you gotten so involved in this murder case that you've allowed it to influence your assignment for the paper? I know your job is to investigate, but do you think you may have blurred the line a bit too much? I do remember cautioning you to let the police department do its job in that regard."

Wendy noted the slight edge to Lyndell's voice, and it was disconcerting to hear. Perhaps there was some truth to what Lyndell was saying, but Wendy just couldn't help it. Her close association with Ross and her father inevitably put her in the unique position of being the beneficiary of leaks that others did not enjoy. Wendy knew that it was in her blood, but also that she wanted the best of both worlds. She wanted to maintain her job as an investigative reporter while honing her sleuthing instincts. Lyndell had just pointed out to her that she was walking a tightrope and needed to be careful not to fall.

"Are you dead set on publishing the piece this coming Wednesday?" Wendy said, trying to negotiate her way out of her dilemma. "I wouldn't want to put the paper in a bad light by running it too soon, as I said."

Lyndell's sigh had an air of resignation to it. "All right, then. Being relatively new to Rosalie, I am going to defer to your judgment here. Your family has been here a long time, and you know the lay of the land better than I do. Just continue to put your article together and get it ready to run. I'll make the decision to release it depending upon how the investigation goes. We've done good work together so far, and I don't want to jeopardize that relationship or your reputation."

"Thank you, Lyndell. I'll get back to work on the piece as if the murder had never even happened. And who knows? Maybe in the end we'll get to have our cake and eat it, too."

Lyndell leaned forward with a wry grin. "Just don't use clichés like that in the feature."

"Done," Wendy said, smiling back.

Then, she finally remembered something very important she had meant to tell Lyndell before she'd been given the original deadline on the RCC article. "By the way, I'm having an intimate little dinner party next Saturday, and I'd like for you to come. It's just going to be my boyfriend, Ross Rierson, and myself; plus my dear old daddy, Bax Winchester, is dropping by for some of my home cooking. I thought maybe you could make a fourth for us, since I do believe you expressed some interest in meeting him. What do you say?"

The suggestion of tension that their earlier conversation about the feature had generated disappeared completely from Lyndell's face, and she brightened immediately. "I'd be delighted, of course. Is it going to be casual or what?"

"No one ever dresses up to have dinner with me in my little bungalow," Wendy told her, and then gave her a wink. "But by all means, wear something inspirational, if you'd like."

"I think I can manage that."

"There's no doubt in my mind you'll manage it well."

Wendy had no sooner sat down in her cubicle and returned to her blinking cursor than the reception desk put through a call for her from Carly Ogle.

"What can I do for you today?" Wendy said, after they'd exchanged the usual pleasantries.

"I wanted you to be the first to know. I've decided to take my son David's advice and put Brentwood on the market. It's time for me to leave."

Wendy was a bit taken by surprise at first but then thought it would be more important to be supportive of the major decision that Carly had just made. "I'm sure your son will be delighted to hear the news. I could tell at the memorial service that he really didn't think Rosalie was the place for you anymore."

"He was absolutely right, but I haven't told him what I've decided to do yet," Carly said. "I was thinking that maybe I needed to pick out which pieces I'd allow to be sold along with the house and which I'd want to save for David. He'll get married someday, I hope, and I'm sure his wife will appreciate acquiring my tasteful things. Brent's stuff is tacky beyond belief, but I have invested in some lovely antiques over the years. If you wouldn't mind, I'd like for you to come out tomorrow sometime and help me go over everything, room by room. Help me clean my house."

The request was an even bigger surprise for Wendy. She, herself, was more an aficionado of flea markets and yard sales. She had a few antiques that she had inherited from her mother, but her house was filled mostly with the out-of-left-field "finds" from those venues. "Well, I have to admit I've never done anything like that, but I'd be happy to give it a try if you really need me."

"I truly would appreciate it so much. I think I need an outside opinion from someone I trust."

"I'm flattered that you think of me that way," Wendy said.

"Then that's all settled. Could you maybe drive out during your lunch hour? I promise not to keep you too long. As I said, it's time for me to leave."

Wendy said she could arrange it without too much trouble. After the call ended, she made a note to herself on her desk calendar and then returned to her cursor. But despite Lyndell's directive that she press ahead with the article for later release, Wendy found herself drifting once again into thoughts about the investigation. She just couldn't seem to help herself.

This time, that opening session of the Bridge Bunch rose up before her with its quick lesson on preempting. Of all the speculations that intrigued her the most regarding Brent Ogle's murder—a handful that included a grand, building-wide conspiracy, two people working together, and everyone except herself having a believable motivation to off the man—the one with true staying power for her was preempting.

She immediately reviewed that relatively short period of time during which she had displayed and then explained a preemptive hand—short on points, but perhaps seven or eight cards long in the same suit. There had been three people sitting at that table taking in her instruction with great interest: *Deedah*, *Hollis*, and *Carly*. Was one of them the most likely to have utilized the concept of preempting after committing murder, then? Why had she not considered this before in terms of who was actually privy to her instruction that day?

Then, she let out a little gasp when she remembered one little detail she had overlooked. There was one other person who had been present during that preemptive bid lesson: *Mitzy Stone*. She had come up behind the table and quietly kibitzed before announcing her presence and offering her services as a barmaid. Then she had asked for a further explanation of the preemptive bid and described it as devious.

That was an odd word to use.

Wendy focused further on Mitzy. She had been extremely cooperative and calm about revealing that she was related to Coach P. J. Doughty; and she had hung his picture on her wall, which seemed to give credence to her genealogical claims. But there had been no hint of rage in her demeanor during their lengthy conversation, and she had eagerly pointed the finger at Gerald Mansfield when asked who she figured for the murderer. Could Mitzy have been the one who was painting a picture of herself as always under control, always being the bigger person when it came to handling the macho posturing of certain males, all the while secretly seething to get the ultimate revenge on behalf of her grandfather?

Finally, Wendy came out of her cerebral exercise and faced the cursor at last. It was time to start putting flesh on the bones of her RCC piece, and getting rid of the blank screen was the first step. Of course, she had to admit that Lyndell had her pegged perfectly. She had indeed become distracted by and obsessed with the murder case, still holding out hope that she would be the one to bring home the solution. Back to work, then.

Wendy had just finished composing her opening paragraph, however, when the reception desk informed her that she had yet another call.

"Who is it?" Wendy wanted to know.

"A Mr. Hollis Hornesby," the receptionist told her.

Wendy frowned while she considered whether to take the call or not. First, Carly. Then, Hollis. Were they all going to call her up, one after another? Whatever the case, her curiosity got the better of her, and she was soon exchanging perfunctory greetings with him.

"What do you make of Carly's decision to sell that monstrosity of a house that her husband built?" Hollis continued. "She just invited me to come out there tomorrow around noon and help her decide what artwork she should keep for her son and what she should let go. She told me she'd asked you to do the same for her with the furniture. It sounds like a pilot for one of those super-specific cable TV shows, if you ask me. They have them for every subject under the sun now."

Hollis's propensity for making people laugh had Wendy doing just that, temporarily pushing aside her surprise upon hearing of Carly's other request. "I didn't think of it that way, but you're right."

"How about *Keep or Sell?* or something like that for a show title. Wait . . . that sounds more like a game show, doesn't it? I've always wanted to get on one of those and win some money for answering stupid questions that everybody knows, but I understand all the shows are hard to get on and—"

"Hollis, you're wandering off the plantation," Wendy interrupted.

There was a brief pause, followed by a giggle. "So I am. Anyway, I think Carly's request is downright weird. I honestly think the murder has had a greater effect on her than anyone's realized. Her instability seems to have gone through the roof. My friend Penny who works at the Hair You Go Salon downtown says Carly came in yesterday to have her hair done as usual but insisted on an entirely different style than she's ever worn. Penny said Carly told her she wanted to get rid of the past entirely. As I said, I have to wonder about her mental state at this point."

Wendy flashed back to that cathartic revelation when Carly could not seem to stop beating herself up for having all those violent, hateful thoughts about her abusive husband. "It does make sense, though, if you put it in context. Selling Brentwood would help her get rid of the past, too. There's a part of her that probably can't get rid of Brentwood fast enough."

"Hmmm," Hollis said. "I see your point. And apparently I will see you tomorrow out there. Are you up for this level of responsibility? I don't want to get into some wicked catfight with her if she disagrees with any of my decisions. Of course, I like to think I know something about art, so maybe she'll defer to me."

"I have to hope it goes that way for me, too. At least we won't have to go it alone, you and I."

"God forbid."

After they'd hung up, Wendy made a halfhearted attempt to pick up where she'd left off with her article. But three words kept bugging her. *Carly and Hollis*. Coupled together just like that. What had triggered that combination in her brain? Yes, the two of them had been at the bridge table with her, but there was something more, and it simply would not surface yet. She decided to let it go for the time being. It was a matter of getting down to the business of her paying job.

CHAPTER 16

Down at the station the next day, Bax summoned Ross to his office and handed over several sheets of a document he had just printed out from his computer. "We finally heard from the ME's office in Jackson. This report is a doozy, and it's why you do autopsies under suspicious circumstances and never assume first impressions are always the correct ones."

Ross took a seat and scanned the first page quickly while moving his lips here and there. When he finally finished, the look on his face was one of utter disbelief, and he said, "My money sure would've been on blunt force trauma as the COD just like Tommy Cantwell said."

"And you would've lost big-time."

Ross put the papers down in his lap and frowned. "But this says the blow from the pestle was postmortem. I didn't see that coming."

Bax managed a shrug. "Nope. I didn't either. But when your lungs are full of water, the logical conclusion is that you drowned."

Ross was still trying to think everything through. "So the deal is that Brent Ogle was dead when someone clubbed him with the pestle, then."

"That's how it reads."

"Something about that sequence just creeps me out," Ross said, unable to suppress a shudder.

"It doesn't do anything for me, either. But I've run across even worse things in autopsies."

"How could you not tell somebody was dead in the water, if you'll excuse the expression?" Ross said. "Unless . . ." He paused, still trying to envision a scenario that would make sense.

But Bax beat him to the punch. "Unless somebody drowned Brent first, then pulled him up out of the water and laid his head back the way he was found by Wendy and Carly and Hollis. In the darkness under those circumstances, somebody could have come along and clubbed him without realizing he was already dead. That would mean one of our suspects thinks he or she committed murder when they actually didn't. They would have been trying very hard all this time to disguise their guilt and hide all the turmoil going on inside. They would have been doing quite an acting job all this time."

"We did consider the possibility that at least two people might be involved in this. Are we back to that, then?" Ross said.

"It seems we are. But I'm leaning toward the proposition that neither of these two people is aware of what the other did," Bax added. "They weren't actually a team in the usual sense of the word. That gives us an edge in that we are the only ones who know what the autopsy has revealed, and I think we'll try to use that information to our advantage."

"What are you thinking about doing?"

Bax leaned back in his chair and thoughtfully folded his arm on his chest. "Round 'em all up at the RCC and tell 'em about the autopsy. It could trigger relief in whoever used the pestle, and they just might give themselves up, knowing that they no longer committed murder. They'd still be guilty of mutilating a corpse and attempted murder, but either one of those would be better than having killed someone. I've seen people lose it before when they're suddenly given a way out."

"Sounds like it would be worth a try," Ross said. "I do have a question, though. Are you gonna tell Wendy about the autopsy results? I know you always pick and choose what you leak to her."

"I might," Bax told him. "I'll think about it."

"You have to admit she's been good about sharing things with us that she discovers in her interviews."

"She has. By the way, do you know her schedule today? I might just drop by the *Citizen* a little later."

"Yeah, we texted a little earlier. She's going out to Brentwood to help Carly Ogle with something about the house. Hollis Hornesby is supposed to help out, too. She said Carly was gonna put it on the market and then leave."

The news caught Bax by surprise. "Is she now?"

"She and her son David aren't crazy about Brentwood. They think of it as Brent's house and not theirs," Ross explained. "Anyhow, I'm going out to the RCC today to talk to Mitzy Stone about her grandfather, who just happened to be none other than Coach P. J. Doughty. We have Wendy to thank for that bit of information, which she got out of her interview with Mitzy. She had obviously been holding that back all along, so it makes me wonder what else Miz Stone is holding back."

Bax sat up straight in his chair and snapped his fingers. "Good move. And why don't I go out there with you? We could round up most of our suspects who're there and tell 'em all about the autopsy. We could very well catch somebody off guard, as I suggested before."

After mulling it over a bit, Bax went with his gut and decided to text Wendy about the autopsy. What could it hurt? he figured.

"How about if I go out with you to Brentwood?" Lyndell was saying to Wendy in her office shortly before lunch break. "I think it would help me get a better feel for how the people of Rosalie think and behave. This town requires a bit of a learning curve, I must say, and I'm just not there yet. I'm fascinated by this idea of picking furniture to keep and let go, particularly letting someone else do it for you."

"Don't forget letting someone else pick the art on the walls to keep and toss," Wendy reminded her. "Something tells me you've never met Hollis Hornesby, one of our resident artists, have you?"

"I've been meaning to drop by his gallery, but, no, I just haven't been able to find the time."

"Well, he's a hoot and a half."

"Yes, I forgot about him for a moment. Anyway, when we get back, I'll treat us to lunch—your choice of restaurant."

Wendy offered up her brightest smile as Lyndell rose from her chair, grabbed her coat off the nearby rack, and the two of them headed out to the parking lot.

The traffic was unusually heavy as they drove through town in Wendy's car, particularly at the intersection of Locust and Fort Streets. Perhaps the light was stuck, because it seemed they ended up staring at red for the longest time.

"I absolutely hate this intersection," Wendy said, nervously tapping the steering wheel with the fingers of her right hand. "It seems like something hairy is always going on here."

"I've noticed that, too. I seriously try to avoid coming this way, if possible," Lyndell added.

The light finally changed to green, but during the long wait something that had been eluding Wendy bubbled up from deep within her brain. *Carly and Hollis*. From the day before. She suddenly knew what had finally triggered the interpretation she had been seeking.

Intersection.

Not in the traffic sense. Not in the sense of the one that had just been holding them up for so long and making them antsy and frustrated. The mathematical version. All those higher math courses Wendy had taken at Mizzou while also majoring in journalism were speaking to her now. Particularly the ones that had appealed to her penchant for abstract problem solving. Finite math, specifically.

Unions and sets. It had not been all that long since Wendy had savored such knowledge in a university setting the way other people savored a finely brewed cup of coffee or an after-dinner liqueur. Now her brain was shifting through various gears as she remembered the essence of that kind of intersection:

the union of two sets is a new set . . . new set contains all the elements in both sets . . . called an intersection.

So how did that apply to Carly and Hollis? Why were they such a source of fascination to her right now?

As she drove along Highway 61 South in silence while Lyndell was enjoying the leaf-turning scenery passing by at a clipped pace, it gradually began to fall into place for Wendy:

Carly and Hollis were two of the four people at the bridge table who had participated in her preempting lesson.

Carly and Hollis were the first two people to discover the body, within a minute of each other, so it seemed.

Carly and Hollis went out to the portico together and had time to discuss whatever was on their minds. Had Brent Ogle been on their minds?

And now Carly and Hollis would be awaiting her—and Lyndell as a tagalong—at Brentwood. Those two, and those two only, comprised the intersection. No one else fit into it that way. And even though it was mathematically correct, something about it all did not feel right to her. Suddenly, Wendy began to feel very grateful that Lyndell had offered to come with her. That sleuthing gift of hers was working overtime. Was she being paranoid or merely cautious? Perhaps a bit of both?

Lyndell finally turned away from viewing the scenery and said, "How much farther is it?"

"Just a few miles. I can picture Brent Ogle insisting his property needed to be a certain distance from town to be referred to as a 'house in the country,' though. That would be so gentrified of him, of course. Everything always had to be about him, what he wanted, and nothing else."

Lyndell adjusted her visor because of the way the sun was slanting in on her face, causing her to squint. Then she said, "I've been thinking about your article, of course, and this business about waiting for the case to get solved first does make sense. But I have to ask again, do you really think Deedah Hornesby or Mitzy Stone could have actually murdered Brent Ogle?"

"At this point, I don't. I have to confess, I'm much more interested in Carly Ogle and Hollis Hornesby right now."

A hint of concern registered in Lyndell's face. "Are you implying that we're on some kind of investigative mission, rather than just helping someone sort out their belongings?"

"I don't know just yet. It's this feeling I have, all of a sudden. I may be close to figuring this thing out once and for all, but I'm not sure what'll come of it."

Wendy considered the possibility that she might be overreacting to hypothetical and circumstantial factors, but she had rarely gone wrong paying attention to her instincts. She needed to apply the full force of her sleuthing gifts to come up with the solution, and be done with it. Meanwhile, they weren't very far from turning off onto the gravel road and then down the fledgling alley of immature oaks that led to Brentwood—less than a quarter of a mile away, in fact.

"I have something to tell you," Lyndell said, turning her way. There was no smile on her face. "I have a permit to carry, and I have a loaded gun right here inside my purse." She gently patted the cool gray suede of her stylish accessory a couple of times. "My father taught me how to shoot, and I'm quite a good shot, if I do say so myself. I don't mean to frighten you by saying that, either. I've used my gun only once to put a bullet in anything besides at target practice, and it was an armadillo that was digging up my beautiful azaleas when I was living in Little Rock. Still, I keep up my skills by going to the shooting range regularly here in Rosalie."

The revelation calmed Wendy somewhat, her stomach muscles relaxing a bit, while she lessened her tight grip on the steering wheel; but her knuckles were still on the white side. "I never figured you for an 'Annie, Get Your Gun' type. You're full of surprises, aren't you?"

"I don't fit stereotypes, that's for sure. But I'm only going by the sense of urgency I'm getting from you all of a sudden in telling you about it."

Wendy was feeling even more comfortable with Lyndell by the minute, and they had already bonded significantly in the relatively short time they had been working together. "I've never been able to get into guns. It's the main reason I haven't joined the police force, much to my father's disappointment. I've told Daddy many times over the years that I like solving puzzles, but not with a gun in my hand—with my brain. At any rate, I'm where I'm supposed to be for the first time in my life—and that's as an investigative reporter."

Now they had reached the gravel road, and Wendy turned off onto it. Then she put the car in park and let the engine idle right beside the huge metal mailbox with BRENTWOOD painted red in all caps. "Let's just wait a few minutes right here. I think I need to settle down before we go any farther."

"I didn't expect our outing would be this full of drama. I feel like I'm in one of those TV police shows," Lyndell said.

"I trust it won't turn out like that, but I can't help the fact that my brain is working through a few things."

During the tension-filled wait, Wendy continued to try to fit every piece of the puzzle that had been presented to her since the first meeting of the Bridge Bunch had begun on that fateful Saturday. She was trying to line everything up carefully—every concept, every supposition, every principle, from preempting to Occam's Razor to teamwork to the intersection of two sets.

Then, she received a text from her father:

Brent Ogle's autopsy in; COD not blunt force trauma; Ogle was drowned; blow from pestle postmortem; keep on down low for now; Daddy

Wendy sat stunned, unable to exercise her vocal cords. She needed time to digest it all.

Lyndell studied her face carefully and said, "What's the matter? Did you get some bad news?"

Mindful of her father's directive, Wendy thought quickly on her feet. "Nothing really . . . something from Daddy that's work related. He's having discipline problems down at the precinct, it seems. He likes to blow off steam from time to time by telling me about it."

"Sorry to hear that. But I'm sure he'll be able to handle it, and I can't tell you how excited I am to finally meet your father next Saturday. I've really been neglecting my social life since I came to Rosalie," Lyndell told her. "I've always been the type of woman where my job came first."

"Now you know there is absolutely nothing wrong with that. You and I, we're two of a kind."

But instead of more small talk, what Wendy really wanted to do was get out of the car and go for a long walk in the woods by herself, thinking about the implications of what her father had just texted her. Carly and Hollis were expecting her, however, and she would just have to multi-task, juggling her thoughts about the autopsy while giving the best advice she could on the subject of antiques and other pieces of furniture. Something about it all seemed wildly improbable and out of sync. The image of getting tangled up in an elaborate spider's web flashed into her head. Was her subconscious trying to warn her?

Nevertheless, she fearlessly put the car in gear and forged ahead, saying nothing further to Lyndell. The sleuth inside was in complete possession of her now, preventing her from seriously considering the possibility that she might be acting in a foolhardy manner. She was driven by visions of solving the case all by herself and all the huzzahs that came with that. She continued to push danger out of her head. After all, she had her gun-toting editor by her side. But none of that stopped her from earnestly working through the puzzle moment by moment. *Carly and Hollis* had become her internal mantra.

Ross and Bax had no sooner pulled up into the parking lot of the RCC than Tip Jarvis and Connor James got out of a black SUV two spots to the right of them, dressed in their gaudiest golf duds. Never had so much plaid clashed with so many stripes. Never had bright colors refused to complement each other with such dedication. Then, Tip caught sight of the police car and stopped in his tracks, and Connor followed his lead.

Ross caught up with them first and said, "Much better weather for golf today than the last time you fellas were out here, I do believe." Indeed, the November sun was out and doing the best it could; and though the air was on the slightly chilly side, there was no wind to speak of—ideal golfing weather—and certainly nothing a sweater or windbreaker couldn't solve.

"Yeah," Tip said, just as Bax joined the group. "We thought we'd give it a shot and work off some leftover Halloween candy the trick-or-treaters left that we just couldn't resist. You know how that goes."

Connor spoke up next while absent-mindedly fiddling with the lapel of his windbreaker. "Are you guys still investigating out here? We haven't read anything in the paper about Brent's murderer being caught or anything. We . . . uh . . . thought you might've given up. Is this place still officially a crime scene? Aren't we allowed to play some golf here today?"

"To answer your questions in order: no, it's no longer a crime scene, and, yes, the RCC is open for all bid'ness as usual. But we would never give up our investigation that easily. The case is still unsolved," Bax told them. "And we came out today to try a little experiment. Would you guys like to delay your game for a just a few minutes and participate? It's a bit of luck running into you both like this, and I promise it won't take long."

Tip looked supremely uninterested. "Uh, we came out to play golf, though. I mean, why should we help you do your job? I don't see you guys teaching us how to swing our clubs."

Ross caught Tip's gaze and then Connor's in turn. "As Captain Bax said, it won't take very long. Just a matter of being a good citizen is all."

"If we don't do this, are we breaking any law?" Tip said. "We certainly wouldn't want to do that."

Ross told him that they wouldn't be.

Tip and Connor exchanged furtive glances, and Ross perceived that something significant might be passing between them.

"What is it exactly that you want us to do that's so all-fired important?" Tip continued, narrowing his eyes.

"Just listen to something we have to tell you," Ross told him. "Nothing more than that."

Again, Tip and Connor locked on to each other, and Tip said, "A lecture? I can tell you, we're not up for that."

Ross shook his head but said nothing.

"So if we hadn't happened to show up here like we did, you wouldn't have come and gotten us?" Tip began. "We're really tired of dealing with this whole thing. People still stop us on the street or come up to us at restaurants and ask us if it's true we were out here when *it* happened. Sometimes, it feels like we're part of a sideshow. It was our bad judgment in the first place that started us hanging around with Brent. Truth is, we didn't like him very much, but we had our cold dranks together, as we called 'em, and played golf with him whenever our schedules meshed. It's actually a relief to us that he's out of our lives now."

Bax noted the intensity of Tip's last comment and chimed in. "A sentiment apparently shared by many. The man's legacy was not one to brag about."

"Let's go ahead and do what they ask," Connor said, though he didn't sound very convinced himself. "The sooner we do it, the sooner we'll get to our golf game and have a little time to relax."

Reluctantly, Tip agreed after shooting Connor a sharp glance, and soon the four of them found themselves inside the great room, where Mitzy Stone greeted them all. Deedah soon emerged from the front hallway and joined them as well.

"Ah, you're here, Mr. Rierson. Oh, and you've brought your captain with you, I see," she said. "Mitzy told me you were coming out today to talk about something. Is there anything I can do to help? Do you need to use my office again?"

Bax pointed to the bar where Carlos was busy wiping off the counter, preparing for the members who would drop by throughout the day to enjoy his famous cocktails. "Right this minute we won't require that, but if you would, please ask Carlos to head on over. And by the way, is Gerald Mansfield here?"

"He's out in the equipment shed, I believe," Deedah said. "Do you want me to text him to come in, too?"

Bax nodded with a smile. "Please."

A few minutes later, every suspect with the exception of Carly and Hollis was assembled in the great room, awaiting Bax's instructions. He quietly surveyed the group standing around before beginning and noted faces ranging from the nervous to the quizzical. Which if any of them might crack after hearing what he had to tell them? Would the surprise element be enough to do them in?

"Ladies and gentlemen," he began, "we've just gotten back the autopsy report on Brent Ogle from the State Medical Examiner's Office in Jackson." He paused for effect, looking for possible changes in expressions, but there didn't seem to be any—at least not yet.

"It seems that the cause of death for Mr. Ogle was not the blow landed to the crown of his head by the pestle. In fact, someone drowned him first, so Tommy Cantwell was mistaken in his preliminary conclusion that the blunt force trauma was the COD. Therefore, someone only thought they had murdered Brent Ogle. I can't imagine what that person has been going through all this time. If that person is standing here among us now, I suggest that they step forward and own up to what they did. Or actually—what they thought they did."

Even though dead silence was prevailing, the element of surprise had presumably served its purpose. There were a variety of immediate reactions from the group: a widening of eyes here, a slack jaw there. Those were unremarkable and expected. But the sharp intake of air and an involuntary jerky hand motion from one particular person drew the undivided attention of both Bax and Ross. Their investigative instincts told them that this was the suspect they needed to question further right away. Perhaps the practiced façade would finally be stripped away and the artful person behind the mask would be revealed at last.

Lyndell and Wendy had just stepped out of her Impala, parked in front of the imposing portico of Brentwood. Another car, an ancient VW Bug presumably belonging to Hollis, was already waiting for them there. Inside the house, Carly and Hollis would be waiting for them also. But Wendy was determined not to be put off by her speculations. She was stronger than that. Nevertheless, she stopped long enough to answer her father's text about the autopsy:

shocked by COD; here at Brentwood w/ Lyndell; head over here ASAP; gut feeling it's over.

In fact, Wendy was certain at her core that it was indeed over. In the last couple of minutes, she strongly believed that she had figured most of it out now, and she kept mentally chastising herself for being so gullible. Face value was something a certified sleuth should accept at her own peril. Her first mistake had been glossing over Carly's emotional outbreak in front of her at Brentwood. Carly said she had invited

Wendy out to confess her guilt over what she had thought about doing to her husband.

But what if instead, Carly was confessing her guilt over *what she had actually gone ahead and done*? Later, she might have been unable to cope with the reality of it all any longer. Perhaps she had learned her lesson well that day at the bridge table and fallen back on the art of preempting—offense through elaborate and exaggerated defense. Anything to help with her pain. Anything to give herself time to find a way out, if that were even remotely possible.

So where did Hollis fit into all of this? About that part, Wendy was less certain. Had he been lying all along about sneaking around to the hot tub merely to call out Brent Ogle? Suppose angry words and wagging fingers had not been Hollis's intended weapon. Had he somehow managed to get hold of the pestle and do the clubbing, thinking that Brent was still alive? Or was Hollis just in too much of a hurry in the darkness to notice the difference?

He and Carly could have plotted this together out under the portico in the darkness with the threatening weather frowning down upon them. Perhaps the lightning and the thunder had stirred them to vengeful heights that had pushed them over the edge. It could have been as simple as the two of them each wanting to end Brent's life in their own separate ways. That, Wendy decided, was profoundly ghoulish and made her want to shudder as if a tick were crawling up her spine on its way to biting her and settling in to gorge itself.

"Stay close to me, and hold on to your purse," Wendy told Lyndell while ringing the doorbell. Even then, even after pressing that bell with her finger, she refused to turn back.

Lyndell nodded and said, "I have to admit, you have my blood pressure up. What are you expecting to have happen?"

"It's just me and my worst-case scenarios. I guess I like to live on the edge. Isn't that the definition of an investigative reporter?"

"I think there are definitely some things you're not telling me. We'll discuss the concept of full disclosure when we get back to the office."

Then the door opened, and Wendy was somewhat startled. It was not Carly's maid who was standing there with a gracious smile, or even Carly, herself. Instead, Hollis was doing the honors, but that was hardly an accurate description. Far from it. There was a look of pure terror on his face—there was no other way to describe it. He swallowed hard, saying nothing. Then he sucked in air. What on earth was the matter with him? Was he ill or in pain?

Then, it all made sense when Carly stepped from behind him off to one side with a gun in her hand. It had obviously been pointed at Hollis's back just a second before she had revealed herself.

"Walk in slowly," Carly said to Wendy while she shot Lyndell a look of disdain. "Who is this with you?"

"This is Lyndell Slover, my editor," Wendy told her, her pulse quickening by the second.

"I only wanted *you* to come. You and Hollis," Carly continued. "But . . . you and your editor, both of you walk in slowly. Then I want the three of you to go into the parlor. Hollis, you lead the way, and none of you forget that I have a gun pointed straight at you, and I know how to use it. If Brent didn't teach me anything else during our trial of a marriage, he taught me how to shoot. He said he wanted to be sure I knew how to dispatch any of the poisonous snakes that crawl around out here. And if anyone would know about snakes, it would be Brent."

As the trio did as they were told with Carly walking behind them, the word *reckless* popped into Wendy's head. Then, it paired itself with *fearless*. She was going to have to

learn how to be the kind of sleuth that could distinguish between the two. At the moment, with her adrenaline coursing
throughout her body, she could only hope that her failure to
do so this time out would not end up being a matter of life
and death.

CHAPTER 17

Having pressed Deedah's office into service again as they had the Saturday of the murder, both Bax and Ross were behind her desk—one sitting, one standing, but both witnessing the emotional breakdown of the suspect who had been believing all this time that she had actually killed Brent Ogle. Now the dam had burst.

"I had somehow managed to deal with running into Brent Ogle at the RCC in the first place. His rudeness toward me, all the disrespect, all the taunting. I could handle all of that. Sexism is something I've always been prepared for. I thought I'd even made my peace with Brent being around all the time. It was enough that I'd come to Rosalie to make a success of myself where Grandpop had failed," Mitzy was saying to them after acknowledging her genealogy. She was sitting on Deedah's couch, dabbing at her eyes with a Kleenex.

"But when Brent told us that he'd done all that bragging to Tip Jarvis and Connor James about the clock operator being paid off and implied that it really was true, something inside me quietly snapped. I could almost hear the noise inside my head—like a tree branch falling to the ground after an ice storm. Just too much weight to bear—for it and for me. When I headed over to this very office with the rest of them, and they were all yammering about what to do with Brent, I did everything I could to rush the meeting so I could make an excuse to get outta there quick. I was in utter turmoil. I told everyone I was going to the ladies' room, and I did head that way. But all I really wanted to do was swipe Carlos's pestle. It just came into my head, 'Club him with that pestle.' I'd figured the rest of it out from there."

"And did you swipe it?" Ross said.

"Yes," Mitzy said. "I ran into a bit of luck, I guess. Carlos was puttering around in the supply closet when I approached the bar, so I slipped it into my pant pocket and hurried into the ladies' locker to think things through. I stayed in there until the power went off, and then I seemed to lose my nerve for a while."

"You were having second thoughts?" Ross continued.

"I don't know if you could call it that. I just think the darkness startled me at first. But I can tell you the pestle was burning a hole in my pocket."

"What did you do next?"

Mitzy had a faraway look in her eyes, and she shook her head. "I ran out of the locker room and down the hallway, right past Brent in the hot tub, and ended up under the deck halfway to the pro shop. It was so dark and I was going so fast that I doubt he could figure out what was going on."

"That makes sense," Ross said, squinting to picture everything in his head.

"And he was profoundly drunk, as we all know. But the longer I stood in the dark up under the deck, thinking about who and what he was, the more my resolve was strengthened again. I think some people are capable of doing anything in the dark. Things they would never consider in the light of day seem doable when the sun goes down. I'd already figured out that I'd definitely not made peace with Brent Ogle, whether I believed what he was saying about The Four-Second Game or not. I knew then that all the brave speeches I'd made to everyone about being too strong to let Brent get to me were just so much 'playacting.' I had the pestle now, and all I had to do was wait for the right moment to put all of us out of our misery where he was concerned."

Mitzy paused, taking a deep breath to keep on going. Every word seemed to be taking something out of her. "Brent *had* gotten to me and reached deep into my soul and possessed it somehow. His nickname was The Baddest Devil of Them All, and it's my belief that he literally became just that over time. So I was determined to put an end to him, not only for myself, but for my grandfather and my grandmother and my parents, not to mention his daily victims at the RCC. Nothing was going to stop me at that point."

There was another pause, and Bax used it to speak up. "Tell us about finally using the pestle. No gory details. Just the logistics, please."

There was nothing but resignation in Mitzy's voice now. "When I'd made my final decision to go through with it, I just ran down under the deck and hurried over to the hot tub. I called out Brent's name. But he didn't say anything, even when I called his name again, and then—"

Bax interrupted. "He didn't say anything to you because at that point, he was already dead."

"I didn't realize that until you told all of us a few minutes ago," Mitzy said, staring down at her shoes. "It shook me down to my roots, and I guess you got what you wanted—a breakdown right here in front of you both."

With no emotion in his voice, Ross picked up where Bax had left off. "Continue telling us the rest of your story."

"There's not much more to tell. I stood over him and said, 'This is for my family, especially Coach Doughty.'" And I hit him as hard as I could, tossed the pestle into the tub, and followed the deck back to the pro shop. But I remember feeling very empty once I'd gotten back to my office after climbing through the window. Then I joined the rest of the group in Deedah's office. It felt like I was under some sort of remote-control spell, though."

"It may have felt that way to you, but you chose to do it, Miz Stone, nobody else. You just told us you had second thoughts, but you didn't let them guide you. You risked everything you've accomplished here in Rosalie, I hope you realize," Ross told her. "And at this point I have to read you your rights and tell you that you are under arrest for attempted murder and the mutilation of a dead body."

Mitzy sat there, stoically listening to the words that resulted in Bax cuffing her. Then she said, "What's going to happen to me?" Her voice sounded like that of a small child wandering around, lost in the woods. Her usual confidence had been manifestly drained from her. In removing Brent from the known world, she had also effectively removed herself.

"The only advice I can give you now is to get a very good lawyer," Bax told her. "And I'm sorry you let Brent Ogle get the best of you the way you did. As it turned out, someone else had already done the dirty work before you got there. You would've been off the hook if you'd just taken a close look and backed off."

Mitzy slumped her shoulders. There was no more fight left in her. "I'm glad it's over. It's been a trial putting up a front and lying to everybody. I'm . . . just glad it's finally over."

Then the text Wendy had sent about Brentwood came through on Bax's phone.

"You stay here and take care of this," Bax said to Ross with a sense of urgency after reading it. "Wendy wants me out at Brentwood. Call for backup."

"What the hell's happening? I'd like to go with you," Ross said, picking up on the alarm in Bax's voice.

"I don't know exactly what's going on, but you need to take Miz Stone down to the station first. You can head out to Brentwood after that. Just call for backup out there right now, okay?"

Wendy couldn't believe she'd walked into such a trap, that she'd allowed her bravado to crowd out her better judgment. At least she'd had the good sense to send that text to her father. For not the first time, however, she realized that there was a significant difference between being an investigative reporter and a law enforcement officer. As a result, she found herself sitting on Brent's purple-and-gold–striped eyestrain of a sofa with Lyndell and Hollis, while Carly stood at a comfortable distance in front of them with her gun still pointed their way.

Carly had forced Hollis to collect all phones and purses and pile them on a table in the corner of the room, so she was in complete control of the situation. "I'm sure you all think I'm insane or have lost my mind," she began, "but I wanted you here for a reason. Well, not you, Miz Slover, but three witnesses are just as good as two."

"What are we going to be witnesses to?" Wendy said. "Why are we being held hostage like this?"

"You're not my hostages," Carly said. "This gun is only so none of you will stop me."

Everyone looked puzzled, but it was Wendy who spoke up. "Stop you from what? Are you going to shoot us?"

But Carly didn't answer, and the silence that followed only filled the three people on the sofa with more anxiety.

"I do want you to help David sort out the art, Hollis,"

Carly said finally. "I know you thought we were going to do it now, but that can wait."

Hollis's hand gestures were all over the place, pointing first in that direction, then in another. "You're going to have to explain things better than that. I mean, I haven't been able to think straight since you greeted me at the front door with that gun. What on earth is this all about? And what's happened to Reeny?"

"I gave her the day off. I didn't want her around for any of this. But to answer your question, this is about me leaving," Carly said. "On my own terms."

Then Wendy spoke up. "Do you want to tell us about Brent? I've already figured it out, you know."

"Then I don't have to explain it, do I?"

"As long as you have that gun pointed at us, I think you owe us that much," Wendy said.

Carly lowered the gun slightly and began. "I'd just had enough of Brent. I was tired, very tired. You have no idea what it's like to live with someone who's always beating you down. He never beat me up, you understand. He never laid a hand on me. He just beat me down with his verbal abuse, with the way he made me feel about myself. It was my bad judgment to stay in the marriage, but I did it for David. If Brent and I hadn't had him, I would have gotten a divorce a long time ago. But I stuck it out, and now I've paid the price."

She caught Wendy's gaze particularly. "And you're right, Wendy. I did drown my husband despite my lies. It wasn't very hard to do. He was mostly out of it when I checked on him. He was practically snoring because he'd had so much to drink. So, I saw my chance, and I took it. I pushed his head down into the water and held him there until there was no more resistance. It didn't take long for him to stop struggling. Then I pulled his head back up and rested it on the edge of the hot tub. I wanted to be sure he was dead, that he wasn't breathing. Then I started walking back to the locker room and froze in place when I realized I'd actually killed him. It was surreal and—"

Hollis interrupted, sounding confused. "And that's when I ran over you? So you didn't hit him over the head with the pestle?"

"No, someone else did that. I guess it could have been anyone."

"It wasn't me," Hollis said. "I found your husband that way."

An awkward silence fell over the group until Wendy said, "So you drowned Brent right after you left me in the locker room, then. When you came back, you looked like you were in shock. But was it real, or were you faking it?"

Carly did not answer right away. Then, she managed a little smirk. "A little of both, I think. I wanted to kill him, and I did, but then I couldn't believe I'd actually done it. Does that make any sense?"

"In a morbid sort of way, yes," Wendy said.

"Of course, I was truly in shock when I returned to the hot tub with you, and you told me Brent had that huge gash on his head," Carly added. "Just know that I got there first with the drowning, but I wasn't expecting this mysterious extra damage. Who had done that? That was what really threw me."

Wendy was nodding. "Yes, I remember that you kept repeating the word 'gash' over and over again. That makes sense now. You knew you hadn't put it there."

Hollis was still trying to piece everything together and offered one of his flare-ups, dramatically clutching at his throat. "This thing is making me dizzy. You mean to say that you drowned your husband, Carly, and then somebody else clubbed him right after, and then I discovered the body right after that, and then I ran over you on your way back to the locker room? Is that the insane sequence? That's more complicated than a dark ops military operation."

"I don't think you could actually pull all that off if you planned it that way. Something probably would have gone wrong. But that appears to be what happened with everyone acting on their own. Let's just say the stars were aligned, and they were not in Brent's favor," Carly told him. "I have to say that I don't think I would've done my part if we hadn't had the power outage, though. I think it emboldened me. Everything came together to push me toward what I did—the darkness, Brent's oblivious, drunken stupor before and after he got into the tub, the memories of the years spent putting up with his ego and his cruelty to everybody, including his own son. I was playing the Devil on his own ugly terms, and it didn't make me feel good to succeed once it was over and done with."

"So when you asked me out here that first time to confess your guilty feelings, was it because the knowledge of what you'd done was finally getting to you, or were you just trying to fool me and buy yourself some time?" Wendy said. "Because you had me fooled, you know."

"My brain was totally out of sync, but, yes, I knew I couldn't handle it. I thought maybe I could deal with it by pretending it never happened. That it was only something I had contemplated but never followed through with. That I could fool you and fool myself at the same time. I found I couldn't sleep at night, but your lesson in preempting came to me again—that I could get rid of the guilt that way. But it didn't work. I can't live with what I've done. If I could take it back, I would, even though Brent had become a monster of his own making. But I can't take it back. And so, when I told you and Hollis I was putting the house on the market so I could leave, I was telling you both only a small part of the truth."

Wendy and Hollis exchanged puzzled glances, and he said, "What's the large part of it, then?"

Carly's stoic façade began to crumble, even as she continued to hold on to the gun firmly. But she could not stop the tears that were forming in her eyes. "The rest of it is that I do want both of you to help David sort through everything when he comes down to deal with the house. I'm not putting Brentwood on the market. I'm just leaving it to him to do with it as he pleases. I'm sure he'll want to sell it and walk away from his life here."

"Why is the gun necessary, though?" Wendy said. "You could have told us all this without it."

"I'm sure you've already figured it out." Carly affixed a strange little smile to her face. There was also a sadness to it that could not be ignored, as one of her tears finally fell.

"I asked you before if you were going to shoot us. I think the three of us are still terrified that you may still do just that. No one considers being held at gunpoint a soothing experience."

"Amen to that," Hollis said, sounding somewhat breathless while bringing his hands together prayerfully.

"You misunderstand me, then," Carly said, pointing to the gun.

In reality, Wendy had not misunderstood. Her instincts had whispered the truth to her, but she wanted to prolong the confrontation in hopes of defusing it somehow. Maybe she could manage to turn it around. Maybe she could find a way for all of them to walk out alive. "How did we misunderstand you, Carly?"

"The part about me saying that it was time for me to leave."

"Then explain it, please."

"I didn't mean that it was time for me to leave Rosalie. I will not be going up to Wisconsin to join my son. But I will ask that you explain everything to him when he comes down. I'm counting on you."

Wendy continued to think on her feet. Anything to distract Carly from her task. "But where are you going in the meantime? Whether you believe it or not, there are options available to you."

Carly's voice was now completely infused with sadness, as if she were already in a faraway place of her own making. "I don't know where I'll end up exactly. I wish I could tell you I knew. Don't we all want to know? But I wanted the two of you, Wendy and Hollis, to understand why I'm doing what I'm doing. I wanted you to know the whole story. You are my witnesses to it all. You are my Bridge Brunch friends. We bonded over that. I trust you." Then she focused briefly on Lyndell. "And you will be a witness, too, as it turns out, Miz Slover. You're a member of the Third Estate, and that puts an official stamp on it all."

Lyndell could barely manage a nod, sitting frozen in place.

Suddenly, the wailing of sirens could be heard in the distance, and Carly glared at Wendy immediately. "You had the police follow you here? Why on earth would you do something like that?"

"I texted my father that I was coming out here. I told him that I was concerned about a few things, and I see now that I was right to be. Daddy is a very instinctual person, like I am."

"None of that really matters now. I will not be stopped," Carly said, sounding very sure of herself. "No one will stop me from leaving. Not you, not Hollis, not your editor."

Wendy began pleading as a reflex action, hoping she still might be able to stumble upon the right words to defuse the situation. "Please don't do this, Carly. Maybe we can get you some sort of help. You just weren't in your right mind that night. There is such a thing as diminished capacity in legal terms. Let it play out, please . . . please. You do have your son to live for, if nothing else. Perhaps he'll get married and give you grandchildren. Think about him and the effect what you're doing will have on him."

The sound of the police sirens grew louder as the cars were getting closer by the second, and Carly said, "David is strong enough to take care of himself. He had to be to survive a father like Brent. He's everything his father was not."

"Don't let Brent do this to you, though," Wendy said, still hoping to get through. "Don't let it end this way."

"I have to pay for what I've done. I just can't live with myself. It's time for me to leave," Carly said, swallowing hard.

Then she smiled at the three people paralyzed on the sofa and put the gun to her temple.

Bax bounded out of his police car, drew his gun, and then stationed himself behind the door, using it as a shield as he focused on the nearby front entrance of Brentwood. His heart sank to his shoes as the report of the gunshot coming from inside reached his ears. During the next few seconds, he was tortured by the worst-case scenario a devoted father could possibly imagine. He had already lost his beloved Valerie twelve years ago to the unforeseen circumstance of fatal pneumonia. He thought he would never recover, but somehow he had managed. To lose his Wendy now would be the nightmare that would make him want to give up breathing. He was positive he could not go on living if the shot he'd heard had taken her out.

At the moment, the words were trapped inside his head. Uttering them out loud was too strenuous and devastating a task even to consider, so they remained unspoken but desperately felt:

Please, please, God, don't let anything happen to that daughter a' mine.

Two officers burst forth from a second police car that had just driven up with its blue lights flashing, and Bax shouted to them, "Gunshot inside!" as they drew their guns and took defensive positions behind their doors as well.

"Rosalie Police Department!" Bax shouted toward the house. "Come out with your hands up!"

The officers did not have long to wait, as the front door opened immediately. Bax's entire body was washed by an enormous wave of relief, moving all the way down to his toes. It was Wendy, his beloved daughter, who stepped out onto the portico, waving her hands in the air.

"Don't shoot. It's my daughter!" Bax shouted, even though practically every officer on the force knew who she was after she had helped solve the Grand Slam Murders case the year before. But Bax was taking no chances with the most precious and finest accomplishment of his life.

"It's okay!" Wendy shouted. "Everything's under control in here. It's safe to come in!"

Bax ran up the front steps and embraced Wendy as if her picture had been on a milk carton for years and she had finally been found against all odds. When he finally let go, he noticed the large contusion on her right cheek.

"Did somebody get shot? What happened to your face?"

"I haven't looked in the mirror, but thankfully, no one was shot." Wendy steadied herself, closing her eyes briefly before continuing. "Carly Ogle tried to commit suicide, but I stopped her. When she put a gun to her head, I just sprang up off the sofa and leapt as far as I could. I knocked her to the floor, but the gun went off anyway. The bullet's probably in the wall or the ceiling somewhere. Better there than in one of us. Don't ask me how I did it. My adrenaline levels were off the charts, and I landed hard on the floor, too." She pointed to her cheek. "Does this look awful? It does hurt a little bit right now."

Bax exhaled and held her hand. "We'll get you fixed up, but my expert opinion is that you'll live."

That brought a smile to Wendy's face, and she said, "Anyway, Hollis and Lyndell have Carly completely restrained on the sofa in there now. She confessed to drowning Brent—all three of us are witnesses to that—so someone can go in and read her rights to her and cuff her."

Bax motioned the other officers to follow him in with Wendy; but after they had all entered the purple and gold parlor to the sight of Carly tightly wedged between Hollis and Lyndell, Bax said, "Let me handle this, guys."

But before he could say anything further, Carly glared at Wendy and said, "You should have let me go. It was time for me to leave, and you denied me that. Why would you want to force me to spend the rest of my life remembering what I did? There could be no penalty worse than that."

Somehow, Wendy found an answer. "It's the high regard for life I learned from my father as a police officer all these years. I don't know what will happen to you, Carly, but there are always specific legal remedies in cases like yours. Your lawyer may plead diminished capacity for you, and there'll be psychiatric help available. I'm no expert, of course, but I didn't want things to end the way you had planned them. I tackled you because I believe in the value of life."

"Still, you had no right to stop me," Carly said, but her words lacked conviction. She appeared to be merely going through the motions. In a sense, she had already left mentally.

"There are some who would say you had no right to take your own life that way," Wendy said. "It doesn't matter now, though. What's done is done. Your husband is dead because of you, and you're still alive. Your lawyer and the courts will take it from here."

Bax moved to the sofa and stood over Carly and the two people restraining her, speaking as gently as possible. "Miz Carly, I need to confirm that you did confess to drowning your husband at the RCC two Saturdays ago. I need to actually hear it from you."

"Yes," she said softly and without hesitation. "I did it. But I didn't hit him over the head."

Matching her soft tone, Bax said, "Yes, we know that." Then he charged her with murder and read her rights to her while one of the officers cuffed her as she got to her feet. The entire process seemed to move in slow motion with an unexpected surreal quality to it.

When Carly was finally escorted out of the room, Wendy took her father by the arm and said, "Well, these are hardly ideal circumstances, but, Daddy, I'd like to introduce you to my esteemed editor, Lyndell Slover."

"It's my pleasure to meet you," Bax said, as Lyndell rose from the sofa to shake his hand. "Though I have to admit my daughter is correct. I never thought it'd be while I was arresting someone for murder after you'd also been held at gunpoint the way you were."

"No, I imagine you didn't," she said, unable to suppress a grin. "Let me just say that it wasn't even close to my normal experience behind the editor's desk. But all that aside, it's also a pleasure to meet you."

"I'm sure things will be much less frantic and stressful when we get together at that dinner party my daughter is planning. No gunshots, no handcuffing and wild antics like this," Bax said. That was followed immediately by a frown. "But how in the world did you get mixed up in all of this?"

"It's my fault, Daddy," Wendy said, jumping in quickly. "I was coming out to help Carly with some business she'd made up about putting Brentwood on the market. She invited Hollis out for the same phony reason. I'm afraid I let Lyndell tag along at her request."

"But that's hardly your fault," Lyndell said. "I came with

you of my own free will, and since I'm your boss, you properly deferred to me. What were you going to say to me, 'No, you can't come'?"

Wendy needed the genuine laugh that followed. Her entire body relaxed, even though her pulse was only now starting to slow down after racing at a breakneck pace for so long. She could still feel it pounding in her ears.

Then Hollis chimed in. "I never would've figured Miz Carly for the murderer, though. Frankly, I thought one of Mr. Ogle's golfing buddies did it. I mean, they almost got into that nasty fight by the bar, and they were all roarin', screamin' drunk. Either one of them did it or Carlos, I thought." Suddenly, Hollis was frowning, too. "So, if Miz Carly did the drowning, who did the clubbing with the pestle?"

"We've solved that, too," Bax told them all. "Ross and I got a confession at the RCC from Mitzy Stone before we came out here. Seems the drowning and the clubbing followed one after the other very quickly, and it was incredible, unplanned timing that prevented both acts from converging. The result was that it was clearly Brent Ogle's time to go. I imagine not many people on this earth have survived back-to-back attempts on their lives within a few minutes of each other."

It was Wendy who seemed the most surprised. "Mitzy confessed? I was convinced she was on the up-and-up with me about everything—the success she'd made of her job here, how she didn't want to let her family down, how she could take Brent Ogle's guff, no matter what. So tell me you're kidding."

"Nope, I'm not."

"I guess I'm two for two in taking people at their word," Wendy added. "It took me way too long to figure out Carly was preempting me with her own little sob story. I'm not exactly proud of that, and what's worse, I didn't even tell you and Ross what she told me. Maybe if I'd done that, you could have figured things out a lot sooner."

"Don't beat yourself up too much," Bax said. "We have your sleuthing skills to thank for uncovering Mitzy's relationship to Coach Doughty in the first place. That led to our testing her and most all the other suspects when we revealed the results of Brent Ogle's autopsy out at the RCC. You helped us bring that to a close quickly. That was on you. Apparently, Mitzy was tired of bluffing her way through it all, and she broke down and finally confessed when the drowning twist was revealed."

"I'm thankful for that much, at least. But . . . I sure fell for the front she put up, didn't I?"

Bax snapped his fingers. "You did important work in the case on your own, but I forgot to mention that there's a catch where Mitzy is concerned, though. Since Brent Ogle was already dead when she struck him with the pestle, she cannot be charged with actual murder. Her blow was postmortem. Still, she's been arrested on attempted murder charges and mutilating a dead body. Ross is taking care of all that now down at the station."

"Wait . . . you can mutilate a dead body?" Hollis said, nearly hyperventilating at the thought.

"Yes," Bax told him. "Believe it or not, corpses have rights, too. They are entitled to be treated with dignity and respect at all times. Funeral homes will be the first to tell you that. But that's the least of Mitzy Stone's worries. It's the attempted murder charge that's gonna do her in."

Hollis pressed on with a flabbergasted expression on his face. "What will happen to her?"

"She'll go to prison, of course," Bax added. "But as for the details of the sentencing, that'll be up to the lawyers and the judge. Her golf pro days will be over for a while. It's a shame, too. She was very good at what she did, according to all my sources. She just went a little bit crazy on the spur of the moment, it seems. I guess you could say the same thing about Carly Ogle. There must have been something treacherous in the air that night besides thunder and lightning and driving rain."

"Brent Ogle was in the air out there," Wendy said. "I wonder if it's possible to poison an entire environment with your mere presence."

Then Lyndell managed a little gasp and turned to Wendy. "What a prescient investigative reporter you are. You were exactly right to suggest holding up on releasing your article until this case was closed. We can't very well tout Mitzy Stone as an example of female accomplishments now, can we?"

Wendy could do little but shrug. "Afraid not."

"So . . . we just focus on Deedah, then? Do you think we'll have enough material to make it work?"

Wendy thought about it for a few moments and said, "Why not? We can concentrate on her accomplishments at the RCC and even include a little bit about the Bridge Bunch as a sidebar."

"If I'm not mistaken, wasn't Carly Ogle a member of your bridge club, though?" Lyndell said.

Indeed, the Bridge Bunch was now short a critical fourth member to make up a table. Wendy mentally cringed at Lyndell's reminder and said, "Unfortunately . . . she was."

It would now be up to Deedah and herself to recruit at least one more new member from the ranks of Rosalieans to keep the fledgling club going. Wendy wondered yet again if her desire to become proficient at playing the game would ever become a reality. Incessant hurdles coming at her from all directions had presented themselves since she had made up her mind to even try her hand a couple of years ago. And with no appreciable success so far.

Before the group broke up and headed in all different directions, Bax stole another heartfelt hug from his daughter and half-whispered in her ear, "I'm so proud of you, I could just explode. You took a huge risk lunging at Carly Ogle with a gun in her hand—and I don't even want to think about what could have happened—but I can't fault you for being brave and putting your life on the line. You're just like your dear old dad. I've done the same thing in my job all my life. You may look like your beautiful, talented mother, but you have my guts and instincts. So I'll say it again for the millionth time: I love you, daughter a' mine."

She pulled away just far enough to reward him with a smile for the ages. "I love you, too, Daddy."

CHAPTER 18

Remembering her promise to Hollis that she would have him and Deedah out to the bungalow some time soon to see her mother's artwork, Wendy decided to increase the number of people coming to her little dinner party by two. It occurred to her that adding extras might also take some of the pressure off Bax and Lyndell to "click," particularly since the conversation would probably center around Valerie Lyons Winchester's famous acrylics on the walls. At least in the beginning. Sometimes, suggesting an interesting subject that fascinated everyone was the secret ingredient for a successful dinner party, and before they knew it, strangers or mere acquaintances had discovered their mutual interests and become friends. For her part, Wendy savored the realization that sleuthing skills were not her only talent.

Once everyone had arrived on a chilly November Saturday evening, the subject of the paintings on the walls kicked things off as expected.

"I positively adore her primitive technique," Hollis was saying while browsing the collection in the living room above Wendy's flamingo-colored flea-market-find sofa. "She really was quite fond of blue, black, and silver in this one, wasn't she? And even though everyone knows the Mississippi River is actually brown, this interpretation really speaks to me. There are times when the sky can make even muddy water look blue. Perhaps it's a bit of a stretch since this is a night sky, but that's what art is all about. You create it through your own filter." He lifted his glass of Chardonnay to the painting and took a generous swallow.

"That's from her *Moon on the River* collection," Wendy said, after sipping her wine as well. "It completely sold out not long after she put it up for sale. She was thrilled to get that kind of support from her hometown, and she immediately turned out her *Sun on the River* collection. That got snapped up just as fast."

Deedah, who was standing nearby in an elegant gold caftan, said, "Don't I know it. I remember that I fully intended to buy one of that first collection myself and hang it in my parlor. But I went out of town for a week to visit your aunt Trudy, Hollis, and when I got back, they were all gone. I don't remember where I was when that second collection appeared, but I've tried to get one of either of them ever since. It's useless. People hold on to them like they were diamonds. It seems their value just keeps on increasing with every passing year."

"I'd sell you one if I had an extra," Wendy told her. "But the one you're looking at is the only one I have from that particular collection, and I doubt Daddy would part company with his, would you?"

From his vantage point on the sofa where he was sitting cozily beside Lyndell, holding her hand, Bax said, "No, I don't think I'd let mine go at any price."

Wendy was encouraged by the sight of her father's hand-holding, as well as the charming simple black dress that Lyndell had chosen to wear. Well, it wasn't exactly simple. There were some sparklies here and there, drawing attention to certain strategic areas of her figure.

"Well, every one of these paintings is just fabulous," Hollis said with a sweeping gesture that included the entire wall. "Such bold strokes, and the way she makes the water pop with those ripples of white from the moonlight. I'm totally jealous. I'm barely getting a trickle of business at the gallery, no matter what I do."

"You need to do another grand opening," Deedah said. "I think some people were out of town when you had the first one."

"Oh, please. That many people couldn't have been out of town, Mother. Besides, I don't want to appear to be pandering too much. I mean, what's next—buy one, get one free?"

As usual, Hollis's hyperbole produced an outburst of laughter from around the room, and on that note, Wendy said, "I think dinner is about ready, folks. Ross just gave me the high sign on the dinner rolls. And let me say, there's nothing like a man who will help out in the kitchen."

"That's me," Ross said, raising his hand with a smile after taking the rolls out of the oven. "I can put on a mitt with the best of 'em."

Over a dinner of roasted chicken with rosemary, dirty rice, and squash casserole at Wendy's rustic kitchen table, conversation had drifted from artwork to the aftermath of Brent Ogle's murder.

"Tell us. Do you have any prospects for a new golf pro yet, Deedah?" Wendy was saying.

"It's a little too early yet," she said. "We've put out plenty of feelers, but I'm sure somebody will jump at the chance very soon. I have to be honest and tell you, though, I still feel bad for Mitzy. I know she'll regret for the rest of her life the moment she struck that blow."

"It *is* sad," Bax added. "It's been my experience that there are some arrests you just hate to make. But the law is the law. It applies to everyone, and we have our moral code as well. I do have an update on Carly Ogle, though. Her lawyer told me that he will plead diminished capacity for her, as we thought. My take is that she'll end up in a psychiatric facility of some kind. Perhaps that's for the best. I doubt she would survive prison very long. It's been my observation that some people just give up and die when they get into that situation. Carly had already tried to commit suicide once, as we all know."

Deedah finished buttering her roll and said, "Poor Carly. I can't imagine what her life was really like on a daily basis, and the whole thing about what kind of man Brent Ogle really was still makes me shudder. He put people on the defensive immediately, and nothing good ever comes of that. You could even say that they were put in a no-win situation. They were forced to deal with him on his terms, not theirs. I don't believe I've ever run across someone like that who produced such bad feelings in everyone. There was no upside to him, and you see the results."

Then Lyndell spoke up. "But maybe there's an upside of a different sort, Deedah. Wendy's just about finished with her article on your directorship at the RCC. We want to support the work you've done and the changes you've made, as you know. Of course, we had intended to include Mitzy's work as the first female golf pro out there, but that's totally out of the question now. We only hope Wendy's article will get people to focus on the positive things that the RCC offers to the community. We don't want them to associate it with murder and mayhem."

"Spoken like a true editor," Wendy said, winking at her boss.

"Shall we make a toast to my daughter's article, then?" Bax said.

Everyone raised their wineglasses and said, "To Wendy's article."

"Thanks, everyone. It'll be out this coming Wednesday with all the grocery coupons, so there's your extra incentive to read it and tell all your friends about it, too."

It was after a dessert of espresso and sherry custard with whipped cream that people started making their manners to leave. But Wendy managed to break away from her hostess duties briefly to take her father aside and whisper, "I need to talk to you in my bedroom for a minute."

Bax drew back and looked at her sideways. "What's this about? Can't we talk about it right here in front of your mother's wonderful paintings?"

Wendy continued to whisper in girlish fashion. "Just humor me, please." Then she quickly turned to Lyndell and said, "Let me borrow Daddy for just a few moments, will you?"

Lyndell smiled graciously. "Absolutely. He's all yours."

In the bedroom with the door closed, Bax showed signs of impatience. "What are you up to now?"

"Nothing," she said, playing up to him by patting him on the shoulder affectionately. Then they sat on the edge of her bed with the shiny blue quilt that was so delightfully cool to the touch. "I just wanted to ask you what you really thought of Lyndell, that's all."

"I see." He appeared to be teasing her by tapping his temple with his finger. "Well, let me think about it for a while."

"Stop it. Just tell me how you think it went tonight."

"I enjoyed it thoroughly. You outdid yourself with the delicious food and the hospitality."

She punched him gently on the arm as she'd done from the time she was a little girl. "You know good and well what I meant. Now, give."

Finally, he stopped playing games with her. "Okay, then. I think there might be something there. I'll admit I'm intrigued. She's very intelligent, of course, but I like the way her hand felt in mine. She wasn't pushy about anything, either, and that's all good with me."

"Translate, please," Wendy said, still not satisfied. "Does that mean you'll definitely be seeing more of her?"

"If you want an answer right now, I'd have to say yes. Is that what you wanted to hear?"

She put her arm around his shoulder and leaned against him. "That'll do for now. But I expect you to keep me posted on all developments."

He turned, straightened his posture, and gave her a mock salute. "Yes, sir. I mean, ma'am. Now, let me get outta here and escort Lyndell home."

"Will there possibly be a good-night kiss at the door?"

He stood up and gave her a firm, fatherly stare. "That's too much information to give you right now, young lady. But if anything significant happens, you'll be the first to know." Then he headed out to join Lyndell and the others.

It was Merleece's Tuesday to clean up Wendy's bungalow once again, and no sooner had the two good friends sat down to their morning cup of coffee at the kitchen table together than Merleece gave Wendy an unsettling stare.

"Strawberry, I don't think you gone like what I have to say to you, but I have to warn you, else you gone be mad with me."

Wendy put down her cup and drew back slightly in her chair. "A warning, you say? This sounds very serious."

"Maybe it is, or maybe not. But I don't wanna see you surprised by it, no matter what."

"For heaven's sake, tell me. You've got me on pins and needles imagining all sorts of horrible things."

Merleece wriggled around a bit in her chair, sounding uncomfortable. "Miz Crystal . . . she say . . . she say . . . well, she say to me yesterday evenin' . . ." Merleece couldn't seem to finish the sentence.

Wendy was both alarmed and slightly annoyed. "*What* did Miz Crystal say?" Then, a worst-case scenario popped into her head. "Oh, no. Tell me she's not going to let you go, please. Not after all the hard work I know you've done for her in that enormous house."

Merleece shook her head emphatically. "No, no. Nothin' like that. I'm prob'ly the one person in Rosalie who'd put up with her and her crazy ways. It just that she find out 'bout that openin' you got out there at the country club in that bridge club a' yours. Knowin' her like I do, she could be on her way out there now to talk to Miz Deedah Hornesby 'bout applyin' or whatever you gotta do to get in and play. I mean, that woman have trouble waitin' for the sun to come up. I just thought you oughta know—and Miz Deedah, too. But I also thought maybe you could be the one to tell her instead a' me since we don't rightly know each other."

Wendy took a sip of her coffee and widened her eyes. "You're right. That is on the order of a warning. You already know how desperate Miz Crystal was to join the Rosalie Bridge Club last year before it met with its disastrous end, despite the fact that she denies ever having made that offer of ten thousand dollars to join up."

"You think she might offer that kinda money again, Strawberry?"

"I wouldn't put it past her." Then Wendy thought about it for a while. "Maybe that wouldn't be such a bad thing. I have no idea how Miz Crystal plays the game of bridge, but I do know that Deedah could definitely use the money to run the country club. We just lost our largest contributor in Brent Ogle, and his wife is out of the picture now also. So an additional source of funding might come in handy, and we wouldn't have to do anything but let Miz Crystal play bridge."

Merleece was almost cackling now. "Her money . . . that is one thing. But lemme tell you, her mouth and her opinions, they somethin' else entirely. I oughta know since I have to lissen to her erry day goin' on 'bout this and that as if any little drop a' common sense ever enter her mind. If you willlin' to put up with that, then you go ahead and let her in. Maybe she act more normal if she finally get to play bridge, but I'm just tellin' you what I see and hear at Old Concord Manor."

Profoundly sobered by Merleece's comments, Wendy decided to excuse herself and immediately talk to Deedah on her cell in the bedroom.

Wendy began bringing her up to speed on who and what was coming her way, but Deedah interrupted her quickly. "I'm afraid she's already been here. As a matter of fact, she just this minute left dressed up like she was going to the opera. I mean, why else would you wear opera gloves to come out and talk to me?"

Wendy was taken aback at first, but it was common knowledge that Crystal Forrest wasted no time in going after whatever it was she wanted next since coming to Rosalie with all of her late husband's wealth a few years ago. "And how did that go?"

"She sort of made an offer that I think the RCC may not be able to refuse," Deedah said. "But I told her I'd have to talk it over with you first. You must be psychic, because I was about to call you."

"Let me guess. She offered you money."

"A great deal of money. Twenty-five thousand dollars."

Wendy wavered between amusement and astonishment. "She's upped the ante quite a bit, it looks like."

Deedah's tone remained serious, however. "But she didn't offer the twenty-five thousand to join the Bridge Bunch. Oh, no. She said she wanted to contribute it to the RCC now that Brent Ogle was no longer with us. She doesn't let much get past her, it seems."

"Correct. I'm certain she pays close attention to what's in the paper every day and does tons of research before she makes one of her social-climbing moves. So, what do you want to do about this?"

Deedah was most emphatic. "I think we should take her contribution and let her play some bridge with us. At this point, she's the answer to our prayer for extra funding. I know Hollis will go along with it—we don't have to worry about that. So, do you have any objections to having her join under these circumstances?"

Wendy hesitated to pass along Merleece's studied opinion of her employer. That might deep-six the deal. Instead, she presented a nonjudgmental front. "I have to confess I've never really been around the woman long enough to see for myself. I mean, I've heard a lot of things, but we're only talking about playing a game with her. So, unless she doesn't know what it takes to make a legitimate opening bid or anything else, I'm onboard with your suggestion. Crystal Forrest is our new fourth. Pencil her in right now."

"Done," Deedah said. Then there was a sigh at the other end of the phone. "There's also an executive decision I've made, and I think it's an important one. So I want to run it past you."

"You sound slightly conflicted. As our esteemed director, you know you don't need my permission to do anything."

"I realize that. It's just the nature of the beast. I think we should remove that hot tub, since I'm uncomfortable with it still being there. Some people might see it and be reminded of the fact that it was an actual crime scene with that tape all around it, and I don't want that image to continue. I'm won-dering if those in the know will even want to use it now." Deedah paused for a little shudder. "I don't want potential new members being given a guided tour of the place and tak-ing a chance that such a hideous thing will be pointed out to them, or they'll bring it up themselves. You don't think I'm being a bit paranoid about all this, do you?"

"Absolutely not. You have every right to want a different image for the RCC. It's supposed to be for getting exercise, playing games, and having fun. A drowning in the hot tub is not something you want to advertise."

Wendy recalled how she had felt about the mere sight of the thing during her interview with her stalker, Gerald Man-sfield, in those rocking chairs. She had even chosen to walk the long way around the deck after it was over just to avoid passing close by to it again. "I completely agree with your decision. Keeping the hot tub would be a creepy thing to do. But I do have a legit question. I understand that some of the members did like to relax in those swirling waters after a long game of tennis or golf. Won't that be a bummer for them?"

Wendy could almost picture Deedah's face lighting up as she answered immediately. "I've already thought of that, too. We'll use some of the money that Crystal Forrest donates to us to buy two serviceable Jacuzzis, nothing as fancy as that hot tub, mind you, and we'll put one in each of the locker rooms. That way, the members can still get their sore muscles mas-saged, and maybe the memory of Brent Ogle's murder will start to fade in time. We can't let that keep us from attracting more members and fulfilling our mission. At least, that's my fond hope."

"You are brilliant, utterly brilliant. A couple of plain old Jacuzzis it is, then."

After their call had ended, Wendy found herself smiling and humming a few random notes that came out of nowhere.

Deedah Hornesby really was a capable and forward-thinking director, and the RCC was all the better for it. It might take a little time for everyone to heal from it, but the Brent Ogle era of negative energy that he had brought to everything he said and did out there was over and done with at last. The Baddest Devil of Them All would be playing his game no more, and no one would be forced to play him on his terms ever again.

Back at the kitchen table a minute or so later, Wendy tried to remain philosophical about the decision she and Deedah had just made together. "I mean, how bad can Miz Crystal possibly be? You know very well that I'm a gracious and tolerant person, Merleece."

"I heard that," Merleece said. But then she leaned forward and pointed her finger with a wary look on her face. "Just lemme say that you 'bout to be tested to the limit, and I wish all y'all some good luck. Me, I finally bought some earplugs, and when Miz Crystal get to rantin' and ravin' too much 'bout somethin' so ridiculous it make me roll my eyes, I just put 'em in when she not lookin' and nod erry now and then to make her think I agree with her. She don't even know the difference, Strawberry."

Both women enjoyed a hearty laugh, and Wendy said, "Well, I went and let my coffee get cold chatting with Deedah, but I thank you for your genuine concern for us. Maybe I'll finally get to play some decent bridge and nothing horrendous will happen to anyone around me. Fingers crossed."

CHAPTER 19

It came to Wendy suddenly that in the relatively short time she and Ross had been dating, he had never set foot inside the house of her childhood, where Bax still lived by himself. It seemed that either Ross had gone to her bungalow or she had gone to his place for their dates, dinners, or other social events. It didn't seem possible that she, herself, had never welcomed him as a guest to the charms of 201 Dulcimer. After that realization, she had even called up Bax to see if he had ever invited Ross over for anything.

"No, I don't socialize that way with my officers," he had told her. "A meal at a restaurant for somebody's birthday party or a drink at a bar after hours, yes. I'll do that occasionally. But getting too close can sometimes cause great pain when certain things happen. My home is my fortress and my retreat."

Wendy had read between the lines and not pressed further. But she had her answer: Ross had never seen anything of where she'd grown up.

The cozy little brick home of Wendy's childhood was painted an eggshell color and set back off the street atop a small hill with two towering pecan trees on either side of it.

Every year, those trees had produced enough pecans for Valerie Winchester to bake plenty of pecan pies throughout the fall. That had long been one of Wendy's favorite memories of both the months of October and November and her dear late mother's prowess in the kitchen.

As for the house itself, it wasn't particularly historic and would likely never qualify for a spot on the Spring Tours. Wendy remembered that her father had once said it had been built around 1920, but there had never been any documentation of it. None of that had ever mattered to Wendy, though. Forget architecture, historical significance, or how many antiques it contained: it was a cocoon of love to her, wrapping her up in warm memories that sustained her every day of her life.

And now, at last, she wanted to share it with Ross.

"I want to invite him to a cozy little lunch in our cozy little kitchen. I assume that's okay with you," she had said to her father over the phone. "Just the two of us now."

Bax was more than delighted to hear about her plans. Was his long-awaited wish for a marriage between his beloved daughter and the officer he had always thought of as a son going to come true at last?

"You didn't even have to ask," he had told her. "Are you gonna use your mother's pecan pie recipe on him?"

"Thinking about it."

"That oughta do it."

That last sentiment from her father had given her pause. "Do what?"

"Uh, well . . . you know. Bring him around."

Wendy could not help but snicker. "News flash, Daddy. Ross doesn't have to be brought around. But I'm not doing this for any other reason than I want to give him some inkling of what life was like for me growing up."

"Uh-huh," Bax had said in a tone just dripping with innuendo. "An inkling. Of course that's why you're doing it."

"Stop that, Daddy. I'm serious, or I mean, you're being *too* serious."

"Whatever you say, daughter a' mine. You know you're always gonna be golden with me."

So finally the day had arrived, and it was with a great deal of pride and excitement that Wendy gave Ross the grand tour, crammed with details of the incidents that had happened only to her. In the living room, which was centered around a sofa set made of a beige fabric, for instance, there was the tale of finding her father's wedding ring behind the cushions when she was on one of her "digging for dimes" expeditions.

"What was it doing back there?" Ross said.

"The one and only time I asked him that same question, Daddy got all red in the face and said, 'Something your mother and I will tell you about when you get a little older. You're too young to understand the concept of spontaneous horseplay.'"

"That's a good one," Ross said, laughing out loud.

"I was pretty smart at the age of eleven. I got the picture even then."

"I bet you did."

In the small, utilitarian kitchen with an outdated stove and a refrigerator covered with magnets and messages that kept making noises like a turkey gobbling with a bad cold, there was this from Wendy:

"I don't actually know how old that fridge is, but it's always made that noise you hear. I remember asking Daddy why he didn't trade it in for a newer model, and he said that the fridge made him laugh and that it was like having a pet in the house that didn't eat anything and never had to be walked. Not only that, it still kept things cold or frozen, so why give it the heave-ho because it couldn't keep quiet?"

"I'll have to remember that one," Ross said, laughing again.

"Yes, Daddy and his sentimentality for appliances."

Finally, Wendy allowed Ross to have a glimpse of her bedroom where she had gone through all the transformations—from toddler to teen to young adult woman. It was not a particularly "girly" room, though the color scheme consisted of pastel blues and yellows. There was a small brass bed covered with a busy pastoral quilt, but there were no frilly ribbons or dolls anywhere to be seen around the room. What pictures there were on the walls were of her parents or herself at various stages of growth, and the ambience overall leaned toward the sensible.

"I like it," Ross said. "It's you."

"It was me at one time," she said. "Daddy's turned it into a guest room and removed some of the things that don't fit in anymore. I took my four-poster to my bungalow, and of course all of my mother's paintings that I worship are now on my living room wall. But I think I outgrew this room even before I got out of high school. I never got to have the slumber parties with girlfriends here or anything like that associated with growing up. My mother's death when I was a sophomore shut down any carefree intentions I might have had. Believe me, that put me on the fast track to adulthood, and I've always felt that I lost part of my youth for good."

Ross put his arm around her shoulder and gently pulled her toward him. "You don't talk about that much, so I figured it was a topic that was off-limits for you. It must have been rough."

"I got through it, thanks to Daddy, and he did it while he was going through his own pain. I can't imagine what it was like for him."

"He's one of a kind to lots of people. Everybody at the station idolizes him, you know."

"You don't have to tell me."

Then it was time for lunch at the kitchen table, and Wendy had created what she was sure would be a man-pleasing menu. She had brought everything she'd prepared in her bungalow in an old-fashioned picnic basket covered with a bright floral-patterned cloth, and Ross's eyes kept getting bigger and bigger as she pulled each item out with great fanfare.

"Ta-da!" she announced, moving her hands about like a magician getting ready to pull the standard rabbit out of the hat. "Corned beef sandwiches on rye with Dijon mustard." Ross applauded as she laid them down.

"And now for my next trick—I offer my chunky German potato salad from scratch." She put the Tupperware container next to the foil-wrapped sandwiches and gave them all a self-satisfied nod.

"And last but not least—a homemade pecan pie made from my mother's treasured, Southern recipe. And every pecan came from the trees out in the yard. It's become my fall ritual to come over and pick them up like my mother used to do. Of course, Daddy lends a hand, so we always make quite a haul together."

After she had gently positioned the pie and pointed to it like a game show spokesmodel, Ross said, "I am totally impressed by the show, and I can't wait to man up and dig in."

"Daddy said he'd have various options for us to drink in the turkey-gobbling fridge, so let me take a peek and see what he stocked." She opened the refrigerator door, peered in, and said, "Aha! It looks like we have some lime-flavored Perrier, a couple of beers, and some sports drinks. What a combination, but that's Daddy for you. You'd think he could manage to—"

"Don't worry about it. No beer for me," Ross interrupted. "I've gotta go back to work. If I have a beer in the middle of the day, I'll get sleepy at my desk or at the wheel. So I'll take the sports drink, please."

"And I'll take the Perrier," she said, bringing both to the table. "I have a lot of work to do at the paper, too. At least Daddy remembered that I like sparkling water."

After they'd enjoyed a few bites and sips of everything, the conversation turned once again to Brent Ogle's murder, and it was Ross who surprised Wendy with his comment. "I have to tell you that you are the hero of heroes down at the station. Your father has made sure everybody knew that you were the one that made the real headway in the case, figuring out who Mitzy actually was and how Carly had fallen apart and given in to her demons—not once, but twice. Ronald Pike keeps elbowing me and saying things like, 'Why doesn't she just join the force and be done with it?'"

Wendy swallowed another bite of her sandwich and gave him a knowing grin. "I hope you told him that I am very happy doing what I'm doing. Because that's the truth of the matter."

"Just what *are* you doing? It appears to me that you're trying to do two jobs at once. But don't get me wrong now—I have to admit that you're exceeding all expectations and doing both of them very well."

Wendy bowed her head graciously. "Thank you for that. I just can't help it, Ross. It's not like I've asked for these horrible murders to happen the past couple of years. But when they did, I just kicked into another gear without even thinking about it—that sleuthing gear of mine. I assure you, I'd be happy doing investigative reports that didn't involve homicide for once and also playing a decent game of bridge every now and then for the rest of my life. Would that be too much to ask? I don't think so."

Ross gathered up a forkful of his potato salad and said, "Anything else on your docket, possibly?"

She looked up from her plate and pursed her lips. There was a provocative aspect to the gesture. She knew exactly what he meant and where he was going. The question was: did she want to pursue it at this time? Had she settled in enough to her position as investigative reporter to feel confident that she could play another role that demanded even more commitment?

Ross waited out the silence and said, "Nothing, then?"

"You had something in mind, I take it?"

He took his hand and slapped his leg a couple of times. "It's happens to be right here in my pocket. Something told me that I should bring it along just in case. We've been through this once, and you thought it would be best to postpone any decision back then. Do you still feel that way?"

She leaned in and lowered her voice to a whisper. "Make me a proposal, and let's just see."

"Really?"

"Yes, really."

"Okay, then. Here goes."

He rose, moved to her quickly, and took the little black box out, placing it in the palm of his hand. Then he got down on one knee in the approved, conventional fashion and opened it.

Wendy gasped as the ring caught the overhead light at just the right angle and shot sparkles straight up to her wide-open eyes. It had the same effect that someone watching a shooting star on a clear and dark night would enjoy, and Wendy could only manage a breathless, "Oh, my," at first.

"Go right ahead, sweetie. Please. Put it on," Ross said, moving the box even closer to her.

She lifted the ring out very gently, as if it would break into a thousand pieces if she didn't, and then gingerly worked it down her finger with a gleam in her eyes. The delicious surprise was that it was not the traditional solitary diamond. Ross had ordered up a circle of diamonds in the shape of small stars, gracing a delicate gold band. He had figured rightly that no woman alive on the planet could possibly resist such a dazzling and unique creation.

"So, Wendy Winchester, will you marry me?" he said, with every ounce of his attention directed her way.

She didn't even have to think about it as she rose from her chair. "Yes, I will. Let's finally do this."

He got up quickly and embraced her with a lingering kiss, even if it was ever so slightly flavored with corned beef and lemon-flavored sports drink. But from Wendy's point of view it was the taste and promise of love. What could possibly be more delicious than that?

"I've just got to know. How did you think of these beautiful stars?" she said, pulling back a bit and still in awe of his thoughtfulness. "I don't think I've ever seen anything like this."

Ross looked extremely proud of himself, almost like a new father seeing his baby for the first time through the nursery window. "I figured, why not stars for a star? Listen, once again, you really do have no idea what a celebrity you are down at the station now. When everybody heard about that open field tackle you made of Miz Carly which saved her life, they were all asking things like, 'Where's the video, Ross? Maybe we could use it for training at the academy.' Or even, 'Let's put it on the internet and see how many views it gets.'"

She snickered and waved him off. "It was just spur-of-the-moment. I promise you, I didn't even think about what I was doing for a second. I probably couldn't pull it off again if I tried."

"You're too modest, and you're fearless. But also too reckless at times. But thankfully, it turned out well this time and you're safely here with me now. So, do you want to set a date right this second or what?"

She did not take long to answer him. "I've always wanted a June wedding. My parents were married in June. So why don't we take six or seven months to do this thing up right? There's so much to decide. Like who will be my maid of honor? Oh, I know. I'll ask Lyndell, because we've gotten so close. I'm sure she'll be thrilled. And then there's the wedding cake. Do you know how much those things cost these days? You would think they were made out of silver and gold with what they charge now, and we haven't even gotten around to the subject of the groom's cake. I mean, will it be one of those chocolate creations or—"

Ross raised and waved his hand quickly as he tried to get a word in. "Wait, wait, wait. You don't have to decide everything right this minute, you know. I think it's a good idea not to rush it, too. I mean, we don't have our mothers to help us plan, unfortunately, but I know there are a couple of perfectly capable wedding planners in Rosalie who can do the job."

"I guess I was getting carried away."

Then, his face lit up. "I can just see your father now when we tell him about this. You know as well as I do how he's been playing the matchmaker for quite a while. Seems like he's mentioned me getting together with you . . . oh, every five seconds down at the station, and I really like the way he's always called me 'son.' I don't miss my own father so much when he does that. So now he can relax and put that to bed, and I'll be going from son to son-in-law."

"Hallelujah. Well, at least you know you won't have any in-law problems," she said, as they both laughed. "There won't be any awkward introductions for me to make, or my father worrying about whether the man I'm marrying is good enough for me. He's always been way ahead of the curve."

Then they sat down and resumed their lunch. But things were already different between them. They couldn't take their eyes off each other as they chewed and sipped in silence. There was probably much more that could have been said, but neither of them felt like saying it at the moment. There would be plenty of time to get to that in the months ahead. This was the time to contemplate each other as future spouses while the glow of commitment was at its most radiant.

Later, as they were clearing the dishes together, Wendy finally broke the silence. "I hope you've saved room for a slice of my pecan pie. I don't like to brag, but I think it's a killer."

"Oops," Ross said, putting his plate in the sink. "Maybe a bad choice of words, ya think?"

"You're right. We don't want to invite any more trouble. We've had too much to deal with already."

Over their slices of pecan pie, which both of them were savoring slowly because of the sugary richness, Ross decided to make an awkward confession. "You know, I was beginning to think you would never say yes to me. I was willing to respect that independent streak of yours, and I thought to myself, 'You've done everything you could, Ross. Let it go and walk away.' "

"I think that's a bit overdramatic. We've never stopped seeing each other, you know. It was just me making sure I could do my new job at the paper, that's all," she told him. "I came around when I'd proven to myself that I actually could. But it didn't happen overnight. It's taken the better part of a year."

He raised an eyebrow but was careful to keep a smile on his face. "Now I coudda told you that. You're not the type to fail at anything you try. So if I knew that, then why didn't you?"

She was up to his challenge and shot him a skeptical glance. "So you came out of the academy with nothing to prove to yourself? There's no such thing as a rookie in law enforcement? You were a finished product? Tell me you weren't actually that sure of yourself."

Ross looked slightly embarrassed. "Touché."

"Anyway, we're on the same page at this point in our

lives," she said. "Six or seven months from now, we'll be walking around the streets of Rosalie hand in hand as Mr. and Mrs. Ross Rierson; and if you want my informed opinion, I think we're gonna make one helluva good team."

"I can't disagree with that," he said. "But you know what? I think Rosalie caught lightning in a bottle when you decided to come home to use that journalism degree of yours."

"I hadn't thought of myself that way," she said, beaming at him. "But you might be right. All the time I was taking all those courses in school, I dreamed of winding up in New York or Washington, D.C., for my beat. I was going to make my reputation in one or the other and never look back. But here I am where I grew up, and Rosalie seems to be bringing out the best in me. Go figure."

Wendy decided to keep the rest of her thoughts to herself, however. She was wise enough to realize that she was not in control of *everything*. There was this thing that kept happening every time she sat down to play a serious game of bridge, you see.

Connect with Us

Visit us online at
KensingtonBooks.com
to read more from your favorite authors, see books
by series, view reading group guides, and more.

for sneak peeks, chances to win books and prize packs,
and to share your thoughts with other readers.

facebook.com/kensingtonpublishing
twitter.com/kensingtonbooks

Tell us what you think!

To share your thoughts, submit a review,
or sign up for our eNewsletters, please visit:
KensingtonBooks.com/TellUs.